M000312124

JATISMAR

BECA LEWIS

Copyright © 2018 Beca Lewis

All rights reserved. No part of this book may be reproduced or transmitted in any form or by any means, electronic or mechanical, including photocopying, recording or by any information storage and retrieval system, without written permission from the author, except for the inclusion of brief quotations in a review.

Cover Design by We Got You Covered Book Design

Published by:
Perception Publishing
https://perceptionpublishing.com

This book is a work of fiction. All characters in this book are fictional. However, as a writer, I have, of course, made some of the book's characters composites of people I have met or known.

All rights reserved.
ISBN-13: ISBN- 978-0-9885520-5-0

Table of Contents

Prologue

Every moment of his life, he searched for peace. He knew that it existed. Once, a long time ago, he had felt it. But back then, he had felt many things. Joy. Love. Contentment.

However, as much as he yearned for at least a tiny flutter of peace, it was lost to him. It was lost the moment the fire claimed the ones he loved, but didn't take him.

His punishment was to relive the memories of that moment over and over again. He could search forever, but he knew that peace would never come again.

Not in this lifetime.

One

It was the trucker who told him.

Another trucker, another day on the road. *How many years had he been traveling the country this way?* Jay wondered. Truck stop to truck stop. Crisscrossing the country. Always searching for something. But Jay Kalan had long ago forgotten what he was looking for or where he was going. Now, he was just going.

The day began like most days began for him. One trucker dropped him off at a travel stop. Another picked him up. If Jay had a chance, he would shower between rides, but often he would step off one truck and step onto another. Jay had been traveling for so long, some of the truck drivers already knew who he was.

This time it was a new driver who invited him to ride along. Jay had been waiting at a rest stop just outside of Phoenix, Arizona. He was ready to head east, maybe see some green trees. No other reason to go. Just new scenery. While he waited for someone to pick him up, he showered, ate, and then sat slumped at a table in front of McDonald's, drinking coffee and looking as presentable as possible.

Once in a while, a trucker he knew would come by, slap him on his back and ask if he wanted to go their way. Most of the guys looked forward to some form of company, and Jay was an easy passenger. He listened more than talked, and he never shared what he heard.

None of the truckers he usually rode with were heading east, so he declined, saying, "Maybe next time." After a few hours of waiting, a trucker he didn't know walked over and sat at his table. Said he had heard Jay was looking for a ride east. Said his name was, Pete. After checking around, he learned Jay was a good passenger, and he would enjoy the company.

They both nodded, shook hands and made last trips to the bathroom before heading out. For a while, Jay was treated to silence, and after asking if it was okay, he napped for a few hours. He knew that after he woke up, he would be expected to listen.

Jay wasn't wrong. As soon as he was awake, Pete started talking. Truckers love new riders. They all had many stories to tell and with a new rider they knew their passenger had never heard them before. Not that it stopped most of them from sharing them over and over again. But the first time was always the best. Jay was used to it. It was the price he paid for the ride.

This one was telling the story of a trip he had taken last year. It had been an exciting job that took an interesting twist. Pete had picked up a girl heading to California and had been paid to do it by the father.

However, it turned out that wasn't true. It wasn't the father who needed to keep track of her. It was a guy named Grant who wanted to get the girl to California so he could kidnap her.

Jay let the words wash over him, nodding when it seemed appropriate, but mostly making grunting noises. It was essential to try to be somewhat social when hitching rides.

That way they sometimes fed you and let you keep on riding with them.

Jay didn't care where the truckers took him because he didn't know where he was going. Searching had been his life for so long that Jay was no longer interested in finding anything. He had almost forgotten what it was that started him on the road. Instead, Jay thought of himself as a fugitive. Always hiding. He wasn't stupid, though. He knew that he would never be able truly hide because what he was hiding from was himself. He was hiding from his memories.

However, this time if the story was true, it was more interesting than most that Jay had listened to. So he perked up which encouraged the trucker to tell more.

"Yep," he said, "They were trying to keep her friends distracted by looking for her, but in the end, it all worked out. She found her daughter. The man who hired him turned out to be a long lost uncle. Then she got married, and I was lucky to be invited. It was a happy ending."

Then the trucker said something about the place where the girl and her friends lived. Farm country, mountains, town, and trees. Just like thousands of places in the United States.

But something Pete said brought it all back to Jay in a rush. The images that had taken over his life. The memories that had sucked all joy from everything for as long as he could remember, which turned out to be a long time. Lifetimes of memories.

For the first time since he had gotten into the truck, Jay turned his full attention to the man who had given him a ride. What was his name? Oh yea, Pete.

Swallowing his natural impulse to be rude, he politely asked Pete for the name of the place. Then he waited with growing impatience while Pete told him about the town called Doveland.

****

A few days later, Pete Mann was still puzzled. He thought that he and Jay had been enjoying their time together. But something had happened. They had only been traveling for part of a day before Jay changed his mind about going east. Jay said that he did that kind of thing all the time. Said that out of the blue, he would have the urge to go someplace else, and since he wasn't tied down to any schedule, he went where his whims took him. It wasn't personal.

Pete dropped Jay off at the next truck stop on Route 80. They shook hands and parted on a friendly note. But something didn't feel right to Pete.

So Pete picked up his cell phone and made a call. Could he stop by on his way home? He would be there in a few days. His face creased into a happy smile hearing Ava's excited answer that they couldn't wait to see him. Was he ready to do some baby cuddling? Assuring her that he was honored to be an adopted granddad, Pete hung up feeling the warmth of belonging to this new extended family.

However, something was still bothering him about his passenger. He had learned enough to know that he needed to follow his feelings and trust his instincts. When he got to Doveland, he would tell them about the passenger who called himself Jay. In the meantime, he could do one more thing. He would ask his fellow truckers to keep a look out for Jay and let Pete know if they saw him or gave him another ride. There was no need for explanations. It was a brotherhood. On the road, you needed one.

Two

Ava hung up the phone and did a little happy dance in her bare feet on the kitchen floor. Pete was coming to town. She couldn't wait to tell Evan. She knew he would be as excited as she was about seeing Pete.

Evan was behind the house, working in the bunkhouse, which meant she would have to cross the muddy yard to get to him, so she slipped on her shoes. They needed gravel paths. She would add it to the list of repairs and updates that were accumulating. The first order of business, though, was the bunkhouse. It had been standing empty since last summer, but they hadn't gotten around to fixing it up. Too many other things took priority.

But in a few months, it would be put to use again when everyone came to visit for Ben's christening. That meant they couldn't put off the fix-up project any longer. When they had bought the property, Ava and Evan knew there would be some repair work needed, but didn't have time to do it before the wedding. No one seemed to notice at the time.

That was my fault, Ava thought, but then stopped herself. Yes, she should have told everyone about the letters and she should have never run away, but it all worked out.

Besides, if she hadn't run away, they never would have met Pete. Or perhaps they would never have found Hannah or Hank. Or Grace might not have moved to town.

There were too many blessings to count and at the top of the list was what she was now. She was Ava Anders. She and Evan had settled into a reasonably peaceful existence after all the excitement last summer. On the other hand, some people might not think that what they had done since then was peaceful. But comparatively, it was heaven.

Evan had officially adopted her daughter Hannah. It was almost as if Evan and Hannah had been father and daughter before, because they had bonded immediately. It was Evan that Hannah went to when she didn't understand something or needed an extra hug.

Perhaps it is because Hannah is sensitive to our new arrival, and wants to give me a break, Ava thought. Ben did take up more time than she ever thought was possible. The past few weeks had been sleepless. But neither she nor Evan complained. No matter how much work Ben was, having him was worth every sleepless night and a house filled with baby things.

They knew that they could have lost everything when Grant had set his sights on destroying their Circle. But Grant had been arrested, and the Circles had only gained in strength.

Ava opened the baby monitor on her phone. Ben should sleep for another hour or so, time enough to slip over to the bunkhouse and talk to Evan. She wasn't sure if Pete was only stopping by, or if they could convince him to stay longer. Either way, she wanted to be ready for him.

****

"Mom, mom," Hannah yelled as she flung open the front door and ran into the house searching for her mother. Ava came out of the baby's room and tried to arrange her face into a disapproving look at the noise Hannah was making. But it was hard. Seeing her daughter so happy and full of energy was just too incredible.

Hannah's grandfather was right behind her, not bothering to hide his smile. Eric Jones counted his blessings every moment of his life. The day he decided to change his life forever by taking Ava's mom home after finding her at the clinic where he worked, was the watershed of his life. He wasn't sure how many more years he had left, but Eric knew they would be devoted to making sure he did whatever he could for Ava, Hannah, and her new brother, Ben.

Her mother's stern look did not deter Hannah. "Is Pete coming, mom? Can I make him his favorite cookies?" she asked while tugging on Ava's t-shirt.

Ava looked at Eric. "How does she know?" she asked.

"You mean he is?" Eric said. Their eyes met over Hannah's head, both of them thinking that perhaps they needed to pay more attention to what Hannah knew and how she knew it. They hadn't discouraged or encouraged the gifts that seemed to run in the family, and now it appeared that Hannah might have them too.

"Yes, he is, and yes you can, but first, I need your help with Ben, and then homework. Perhaps we could talk your grandfather into staying for dinner."

Eric nodded. Of course he would.

After the wedding last summer Eric had gone home, packed up his apartment in Carlsbad, and moved to Pennsylvania. It was the right decision. He hadn't known how lonely he had become after Ava's mother, Abbie, died.

In a way, he was coming home. Concourse, the town where he had met Abbie, was less than thirty minutes away. Coming back to the area was like closing a loop.

Ava and Evan had said he could live with them. They had plenty of room. But he turned them down. Instead, he had moved to a small house just a few miles down the road in the village of Doveland. Eric liked his privacy and his quiet time. But he took every chance he got to spend time with his adopted family.

Eric was happy Pete was coming, but he wondered about the reason. Eric might not have those extra spidey senses that his adoptive family seemed to have, but he could tell when something was coming their way that they needed to pay attention to.

Pete was bringing more than himself. He was bringing a warning. But of what?

Three

Grace closed the door behind her and took in the room. Perfectionist that she was, she knew it would never be finished, but was it ready enough for the opening the next day? Her favorite day of the year—May 1st. Her eyes rested on the cherry wood bookshelves that lined the walls, each one filled with books waiting for someone to take them home and read them. A potbellied stove stood in the middle of the room burning with a small fire. It glowed with just enough heat to take the chill out of the store, and provide the welcoming look she wanted. It was still cool enough outside to need the heat, and in the summer, she would light candles inside.

She had placed round wood tables around the room, with plenty of room for the three small chairs set around them. Booths with wood seats made from old church pews lined one wall. Every booth and every table had access to free internet and a plug for their laptops. She envisioned a book or two being written right there in that room.

Tables and booths all had a sprig of fresh flowers in the middle. It meant changing the vases every day, but it would be worth it. In the back of the room, on the right, Grace had arranged two large deep-purple chairs divided by a small table and a reading lamp. The same set-up was duplicated in the front of the room, on the left, by the windows. They were perfect for small talk or reading on your own.

Each wall was a different shade of mauve. Grace and Mandy shared their love of that color. The entire front span of the store was heavy glass facing out into the village square. No one would know by looking, but the window was bullet proof. See-through pull-down shades would help with the late afternoon sun. Although the store sported a tin ceiling, Grace had made sure that a substantial noise damping system was in place behind it and in the walls. There would be no echoing of voices in this room. Instead, it felt like a library with coffee and food. It wasn't a big space, but it felt spacious and cozy at the same time. *The power of color and design,* Grace thought.

Taking a deep breath, she filled her nose with the heavenly scent of baking cookies being prepared for the opening. Cookies would be their first bakery product. They were starting with cookies because they were easy to make and universally loved. However, if all went well, they would expand into a variety of delicious treats.

Tomorrow, the deeply satisfying smell of coffee would join the aroma of baked goods. The scents would not just be inside the shop, they would also waft out into the surrounding area. A friend of hers who worked on the construction crew that came to town last summer had installed a discreet vent that blew the aroma outside. It was their little secret. But she was sure no one would mind that the town square carried the smell of home.

"Is that you, Grace?" Mandy asked coming out of the small kitchen wiping her hands on her apron. She is a sight to behold, thought Grace.

Mandy Mink's auburn hair was still pulled back into a ponytail, and her jeans still had stylish holes in them, but instead of the drawn and worried look she had last spring, her face had returned to its natural beauty.

Today, though, flour spotted her face and bits of hair were falling out of her ponytail. But her smile was all that Grace cared about. Mandy was happy. Or happier. Happier than when she had first brought Hannah to Ava, having kept her safe for years before returning her to her mother.

It didn't take much to persuade Mandy to move to Doveland. She had nothing left in California. Some people were worried about Grace taking Mandy under her wing. But Mandy had been broken, and Grace knew how to fix broken. She only picked the ones she knew wanted to be whole again, and Mandy definitely qualified for that. So last summer, Grace told Mandy a secret dream that she had carried with her for years.

Grace had decided that she was old enough, and in the right place to fulfill that dream, but she needed help. She couldn't do it by herself.

She asked Mandy if she would be interested in helping her achieve the dream, and do it in Doveland. At first, Mandy said, no, thinking that Grace was offering her charity. But when Grace brought her to the abandoned store front that faced the town square and described the plan, Mandy had only one question; "Who is going to pay for this?"

And that's when Grace told Mandy another secret. For years she had stashed away money in an account she called her "dream account."

Over the years, she had added to it. Not because she thought it would come true, but because she believed in the principle of being prepared in case the dream showed up at her door. She wanted to be able to open that door and say, "Yes I can."

Eight months ago that dream had knocked, and Grace was ready. And it turned out so was Mandy. It took every bit of their time and Grace's money to get it right. They wouldn't have it any other way.

Grace had the business designed so that there were two apartments above the store. She had one. Mandy had the other. Mandy had saved a tiny bit of money to help build the store, but Grace still made her a fifty-fifty partner. Grace wanted Mandy to know that she was trusted. And it was true. Grace could never have done it by herself. Besides, she wanted Mandy to have a future, and it gave her a deep sense of satisfaction to give it to her.

Mandy walked to the front of the store, stood next to Grace, put her arm around her and held her close. Together they surveyed what they had done. They had built a business and a home. It was perfect.

Tomorrow, the first day of May, the doors would open. Their business and Grace's treasured dream, a coffee shop and bakery within a bookstore, would come to fruition. The sign was going up the first thing in the morning. It was simple and true. In bold white lettering across a turquoise blue background, it would read, "Your Second Home."

Four

Pete had done what Jay asked of him. He dropped him off at a truck stop. Jay wanted Pete to think that everything was normal, that he had just decided to go in a different direction. But it wasn't true. He didn't want to go in a different direction. He wanted to head straight to the town that Pete called Doveland. Everything Pete said about Doveland felt like the place that he had been dreaming about for as long as he could remember. People say that you can't remember what you did as a child, but Jay knew that wasn't always the case.

He remembered his childhood. He remembered more than one childhood. Some people might think that was a good thing. Jay knew it wasn't. It was a nightmare. Each day he had to figure out what lifetime he was living.

Was it this one, the one he was living now? Or was it the one before, when he looked the same and felt the same? It would have been easier if he remembered himself as a woman, or a Chinese man, or something entirely different. No, he remembered himself as this person.

What made it even more difficult, was that the world was much the same. He had died only thirty years before. Some people were alive now that were alive then.

Except for advances in technology, many things had stayed the same.

So as a child, Jay had felt as if he was one person living two existences. Figuring out which one was which—and when—made him angry and withdrawn. If he made a mistake when he talked to his parents, thinking it was the parents or times that he had before, they believed either that he was crazy, or trying to make them crazy. In the end, they decided on both. And that meant his parents didn't like Jay or want him. To save himself, Jay learned some extra skills, ones that he hadn't learned in the last lifetime.

The first thing he learned was how to fight. It started young. His older brother thought it was funny to push him over as he learned to walk. It progressed from there. Every chance he got, his brother made Jay cry until he learned not to complain—which only made the beatings worse.

His brother got more and more violent. Jay always felt that his parents knew what was happening, but they didn't care. Perhaps they hoped an accident would take place and they would be relieved of their burden of this unwanted son.

Even in school, the kids called him names because he would get confused about where he was and what was happening. Eventually, they took the cue from his brother and started beating on him until he cried or passed out. That lasted until he was eight, and then he learned to fight. More accurately, Jay remembered how to fight. Once that happened, he loved fighting and would seek it out at every opportunity.

By then, his parents were afraid of him. He knew things he shouldn't know, and he had a hair-trigger temper. After one outburst too many, they passed him off to the system. A system that didn't like Jay or want him any more than his current parents did.

This only increased his hatred of the people in this lifetime. As he fought his way through childhood, Jay was passed from person to person, institution to institution.

When Jay neared his middle teens, he learned something even better than fighting. He learned how to retreat into the other life that he remembered. He retreated as often as possible into those memories because in that lifetime he was loved and cherished. No one taught him to do it. It happened because he was desperate for relief. It became the only solution to an increasingly terrible existence.

Jay discovered that in his retreat, he could get along with people. Not get to know them, not like them, not have a life with them, but get along with them. This new skill made his last year in high school tolerable. Jay never had a problem with school work. After all, he remembered everything he had learned in the last lifetime, so there was very little to learn.

If he had had parents that appreciated him in this lifetime, he would have been hailed as a prodigy rather than a terror. The only saving grace in Jay's young life was the teacher or two who saw beneath the fighting and belligerence and recognized a confused, but talented child. To those teachers, he was a model student. To everyone else, he was the freaky outcast.

As soon as Jay turned eighteen, he left the latest home he had been assigned to behind. He left the dirt and the grime and the fighting and the hatred, and started walking. He had a memory in his head of an event and a place, and he wanted to find it. Walking provided an outlet for his confusion. He began to learn how to truly separate the lifetime he lived in now from the lifetime from the past, that he remembered so clearly.

Jay realized that he could remember more than one other lifetime, but he learned to wall the other ones off. It was hard enough to remember one and live in another.

He had the life he was living now, where every moment held the potential of a nightmare, and the one he lived in before which had turned from love and happiness into a nightmare.

He supported himself by doing odd jobs along the way. He could repair anything, especially old farm equipment. Some of it he had learned in his last lifetime. He could cook, build houses, and even play the guitar when someone had one nearby. Jay chose not to learn the new technology of this lifetime.

He liked his last one without that complication so much more. With lifetimes of memories already in his head, he didn't need or want all the information that came people's way through technology.

If Jay couldn't earn his way honestly, he stole what he needed. Usually, he got away with it without being noticed. But if caught, he fought his way out of it and would disappear down the next road.

Eventually, he got tired of walking and started hitchhiking. It was when he got picked up by his first trucker that Jay learned he could travel mostly for free, if he were willing to listen, and to never give away the fact that he was a person who had two lives. One he had loved. One he hated.

When Pete told him about Doveland, Jay's past life moved to his present one. It sounded like the place he had been looking for as long as he had been living in this lifetime.

But Jay had wisdom born of experience. He knew that Pete picked something up from his reaction, and it would be dangerous to go directly there. That included not hitching a ride on any more trucks. So he was back to walking. It didn't matter how long it took him to get there. The place would still be there when he arrived.

Jay knew that the people he loved were long gone. Jay also knew that something else would still be there. Something that scared him. The pain would still be there. He wasn't sure he could take more pain. He didn't know if going there would take it away. He didn't know, but he had to try.

Five

Pete arrived in town just in time for Your Second Home's grand opening. He had to park his truck in the town's parking lot behind the bank. Not only because he was driving a big rig, but because he was sure that every parking place around the square would be filled. Ava had warned him that there would be a significant crowd, something he found hard to believe.

Why would there be a large crowd for the opening of a coffee shop? Then he remembered who was opening it. Grace, the town's adopted busybody. Everyone loved her, and she appeared to love everyone back. She had an over-flowing abundance of kindness and wisdom, which, even though she had only been in town for a few months, had been felt by everyone.

Sarah Morgan had sent Grace to Doveland to watch over her friends. Pete laughed to himself, remembering that no one actually sent Grace to Doveland. Grace had firmly decided that she was needed and she came to help. She wanted to be part of whatever they were up to. Sarah knew that she would never be able to stop her, so she sent Grace to Andy and Sam who were running the Diner. It was the perfect cover to discover everything about everybody. Which Grace did magnificently!

I guess Grace really loves it here if she opened a store, thought Pete as he parked. Getting out of his truck, he could hear laughing, talking, and what sounded like singing coming from the town square. Rounding the corner, Pete couldn't believe what he was seeing. *Everybody in town must be here,* he thought. There were balloons, lights, and three women were singing on a makeshift platform in the middle of the square. Traffic was moving slowly around the square because people had flowed out into the street. A few police officers were trying in vain to shoo them up onto the sidewalk. But no one, including the drivers, was paying much attention.

The crowd was so thick he couldn't see Grace's new store and wondered which direction he should go to get there. Then he heard Hannah calling his name, "Granddad, over here!" and following the voice, saw her running towards him ducking under arms and through legs to get to him. Reaching him, she jumped up into his arms and kissed him on the cheek.

"Come on, mom and dad and grandfather are waiting for you."

Grabbing his hand, she pulled him effortlessly through the crowd which seemed to part for her, and headed to where a group of small tables had been set up on the green.

As Pete had grown older he found it harder and harder to contain his emotions, so he wasn't surprised to find tears in his eyes when he saw Ava with a baby in her arms, surrounded by the two men that adored her. *Well, make that three,* he thought as he hugged her and Ben at the same time.

"I know, it is a little loud to talk, Pete, but I wanted you to see the support that Grace and Mandy are receiving for their new place. Of course, Mandy knows how to put on a show, and everyone loves free food and coffee, but they are bringing this town back to life, don't you think?"

Pete nodded and reached for the baby, and Ava happily handed Ben over to him.

"We'll get you a coffee and some cookies at the free table." Ava pointed at a long table set off to the side, which had a surprisingly orderly line of people making their way around it. "See, free," she said and went off with Evan and Eric to get food for all of them, leaving Hannah and Ben with Pete.

"Mom has something to talk to you about Pete," Hannah said. "It's a surprise."

"She does? Do you know what it is? Did she tell you?"

"No, she didn't tell me, but I know anyway. I know I can tell you these things, Pete, but with most people I pretend that I don't know things that no one has told me."

"Yes, Hannah, you can always tell me these things, but probably it will be best to let your mom tell me this time. We don't want to ruin her surprise, do we? Does your mom know that you know things?"

"Well, I think she has started to figure it out. It's how I knew her before I met her. I told mom I knew her from the pictures that Auntie Mandy showed me, but that wasn't completely true."

"I am sure everyone in your family will understand and want to know more, Hannah. I wish I had these gifts that all of you do."

"Oh, but you do," squealed Hannah.

"You do what?" asked Ava, as she slipped into the seat beside Hannah.

"Mom, could I tell you later?" Hannah asked.

Ava looked back and forth between Pete and Hannah and nodded. Pete smiled at her, looking happier than she had ever seen him.

Little Ben lifted his wobbly head and stared directly at him and smiled, and then laid his head back down on Pete's shoulder and fell asleep.

"He smiled at you, Pete. I believe that is the first smile he has given. He is as happy to see you as we are."

"You got that right," Evan said giving Pete a gentle slap on the back.

*****

The crowd hung around for another few hours. Grace and Mandy eventually made it out to see their friends in the square but could only stay a few minutes. Even with all the volunteer help, they were overwhelmed and too busy to do more than hug everyone and thank them for coming.

Afterwards, Ava, Evan, and Ben went back to the house leaving Hannah with Pete and Eric. Hannah couldn't get enough of the crowd. It was if she absorbed the energy and joy and made it her own. By the time Pete and Eric convinced her to leave, by reminding her that she could ride in the truck, they were both drained and ready for a nap.

Hannah thought it was the best thing ever that she and Eric could ride in Pete's truck. Pete and Eric had to hold her hand to keep her from skipping ahead. Once they got there, she had to be hoisted up to the seat, and even Eric needed a bit of assistance to step into the cab.

As they pulled out of town, Hannah said, "So was that last guy in here a nice guy?"

"Why do you ask?" Pete said.

"Cause he is coming to see me," Hannah replied.

As if realizing that she had said too much, she added, "Just pretending. I figured there must have been someone riding with you cause you always pick up hitchhikers. Didn't you pick up my mom and that's how you met?"

Hannah didn't miss the look Pete gave Eric over her head before answering. "Yep, that's how I met your mom, and I do think the last guy was pretty nice. He did seem interested in Doveland, so perhaps he will make his way here someday."

"Cool," Hannah said, but reminded herself not to say more. Yes, she knew who was coming, and he wasn't a happy guy at all. In fact, Hannah was more than a little scared of him because he was so angry. If she needed to, she would tell everyone, but since she was only nine, almost ten, she wasn't sure anyone would believe her.

On the other hand, she could contact Sarah and talk to her. Hannah loved having a direct line to Sarah and Leif. They had told her they were always there for her, but to use the direct line sparingly. Otherwise, the phone worked just fine.

Pete had Roy Orbison songs on a continual loop in his truck, along with The Traveling Wilburys albums. He and Eric appeared to be completely distracted by the music. *It's good stuff,* Hannah thought, remembering how much she and her mom had enjoyed them the last time she lived here. That information was indeed something she was going to keep to herself.

Six

Back at the house, Hannah remained a bubbling fountain of joy. Everyone else was ready for a nap, so Ava asked Hannah to play in her room while they all got some rest. They agreed that they would convene on the back deck for dinner in a few hours. Ava had arranged for food to be delivered from the Thai restaurant in town so that she could rest while Ben slept, instead of cooking. Everyone agreed that it was the perfect solution.

With a promise to see each other in a few hours, they all headed off to their rooms. Even though Eric had a home in town, he also had a bedroom at the house. It made it easy for him to stay overnight when he was needed, or to take an afternoon nap in times like this. Pete had his favorite space in the bunkhouse. Evan and Ava headed to their bedroom with Ben, and Hannah went to her room. She loved that she had been allowed to decorate it herself with a little help from her mom.

As quiet settled over the house in Doveland, Pennsylvania, Jay was busy walking down a small back road in Kentucky where his last ride in a pickup truck, filled with farm equipment, had dropped him off. It wasn't taking him as long as he thought to get where he was going.

Jay had found it almost impossible to be patient about getting rides. Instead of meandering through life as he had been doing for the past few years, he had a clear direction. He knew he was heading for his destiny, and it both scared him and focused him. There was no turning back now. One way or another he would find out what happened and do what needed to be done about it.

Hannah lay quietly on her bed. She was thinking about the man that was heading towards them. There was nothing to do but wait. Turning over onto her side, Hannah closed her eyes. A nap wasn't a bad idea after all.

****

A few hours later everyone had trickled out of their rooms and started gathering on the back deck. Pete had awakened earlier than everyone else and had spent an hour walking around Evan and Ava's property. He loved the open fields surrounded by woods. It was the perfect blend of peace and quiet, and the perpetual motion of nature. The birds were still in their mating season, so the woods and the fields rang with their calls.

Evan had installed bluebird boxes, and Pete couldn't believe how beautiful the birds were as they flitted through the fields and sat on top of the tiny houses surveying their territory. Sitting on a rock on the edge of the woods and looking at the beauty surrounding him, Pete starting thinking about his life.

His wife, Barbara, had recovered from her illness, but it had shocked them both into realizing that their time together could be over at any moment. He had already reduced his driving time away from home, but perhaps it was time to do something different. Something that he and Barbara could do together. But what? Almost all their savings had gone to medical bills.

Now they would only have their small social security checks to live on. Being an independent trucker his whole life, he didn't have a pension, and Barbara had stayed home and raised the kids working as a waitress when they needed extra cash.

They wouldn't change a moment of it, but it left them with very few options. Pete decided if he were willing for there to be something for him to do, something would come to him. And he was definitely willing.

By the time he got to the back deck, everyone was there, including Mira, Grace, and Mandy. They said they were too wired to stop for the day, and besides, they couldn't wait to see Pete. Ava had ordered plenty of food thinking that the three of them would probably stop by.

As they ate, they caught up with each other. Mira and her twin brother Tom had each bought houses with a few acres adjacent to Evan and Ava's property. However, Tom got restless within a few months, so after fixing up his property he had gone back to traveling the world with his Good Old Dudes club—formally known as Good Old Boys. Mira had insisted on the name change, figuring women could be dudes and now there could be women in the group, beginning with her. Besides, the anagram was just too perfect to pass up.

Mira was in charge of the administration of the group which had become much more organized since she took over. Mira had a purpose, and she was happy in Doveland, so their arrangement was perfect for her. She watched over both their homes and their friends. Tom came back every few months to see everyone. But Mira was sure that Mandy was one of the biggest reasons for his checking in.

After eating, they all settled back to watch the sun glide lower in the sky. It had grown cooler, but jackets and a fire took the chill off.

Finally, not being able to keep still any longer, Hannah blurted out, "When are you going to tell Pete the secret?

Ava laughed, "Well it's not really a secret. It's an idea."

"And a darn good idea too," Eric burst out. "Just say yes!"

"Hard to say yes to an idea that I don't know, but since I trust you all, okay, yes!"

"Yay," Hannah said leaping into Pete's lap. "Now I will see you all the time."

Pete hugged Hannah and turned to the crowd, "What did I just say yes to?"

Ava paused, and Grace, tired of waiting for her to respond, blurted out, "Opening the Diner!"

"Wait. What? First, I don't know anything about opening diners. Second, I don't have the funds to do something like that. And then third and most importantly, isn't it open now with Sam and Andy running it?"

"Excuse these excited people, Pete. They have been planning this idea for a long time," Evan said, "Let me give you some answers. First, the fact that you don't know how to open a diner. That's okay. We are going to bring someone in to teach you and get it started. As for funds, we are your partners. All of us."

Seeing Pete start to object, Evan continued, "Wait, don't stop me now. It's more than the fact we want to thank you for bringing Ava home to us, along with Hannah and Eric. For that, I will never be able to repay you. This small thing is a drop in the bucket for us.

"It's more than that. We want to help rebuild the community of Doveland into a place that the current residents can thrive within, and we, the new kids in town, will be safe and happy. So that's why we will be your partners. You will own the Diner, but we will help with funds and labor as needed. It's a big picture, and we would love for you to be part of it.

"As for the Diner being open now. No, it isn't. Sam's cover as a cook was blown after the operation to take down Grant's organization took place last summer, and the FBI needed him back in the field. He and Hank are working together. That's another story that we promise to share. However, you will see Sam in town once in a while. There appears to be an attraction here that keeps pulling him back."

All eyes turned to look at Mira who turned bright red and looked away.

"What about Andy? Where did he go?" Pete asked.

"Andy went back to his real name of Gillian and returned to the Forest Circle, and that was the end of the Diner. Until now. Or at least we all hope, until now."

Pete looked around at the family he had acquired in the past year. Every one of them someone he felt drawn to and trusted. "Best make a call to Barbara," he said and started walking to the bunkhouse. As soon as his back was turned, tears streamed down his face. "Thank you, God," he whispered. No other words were needed.

Seven

The next morning Hannah woke filled with just as much excitement as she had when she went to sleep. She wanted—no needed—to ask Pete if he had decided for real, and she didn't want to wait for breakfast to hear the answer. Instead, Hannah decided that she would slip outside and confront Pete in the bunkhouse. She thought it was better that way because if he had changed his mind, he might be embarrassed to say so around other people.

Hannah didn't believe that would be the answer, but still, she thought it was best to be direct. She dressed quickly for school, marveling at the beautiful collection of clothes in her closet, and slipped on boots so her shoes wouldn't get wet as she crossed the lawn that was still damp from the dew. She agreed with her mom. They needed gravel paths.

She hoped that Pete was awake, but if he wasn't, she knew how to get him up. It worked with Evan every time.

But she didn't get a chance to try it out because Pete saw Hannah crossing the lawn. Pete flung open the bunkhouse door and nodded yes.

Ava, watching through the kitchen window, saw Hannah running, and Pete scoop her up and then swing her around in circles with both of them laughing. She knew what that meant. It was her turn to say, "Thank you, God."

Breakfast was a joyous but slightly rushed affair, and everyone worked together to get Hannah ready to go to school. Homework needed to be collected and arranged in her backpack along with her books. Evan was in charge of packing the lunch box. Hannah liked that he was the one who made her lunch because he would always tuck a treat in under the napkin. And he wrote notes, too. She would often find a little message or picture drawn inside the napkin where only she could see it. Hannah didn't carry grudges or wish things had been easier when she little. She knew her adopted mother didn't want her. But that taught her how to recognize love, and instead of being sad that she had not been loved, she was happy because Hannah knew that now she was, without question.

There was a bus that would pick her up to take her to school, but Eric always insisted he would drive her, claiming that it reminded him of Hannah's grandmother Abbie. Then he would add that he didn't have that much time left to do this kind of thing, so he was enjoying every moment of his time with his adopted family. Everyone's habitual response to his claiming to be old was to say something about his living forever, but Ava saw something in his eyes that told her that he knew otherwise.

After breakfast, Evan and Ava invited Pete into Evan's office to talk about the details of opening the Diner. Some questions needed to be answered. Some were simple. To the question, would he keep the same name, the answer was, yes.

The Diner had been a staple in Doveland for years, and Pete wanted to continue the tradition. He also wanted to replace anything broken and worn with the same vintage look.

The exception was the appliances. Evan insisted that everything would be brand-new and the best on the market. But those things would not be seen by the public. Pete would get his wish. The Diner would look and feel the same as it had for the past sixty years. It would just have a little face-lift.

Mira, Grace, and Mandy would handle the marketing, mostly by word of mouth. It would be easy. All they had to do was start talking about it, creating anticipation, and letting the news spread through the village.

Pete had the most significant questions. How would he know what to do? He knew nothing about running a diner. Evan assured him that the consultant he had hired was ready to help him with everything. Pete would have twenty-four hour access to him using the internet for the lessons, and text and phone calls for details.

What they needed the most was a short order cook, or Pete would need to learn to cook. "Might not be that hard," he said when Evan asked him about it. "Let me give it a try and see how I do."

Barbara, of course, would wait on tables, and get help from the local young population. Pete had an idea he would be a decent mentor to kids wanting to learn about the world. He had seen enough of it.

The financial details were the hardest for Pete to handle. Not because he had to come up with money, but because he didn't. Evan and Ava's plan was simple. They had already purchased the Diner from the previous owner. For a year they would continue to own the Diner and pay all the bills associated with running it, including buying food and paying for any additional staff that Barbara and Pete would need. Pete and Barbara would keep all the profits.

Each year they would turn over twenty-five percent ownership and twenty-five percent of the cost of the restaurant to Pete and Barbara. In four years, the Diner would be entirely theirs. If along the way, they decided that running a diner was not for them, they could walk away, owing nothing.

Pete was stunned. "I know you are grateful to me for driving Ava and then bringing her home, but I didn't do anything more than that. You really don't owe me anything, and I find it almost impossible to accept this offer."

"I've told you, Pete, that what you did can never be repaid, but the terms of this deal are not as much for your benefit as it is for ours. We have the money to do good things, and we want to do it for this village, and the people we love. It's a selfish motive because we get the emotional high from doing this. And because it's close to home, we can see and experience the results.

"If you could, wouldn't you do the same thing for those you love? Please give us this gift and say 'yes.'"

Pete looked at Ava and Evan, so earnest in their desire and nodded yes, "Where do I sign?" he asked.

****

Before Pete left town, Evan and Ava arranged a date for him to return to Doveland with Barbara. The plan was to pack what they needed, put the house on the market, and come back in time for the summer solstice celebration that was being planned by the village. It would be a quick turnaround since it was only seven weeks away, but Pete thought it was possible.

What he hadn't told them was how happy his call had made Barbara. Her reaction took him entirely by surprise. He had no idea how lonely she had been since the kids had grown up and moved away.

His call answered her prayers. She wanted more time with her husband, and she wanted friends.

Last summer when they had visited Doveland for Evan and Ava's wedding Barbara had fallen in love with the area and the people. But not wanting to pressure Pete, she had only said that she hoped they would visit again soon.

So Pete's call made her happier than she had been in a long time. She told Pete she would have the house on the market by the time he came home, and he believed her.

Pete was so excited by the prospect of building a new life together with his wife and his new friends he forgot about why he had stopped in Doveland in the first place. His passenger, Jay was completely forgotten.

Eight

Pete might have forgotten Jay, but Jay had not forgotten Pete.

For the first time in this lifetime, Jay had a lead that would enable him to complete his mission. Find the life he remembered, and take revenge against the person who had destroyed it.

Jay had heard about people who remembered their past lives. But none of them ever described the hell that he lived in every day. Every morning two lives greeted him. Both of them felt real. Each morning he had to remember which one was the one he was living, and which one was a memory.

Other people described remembering their past lives in flashbacks, or like a dream that would poke its head up once in a while. Or being able to do a skill better than anyone could expect. Child prodigies. "Perhaps they are accessing past lives" people would say, and think that it would be a fantastic thing to have happen to them.

Jay's experience was different. His memories didn't fade. They didn't poke up into his life to be helpful. His past lifetime was always present. His memories were relentless. It was not wonderful. It was not fantastic.

As a child, he was constantly confused. He remembered himself as a grownup, but when he looked at himself in the mirror, he saw a little boy. It was the same little boy that became the man. Jay was sure that if he found a picture of himself from his past life, he would look the same as he had throughout this lifetime.

But one thing would be different. Jay would look happy. He wouldn't look as if he had been beaten with a stick that day, which was a regular occurrence. Sometimes physically, always mentally.

Jay remembered parents that loved him. Parents who doted on the little boy that had come along late in their life. He remembered warm breakfasts, flannel shirts, a fishing pole in one hand, and his father's hand in the other. He remembered laughter.

He learned hard work in the past lifetime. His parents owned a farm, and the gift of a son was also a gift of another worker on the farm. Sometimes, the fact that he had so many chores to do before school would make him grumpy, but the chickens talking to him as he walked out into the yard with their soothing clucks, always brought him out of his mood.

Now, he would give anything to be back in that lifetime. Because in this lifetime, he grew up in a city with parents who didn't like him or want him. There were no warm breakfasts, laughing, or hand holding. There were only angry voices, dirt, and lonely days when he was locked in the house while his parents went out to a party or just to punish him for existing.

Before he learned better, he would tell them stories about growing up before. They thought he was crazy. Perhaps he was.

Jay thought that since he couldn't get back to the other lifetime, it would be heaven to forget. He tried everything.

Jay used every kind of drug that he could find. He tried drinking himself into a stupor. In his last lifetime, that abuse killed him. In this lifetime, none of it helped. It made it worse because when the drug or alcohol wore off the memories would still be there.

Some days he would stand in front of a mirror and try to fuse the two people together. He saw a man who was neither handsome or ugly. The description that came to mind was standard issue.

On the short side, but wiry, just as he remembered himself from before. He even had the emerald green eyes that he had the last time around. Green eyes and dark curly hair. Girls liked his look. One girl in particular. But that was the last lifetime. This one, he stayed away from them as much as he could. He couldn't take any more heartache.

Jay couldn't understand why he had been chosen to be tortured with these memories. The worst part was, he couldn't remember the important things. He couldn't remember where the farm was located. He couldn't remember his past name or his family's name. It made him so angry sometimes it felt as if his head would explode from the pressure that was always building up inside of him. What good were memories if they didn't help you find who you were?

Eventually, traveling helped. New places each day. New faces, no friends, no one who knew him so if he made a mistake about which lifetime he was in, no one would lock him away.

After traveling randomly for a few years, Jay realized that even though he couldn't remember the name of where he came from, he remembered the feeling. If he saw the same rolling hills, he would know them. So Jay's traveling became more focused as he looked for places with rolling hills and farms.

But nothing rang familiar until Pete picked him up. Then everything changed.

Doveland sounded like the place he used to live. If it turned out to be the place, he would find out who had killed his family, and he would take his revenge. He would release the anger, so it no longer ran his life. That's what he wanted. It was what he needed. Nothing else mattered.

Jay thought it was strange that on July 1st he would be the same age he was in the past lifetime when he died. It took him five years to kill himself with drink and drugs after his family was taken from him. He would be thirty years old. Time was closing in on him.

After over a week of taking his time getting there, he had arrived. He rented a room in a motel thirty minutes away from Doveland. He was allowing himself to be hopeful because the countryside felt like home. He was almost positive this was the place. Of all the memories he wished that he had, it was the one of home.

It was ironic that he remembered everything that happened before in that lifetime. But when that terrible fire occurred, he forgot all the relevant details.

The name of the place was erased from his memory along with what led up to the tragedy and most everything that happened after that. But then, not remembering after the fire, was on purpose.

It was if his life ended at twenty-five, thirty-five years ago, and now he was going to have a chance to both remember it and fix it. Then he could go on with this life, hopefully without the anger that burned inside of him every moment of the day.

That meant he would have to kill that person first. But he didn't care.

He would send to hell whoever did that terrible thing to his family, and if that person deserved to have forgiveness, he could find his way back in another lifetime. If not, too bad. Jay knew what hell felt like. Let him feel it too.

But it would take planning. Jay couldn't head directly into town without a plan. Being dumped from one foster home to another in this lifetime had taught him well about getting the lay of the land before being seen.

He had to find a job first, and become just another person who lived there. Then he could start finding out what he needed to know. Plus, he needed to make money so he could find a place to stay.

In the meantime, he would stay as invisible as possible while checking out Doveland and the surrounding areas. If all went well, he would find his past and create a new future for himself.

Nine

Hank was careful not to be seen. It was the story of his life, he thought. Don't be seen. As a child, stay away from the abusive father. Then hide after killing him. Hide as a bad guy after Grant picked him up out of the streets and taught him how to be evil on purpose.

Now he was hiding to be good. Not that he thought he would ever truly be good. Perhaps he was born bad, but at least he was good enough to save his little sister. Where was the line drawn between good and evil? If you did evil things for a good reason, did that make it good?

Hank had no idea. All he knew is that once he found Ava, his sister's daughter, another switch flipped in his life. No longer was Hank running away. No longer was he trying to be the worst bad guy he could be. Now he was running towards something. Now he was choosing to be as good as a person with a horrible past could be.

Which was why he was being extra careful. He couldn't take any chances that Lenny or another of his goons he collected would see him meeting Sam.

Usually, he and Sam didn't meet at all. They used encrypted software on public computers. The fact that they were taking a chance of being seen together worried Hank, but he knew that Sam would not risk it if it weren't important.

It took Hank two hours to get to the meeting place. He drove in circles to see if he was being followed. Then he walked in circles to check again. He waited in coffee houses and browsed in bookstores.

Once he was satisfied that he was alone, he headed to the address that Sam had sent him. It turned out to be a hole-in-the-wall diner. Good, he was hungry. Knowing Sam, he would be in the last booth with his back to the wall, facing the only door, and that was where Hank found him.

Last year, Hank had helped Sam and his FBI team capture all of Grant's crew except for Lenny. In return for his help, and his agreement to remain in Lenny's organization to be an informant, Hank's past was forgotten. *Forgotten, not forgiven,* Hank thought as he made his way back to Sam. No matter what happened in the future, Hank would never forgive himself for his past, and he was sure there were people who would agree with that assessment too.

Hank slid into the booth opposite Sam, answering the waitress as he did so that, "yes," he would like coffee. And then he took a look at his friend. Yes, friend. Sam had become more than the person he reported to. Sam had become his friend. It seemed impossible to Hank. Impossible that a goody-two-shoes like Sam would consider him his friend too, but he did.

As different as they were in temperament, they were in looks. Hank allowed himself to look older than he was. He was balding and enough of a sloppy dresser to be as invisible as possible. Underneath his loose clothing, he was a fit fifty-five year old, but he kept that fact well hidden.

Sam, on the other hand, stood out. Not intentionally, but he was too good looking to blend in. Military training gave him a bearing that couldn't be erased. He was tall and rugged looking with short cropped brown hair and dark blue eyes. Sam loved to dress well, so even dressed down he looked put together. Twenty-five years younger than Hank, Sam was just beginning his life. Hank knew that Sam hoped that Mira Michaels would become a bigger and bigger part of that life.

All the more reason to get rid of Lenny and allow Sam to go back to something a little less dangerous. Mira was Ava's friend. Hank planned to help them both have a happy, peaceful life. That he could have a happy and peaceful life seemed impossible. But that didn't mean the people he had grown to love couldn't.

The waitress appeared and took their order. They both ordered the Eggs Benedict with the works.

"Okay," Hank said. "What's so all-fire important that we need to see each other."

"Nice to see you too," Sam answered. They lifted their coffee cups towards each other in a salute.

"It's Grant."

Hank's heart skipped a beat. He knew no one as evil as Grant. It was too bad they didn't kill him when they found him. Instead, they had him locked away in solitary waiting trial. There was no chance he wouldn't be convicted of multiple crimes, including murder, but no one was in a rush to convict him. They were gathering enough evidence to lock him away forever. He would never get out on bail. He was as good as tried and sentenced.

Hank put his coffee cup down so hard that it sloshed over the edge, "What about Grant?"

Sam paused as their waitress put their breakfast in front of them. "Let's eat first. Tell me about Lenny."

Hank cut through the egg and watched it seep out. Perfect. "As we suspected, Lenny doesn't have the evil destroy-everything-good-in-the-world focus of Grant. He is more into making money. Perhaps if he lives long enough, he will become another Grant, but right now he is trying to make deals with at least one drug cartel to be a distributor.

"I think his long-term plan is to take over once he gets powerful enough. But I doubt that he will make it. Either you guys will take him down, or someone in the organization will. He is too quick tempered, and not wise enough. Grant didn't have time to adequately train him, I guess.

"It's good for me though. Lenny isn't asking me to do the evil things I did for Grant. It would be hard to fake that I won't do that anymore. Instead, I am the liaison between him and the people he wants to work for. Which means, you guys can choose how many of them you want to take down at one time."

Sam swabbed the last bite of his breakfast around the plate to get every bit of goodness and took a sip of coffee before answering.

"Hank, you are still taking him seriously, aren't you? He could be putting you out as a liaison to get rid of you if the deal goes bad. We can't take the chance of leaving you with him much longer. We'll take him down, and then find a way to make you safe.

"The problem is, we aren't the only ones who are out to take Lenny down." Sam stopped and looked at Hank. "It's Grant, Hank."

"What can Grant do? He's in prison."

"Was."

Hank slowly lowered his coffee cup trying to keep it from spilling, but his shaking hand gave him away. "Was?"

Sam nodded, his face etched with worry. "Was. Grant somehow faked an appendicitis attack. The ambulance drivers turned out to be members of some gang that he coerced to get him out. They put him in the ambulance and drove away. They found the ambulance with the dead attendants about fifty miles from the prison. No sign of Grant.

"We figure he is going after Lenny, either to take over or to kill him, depending on his plans. And then, Hank, you know he will come after you, and your family."

Hank pushed his food and coffee away. His face had gone from pale white to bright red. Grant again. "Have you told them?"

"No, it just happened last night. I wanted to tell you first. We have already sent protection to Doveland. I will talk to them after this. Mira is expecting me this afternoon.

"You're going to go to Lenny and tell him about Grant's escape. They'll ask how you know, and you'll explain that you have a source. Lenny's reaction should help us gather more info about him and his crew so we can pick them up. It's tempting to let Grant get to him, but that's not the way I work.

"And then Hank, you will have to disappear."

"Sure, disappear. To where? Grant will find me no matter what I do. Let me decide what to do after we deal with Lenny."

"It's good they all have ways to sense danger, isn't it?"

Hank knew that Sam was talking about the Forest and Stone Circles. Sam and Hank didn't understand how they knew things, but they were aware that they did.

"Yes, good and bad. It's what makes Grant hate them so much. But you're right. Sarah and Leif probably already know and have gathered the Circles to help."

"Have you ever stopped to think, Hank, that we are part of the Circle too? Part of their Karass?" Sam asked.

Hank nodded. They both stood to go. Sam reached out to shake Hank's hand. Instead, Hank grabbed him into a hug, surprising them both. He put a fifty on the table for the waitress and quietly left by the back door leaving Sam feeling both hopeful and bereft. *Get through this Hank and perhaps we can both start new lives,* he thought.

He added another fifty to the table, winked at the waitress who, seeing the cash on the table, blinked back tears. Sam left by the front door. Hank would be long gone. It was time for Sam to put his team to work before Grant found them both.

Ten

Sarah slammed the drawer shut, swearing under her breath, and then burst into tears. It wasn't fair. They had never done anything to him. *Take deep breaths and calm down,* she told herself. *This kind of behavior will never help Hank or the family.* But it did feel good. Sarah wasn't sure if it was the outburst of anger or the release of tears, but yes, she felt better.

Certainly not yet ready for prime time angel work, she thought.

"Well, no one said angels don't get angry. Look at the angel Michael who fought evil or Jesus who overturned the money lenders' tables in the temple," Suzanne said.

Sarah turned to see Suzanne floating around the living room. Present and not. Here and there at the same time. Dimension shifting was the name she and Leif had finally come up with to explain what the Forest Circle could do and what she and Leif were practicing. *There are probably many circles that have those skills,* she mused to herself.

"Yes," Suzanne answered, hearing her thoughts. "Lots of circles with many kinds of skills and some of them are good at dimension shifting too, as you are calling it. But you know that's not why I am here. It's the same thing that brought on the swearing and tears."

"Grant's escape. I don't suppose it will do any good to rail against the idiots who let this happen."

"No, they were easily deceived. Hypnotism is not just something done in shows. Many skilled practitioners are using it for their personal gain. It's best that we concentrate on keeping everyone safe until they, or we, find him. It would be better for Grant if the law found him first. He would have time to repent. Not that I anticipate him doing that, but at least he would have a chance."

"What happens if you find him first?" Sarah asked.

"I thought I heard voices," Leif said as he came into the kitchen and hugged Sarah. "It's about Grant, isn't it?" he asked Suzanne.

"It is," Sarah answered for her, "And Suzanne was just going to tell me what they will do to, or with, Grant if they find him first."

"I think we will save that answer until later," Suzanne answered. "But, if Grant knew, he would surrender to the police the first chance he got."

"Yikes," Sarah said.

"Exactly," answered Suzanne. "I just wanted to let you know that we will be helping, even if you don't see us. On a happy note, everyone wants to come to the summer solstice in Doveland. That's less than five weeks away, so let's hope we handle this before then."

Without waiting for a reply, Suzanne vanished, leaving as she always did the slight hint of the woods behind her.

Leif took Sarah's hand and led her to the sofa. "Let's call them now. Sam has told Hank. It's time we let everyone else know why there are more people in town, before they start worrying about the wrong thing," Leif said.

"Is there a right thing for them to be worrying about now?" asked Sarah.

"Well, maybe worrying is not the right word. Let's say it's time to be super alert. Again."

Grimly, they nodded at each other and called Ava and Evan.

******

Ava was in Ben's room when she heard the skype call on her laptop where she had left it on the kitchen counter. She heard Evan answer and then Sarah and Leif's voice. A prick of panic seized her.

Seeing Evan's face as she came into the kitchen holding Ben her fears were confirmed. "Grant's escaped," he said, as he pulled out a stool for her to sit on. Listening to the explanation of how he escaped and the assurance that they were safe did nothing to stop her heart from racing.

"Why, why is this happening?" she wailed. "Please tell me that someday it will stop."

"I could tell you that, Ava," Leif said, "Because someday it will. Someday. But none of us know when people will wake up, so until then we are always alert. Now, we are just doubling our watch."

"Should I have the village cancel the Solstice Festival?" Ava asked.

"No, please don't." Sarah said. "What will help drive away fear is love and play. The best thing to do besides remaining aware is to celebrate joy and happiness. Plus, isn't Ben going to be christened that day too? And we can't wait to come hug him."

Seeing Ava's face, Leif added, "Sam and Hank are already doing their part. You will be safe. This is just a precaution.

"Could you please quietly alert the rest of your Circle in town? Have Grace pay attention to the new people you see. Some of them are Sam's. Some might not be. Sam will be there in a few days to see Mira. It's both the excuse and real reason of course," laughed Leif.

After the call, Ava and Evan played with Ben who cooed at both of them before snuggling into Ava's shoulder. For a moment, everything felt normal.

"So, should we have everyone over for dinner, or have everyone meet us for dinner?" Evan asked.

"Everyone come here," yelled Hannah as she skipped through the door with Eric right behind her. "It's more fun. That way grandfather will stay over tonight too. We can play games together."

Looking at Eric's face, she added, "After I do my homework of course."

Ava handed Ben to Eric, grabbed her cell phone, and texted everyone to come to dinner at the house. The phone pinged back as Grace, Mira, and Mandy responded they would be there and would bring something to share. Since Tom and Craig weren't in town, she would let them know later.

Eric sighed. He didn't have the gifts that his adopted family and friends had, but he knew something was wrong. He also knew that Hannah knew that too. He wondered if Ava and Evan had discovered that Hannah knew things before they happened. They were so busy with Ben, they might not have noticed. Since Hannah seemed to want to keep it a secret, he would keep it a secret too. For now anyway. Hannah came over to sit beside him on the couch. He hugged her close and kissed the top of her head.

"I love you, Hannah."

"I know you do, and I have always loved you, too."

Eric knew that she was telling him something, and he trusted that someday he would find out what it was. Together they watched Ava and Evan pretend that everything was okay when both of them knew that it wasn't.

On the other hand, Eric thought as he looked around at what had been created in the past few years, all the love that was shaping their lives, perhaps it is.

"It is, grandfather. I promise," said Hannah.

Eric kissed her again on the top of her head and answered, "I believe you, Hannah."

Eleven

Jay's new job wasn't bad. He found it the same way he always found work. He walked. The walking started because he didn't have a car. What else could he do? Eventually, he learned that walking not only helped him get rides, but also get jobs.

Where he walked depended on whether he was looking for a job, or a ride. If it was a ride, he stayed close to the main highways so he would end up at a truck stop somewhere.

If it were a job, he would walk the back roads of town and talk to everyone he saw. For the most part, he was looking for farmers. Even if the farmer was in the field, he would walk out to meet him and ask if he could help. He always offered his help for free.

When they hesitated, which they usually did, Jay would ask him to give him one job that was really hard and see how he did with it. Two lifetimes of knowing farm equipment meant there was almost nothing he couldn't do to use it or fix it.

The result of his free labor would usually end in a meal. Sometimes he would be given a referral to another farmer looking for help, or when he was lucky, he would be offered a job right then and there.

He worked for cheap. He didn't need much. If it were a nice place, they would offer him a place to sleep. Usually, it was a barn or a shack on the property. On rare occasions, it was a bunkhouse. Bunkhouses were a luxury. If he wasn't offered a place on the farm, he stayed at the cheapest motel he could find.

The job he found was a good one. On his third day of walking, he saw an old farmer struggling with his tractor that looked even older then the farmer. Jay offered to get it running. The farmer was so desperate he gave him an hour to try. It only took him forty-five minutes. The farmer shook his hand and gave him a job and a place in the barn.

The farmer's son had gone off to college and never returned, and he was fighting a losing battle keeping the farm running, but he didn't know what else to do or where else to go.

He offered Jay food along with the lodging in the barn. Since it was almost summer, it wasn't bad. Plus the farmer had a cot, sheets, and blankets. Luxury to Jay.

On the second day of work, the farmer introduced himself. He stood up at the dinner table, patted Jay on the shoulder and told him his name was Melvin Byler. Jay reciprocated by introducing himself as Jay Kalan. A small but essential bond of trust had been formed.

The most important part of finding work was it enabled him to become a fixture in the community. Jay never asked direct questions, and this time it was even more important not to look too curious. Instead, he would listen, and maybe prompt more information or gossip just because he was a newcomer and all the stories were fresh to him.

Jay was aware that he might also be in danger of being recognized. Someone who lived in the area their whole life might remember someone who looked like him from before.

He had died at thirty, and now he was almost thirty, so he had been gone only thirty years.

In fact, when Melvin first looked at him, he did a double take. Jay worried that he had recognized him. But the moment passed. However, if Melvin had asked him, Jay was prepared to say that he had a cousin, many times removed, that looked a lot like him.

Jay wasn't really worried that people would think he was the same person. Who would ever believe it anyway?

After being in town just a week, Jay was sure he was in the right place. Not only did the area feel familiar, but so did the people. Something he hadn't considered was that he might recognize someone he had lived with in the last lifetime. Thirty years didn't always change people that much.

He hadn't considered that possibility because there was only one person he was hoping to see. He wanted to find the person that burned his house down. That person was burned into his memory forever.

Jay had gone to town to get some milk so he could make his daughter hot chocolate for breakfast in the morning before she went off to school. In town, he ran across a few friends, and they had a few beers together. Jay wasn't concerned. His wife had said there was no rush getting home; she was going to bed when their daughter went to bed. "Besides, it is your birthday. We have already celebrated together," she said. "Go have some fun!"

A few hours later he headed home, thinking of his daughter snuggled in bed and his wife waiting for him. Probably sound asleep. Both were such sound sleepers that they had a running joke that someone could take all the furniture in the house and they would never wake up. That's why Jay had expensive locks installed. They were safe.

Except they weren't.

Their farm was ten minutes from town. As Jay's old truck climbed the hill, he could see smoke over the rise. He didn't think anything of it, just a neighbor burning his trash pile. But, cresting the hill, he saw his house. Burning.

His memory of events after that was hazy. He knew he drove as fast as he could, but even though it was only a few minutes later, by the time he reached the house, it was completely engulfed in flames. Before he collapsed from the smoke, he saw him.

He saw a man standing at the bottom of the hill. Watching the house burn. That was the man that haunted his dreams. The man who fell to his knees and buried his head in his hands.

Later the fire department told him that his wife and daughter didn't suffer. While asleep, they inhaled enough smoke to kill them before the fire got to them. He knew they thought it would help. And it did. It took away one percent of his pain. The rest never left.

Twelve

Thirty miles away, the village of Doveland was preparing for their annual solstice festival. They had a little more than a month to do everything on their list to make it the best celebration yet.

The standing committee for the festival consisted of all the store owners located around the village green. They saw it as a chance to both promote their businesses and to give back to the community at the same time. Other villagers were welcome to join the committee, but they rarely did. It was too much fun to participate without doing any work.

Four new members had joined the committee this year, Grace and Mandy with their new store, and Pete and his wife Barbara, who were in the process of reopening the Diner. The old timers warmly welcomed them all. They were fresh bodies! That meant less work for them.

The committee met in the town hall located in an old two-story building. It used to be a hardware and feed store, but the town took it over when the previous owners went into bankruptcy. The bank ended up owning the building, and they were all too happy to sell it to the town of Doveland for a minimal fee.

It didn't look like a store any longer. Some of the local carpenters had donated their time, and the village had raised enough money for materials. In less than a month, they gutted the entire downstairs and turned it into one long room, ready to be used for gatherings of all kinds. It was not fancy. But the old windows let in plenty of light, and the original dark hardwood floors looked good against the plain off white walls.

Half of one wall was painted with chalkboard paint and people of all ages loved coming in to draw on it. Once a month it was washed clean and new drawings appeared almost immediately. On the other long wall were multiple bulletin boards. These too were cleared off once a month and quickly filled up again with work opportunities, artwork, and lost cat and dog notices.

The farmer's market was hosted twice a month in the hall during the winter when it got too cold to be held in the town square. Other times, the hall was filled with seniors practicing their latest dance steps. Tap and belly dancing were favorites. Every month there was a community dance. Free lessons were given at 6:30 P.M., followed by the dance. It was very popular.

Upstairs the atmosphere was very different. It housed Doveland's planning and building offices. A staircase located on the left of the front door provided access to the offices. Sometimes the music, laughter, and gaiety drifted up to the rooms, and if a visitor looked closely, they could see the sensible shoes of the town clerks tapping along with it. However, mostly it was a quiet place with only the rustle of papers, or the ringing of a phone breaking the silence.

Today was different.

Everyone was downstairs ready to be part of the solstice planning. Permits had to be filed, and all the details of a gathering had to pass through town rules and laws.

There weren't many, but they needed to be taken care of by people who knew what they were.

The large table that was usually pushed up against the wall was pulled out into the center of the room. The wood folding chairs that surrounded the table were all filled. A second smaller table had to be added as committee members drifted in on their own timing. It was a full house.

Grace glanced around the room and realized that she knew everyone's name. It wasn't just wise marketing that drove her to remember names; it was a sincere desire to know people. A new village gave her many opportunities to test her theory that there was one of every kind of person in every meeting, in every town, in every class. She giggled to herself and was poked by Mandy who knew her friend quite well.

Mandy knew Grace was attaching characteristics to each person. Mandy had to admit that Grace was often accurate and that her knowledge of human behavior had come in handy many times while getting the permits necessary to build their store. Plus, she knew that Grace was always on the lookout as part of her determination to keep them all safe.

No, Mandy said to herself, I am not going to think of those things now. Today, I am going to be part of a group of people who could not possibly be wishing any of us harm. Turning to her right, she spotted Mr. Jacks, the owner of the gas station on the corner who leered at her. *Well, she thought, maybe I am wrong about that.*

As if reading her mind, Grace shot a glance at Mandy, and they both giggled enough to draw another leer from Mr. Jacks.

At the front of the table was the head of the town board of trustees, Valerie Price. Grace and Mandy both liked her. She and her husband, Harold, also owned the Bed and Breakfast Inn.

There was no need for a fancy name since it was the only one in town. Barbara and Pete were staying there until they could clean up the top floor of the Diner enough for them to live above the restaurant. Pete assured Barbara that it was not that far away.

Everyone was buzzing, talking about their health, their neighbor's health, the cat in the garden, the trouble with the son-in-law, everything but preparation for the event. The table was covered with coffee cups and treats from Your Second Home. It looked like a party.

Grace thought it was going to be impossible to get everyone's attention, but then Valerie, who was the principle of the school, whistled.

The newcomers had never heard anything like it. Everyone else had heard it before because they had either been one of her pupils or one of the teachers she ruled over with an iron hand covered with a velvet glove.

The room became silent in a second, all eyes to the front. Hal just stared at the table, pretending that it wasn't what she did when she called him in from their garden.

Satisfied that she still could quiet a room, Valerie asked for reports. A few hours later, everyone had projects to complete for the next meeting which was exactly four days away.

"Same time, same place," said Valerie. "And be sure to have all your work completed. No excuses." And then she smiled and hugged everyone as they gathered their papers and left the room.

Grace and Mandy thought they had never seen anything quite as astonishing. "Whoever elected her to be the head of this, knew what they were doing," Grace said as they stood outside surveying the beautiful spring morning. "If everything was run like that there wouldn't be any problems in the world at all."

"Amen to that," Pete said as he and Barbara joined Grace and Mandy. For the moment all that was on all their minds was the joy of living in such a beautiful place, together. There would be plenty of time to discuss what they had learned at Ava and Evan's house a few nights before. For now, they merely stood in the sunshine and took in the beauty of the world.

Thirteen

Sam Long snapped his gum while drumming his fingers on his desk. He was waiting. Not patiently. The reports should have arrived hours before. Not having them to read gave him too much space to speculate about what was going wrong. They had been looking for Grant for over a week and found nothing. At all. Grant had vanished.

Sam knew that was impossible unless Grant was dead. But until he saw Grant's body on an autopsy table Sam would never believe it. No, Grant was out there somewhere, hiding. Even the Forest Circle, which had returned to help, had no idea where he went. That meant that either Grant had become aware of the group who lived in another dimension and knew how to hide from them, or he was just plain lucky.

Sam was choosing lucky. As far as he knew, Grant despised the people who had extra gifts in the world and used them for good.

But Grant didn't believe in anything other than what he could see. Since Grant couldn't see the Forest Circle or any of the other circles living in various dimensions, but still able to exist in this one, it was unlikely Grant knew how to hide from them.

Sam didn't see them either. But he knew they were there. He felt the results of their work. In addition, Mira kept him up to date with what was going on with those he couldn't see. He wished he could. That way he wouldn't always feel so crazy when he tried to explain who they were to his superiors.

The one time Sam tried, they told him that he probably needed to take some time off. When he realized that they were never going to believe him, he claimed extreme tiredness and took a day off before coming back looking refreshed, and not out of his mind.

Mira told him that everyone could know beyond the five senses, but the desire and belief that it was possible had been trained out of them. Some people had a natural gift, just as some people have a natural gift of a sport, or art, or language skill. But a natural gift was not enough. It took practice.

However, even without the natural gift, it was still possible. Some of the best people in their fields of expertise were those who practiced and learned to make up for not having it come naturally.

Well, Sam thought, *I am willing, and I do have the desire, so I will remain open to the possibility that I too will be able to see and understand past my five senses someday. It would definitely be helpful in times like this. I wouldn't feel so blind.*

Just then his cell phone pinged. Hank was checking in. There was no sign of Grant anywhere near Lenny. When Hank had told Lenny about Grant's escape, Lenny had turned pale and walked out of the room.

He returned with two of his bodyguards and had Hank tell them about Grant. Since then Lenny had established a twenty-four hour watch. He was taking no chances and was sticking close to home. Hank had already told Lenny that he would go to the summer solstice in Doveland, and watch for Grant.

Lenny had fully agreed, telling Hank that he was a genius for thinking that Grant might show up there.

Sam and all his reinforcements would also be at the celebration. If Grant appeared, they would be ready for him.

****

Grant grunted in pain. Who knew that plastic surgery could be so painful? But worth it. Holding a mirror up to his swollen face, he could see the results of the changes even though the swelling was still present. It wasn't much, but it was enough to transform his face from the one being shown everywhere to a look no one knew.

The side benefit of a new face was he also looked at least ten years younger. Plus prison had forced him to lose weight; the food was horrific. And a week of throwing up from the antibiotics needed after the surgery took off another ten pounds. Another week and he would look terrific.

If he could stand the pain of laughing, Grant would have laughed. If he could move his face. He knew everyone was looking for him, but in all the wrong places.

Instead of heading towards Lenny in Ohio, or those fanatical do-gooders in Pennsylvania, he had crossed the border into Mexico hidden inside a produce truck. It dropped him off a hundred miles from his destination. After killing the driver and hiding the truck, he walked to the next town where his next ride waited for him. It took three separate rides to end up in the bunker where the doctor waited with his small medical staff to transform him.

Years before, aware that someday he might be caught, Grant had set up multiple scenarios for escape and the remaking of his life. Everything had been prepared in advance.

The minute his capture was released to the media the plan was put into action. A network of people bought and paid for, alerted the next person in the chain.

Each one was necessary to free him and remake his face. No one knew more than their one step. They didn't know each other. They didn't know the outcome. They just knew that if they didn't do as told, their family would die.

Of course, they probably had heard that he had killed the ambulance drivers because it had been on the news, so now they were aware that they would die.

But they also knew that their families would be spared if they still did the work. He would never be able to use the network again. He would rebuild with a new face and a new name.

Grant did not intend to go back into the business. He had money stashed all over the world. Once he took care of his enemies so they could never come after him, he would disappear.

He knew that they were expecting him in Ohio and Pennsylvania, and they were right; he was heading there eventually to take care of that unfinished business. However, first he would wait until he didn't look like a puffer fish, and then he would take his new identity as Jim Smith on the road.

He counted on the fact that they would all be tired and frustrated before he showed up, while he would be fresh and focused. Plus, for them it was work, and they were afraid. For him, it was fun. Fear never entered the picture.

Putting down the mirror, he picked up the book he was reading. It was a luxury to be able to read all day, and if his eyes got tired, a beautiful girl came in to read to him.

He was reading "Autobiography of A Yogi." He thought it was complete and utter bullshit, but he believed that it helped him understand the do-gooders. It gave him a common language in case he had to fool one of them with words to carry out his plan to eliminate them.

The other benefit was that the people taking care of him thought he was a sweet man, with goodness in his heart. He snorted thinking about it. *Stupid people.*

Dinner would be in an hour; he could already smell it. It was worth it to bring that chef down from New York to serve him. It was a waste to have to kill him when this was over, but he couldn't take any chances. *Life is good,* he thought, *and it will just get better.*

Fourteen

One day Melvin asked Jay to drive into Doveland and get some groceries. He had asked before, but Jay had demurred saying he didn't have a driver's license. Melvin looked Jay up and down and told him that if he wanted to work at the farm, he would have to drive so stop dicking around, and get a license. There were no ifs, ands, or buts about it.

The next day Melvin drove Jay to the DMV located in a town an hour away, and Jay returned with a temporary license. The new one would have Melvin's address as Jay's home. A week after starting work, Melvin had suggested Jay move into the spare bedroom, saying if Jay intended to murder him in his sleep, just let him know, he would get all his affairs in order first.

Neither laughed. But when Jay looked into Melvin's eyes, sunk so deep into his wrinkled face that they were barely visible, he saw a sparkle, and something else—understanding. It was overwhelming. No one had looked at him that way in this lifetime. Jay acknowledged what he had seen with a curt nod, and headed up the creaky and narrow stairs to bed.

Melvin watched him go, shaking his head. Perhaps there was something that could be done to stop what was coming, but he doubted it.

The next day Melvin showed Jay how to keep the rusted truck going so that it wouldn't stall on the road. Or if it did, how to start it again. "How long have you had this beat up truck, Melvin?" asked Jay, as he pushed hard on the clutch peddle and jiggled the stick shift.

"Longer than you've been alive, but it's the only one I have and there ain't going to be another, so don't go horse playing around out there. Get the stuff and come home. I got work for you."

Jay smiled, saluted, and eased the truck out the unpaved and pitted drive to the old road that led to Doveland, and possibly his past.

The thirty-mile drive took almost an hour. The truck spit and sputtered the whole way and Jay spent most of the trip frozen in his seat hoping nothing would happen and no one would recognize him when he got to town. That is if it was the right town. Since moving in with Melvin, Jay had let his hair and beard grow and changed into clothes that had belonged to Melvin's son. They smelled old and musty, but they were clean and not something that he would have worn before.

This new look was the same one that his picture would show on his driver's license. Jay hoped that if Pete was around town, that he wouldn't recognize him. But if he did, he had a story ready to tell. What he worried the most about was that someone would see the slow burning flame of anger inside of him. It propelled him forward, but he didn't want anyone to know that. Jay knew how to be charming and gracious and one of the boys, and that is how he was going to be in town.

Even though he was busy staying alive in the tin can of a truck he was driving, Jay was also aware that the road he was driving was familiar, but it was not the road to his old house. This road was as curvy as his road, but it was flat.

He remembered cresting a hill and seeing his home on another rise a few miles away. However, he wasn't worried. There would be more roads to explore. He had time. The person he was looking for was running out of it.

A few miles outside of Doveland the hair on Jay's arm stood up, and he felt as if an electric current was passing through his body. It was so shocking he almost ran into a tree that leaned out over the road. Righting the truck, he slowed down to a crawl, breathing slowly, not knowing what he expected to see.

There wasn't anything that stood out to him. A few yards back, where the jolt had happened, Jay saw a small side road, or perhaps a driveway curving up the rise, but there was nothing else.

Jay knew not to discount weird feelings, so he decided that once he got to town, he would try to find out who lived up that drive. It would be a start towards understanding what had happened.

Not long after that, he began to see homemade signs along the side of the road reminding people about the solstice celebration coming up in a few weeks. By the time he reached the park in the center of the village, he had seen at least ten homemade signs plus a banner that hung over the street entrance to the square. As he drove around the square, he saw there was a banner hanging over every street. In the center of the square, a crew of carpenters were building a gazebo. *These people are taking their celebration seriously,* he thought. Maybe he would attend. It looked as if the whole town would be there, perhaps even the man he was looking for.

It took him two trips around the square before he found the turn-in to the small grocery store. On the way out, he would stop at the gas station next to the store and fill up the truck for Melvin.

It wasn't because he was a nice guy. He wasn't. It was because it would give him a chance to chat people up.

The question was if this was the town he lived in before, why didn't anything feel familiar? A deep sense of frustration tried to creep in and tell him he was wasting his time, but the memory of the jolt of electricity on the road to town made him think that he was on the right track.

He would stick it out, wait and watch for more signs. As he had for years. He promised his wife he would avenge her death.

What he never admitted to himself is that he would hear her tell him it wasn't what she wanted, that revenge wasn't the solution. But his wife was dead, so he was just imagining it. What was real to him was the sweet revenge that was waiting for him.

As he pulled into the grocery store, he glanced across the square to a diner. It looked closed, but he could see workers inside fixing it up, so maybe next time he would stop in there for food.

As he watched the workmen, he felt drawn to the building across the street from the diner. On the turquoise and white sign hanging above the door, it said Your Second Home. Through the window, Jay caught a glimpse of three people sitting at a table. The little girl seemed to be looking right at him, and once again, he felt that jolt.

Good god, he thought, what is happening to me? When he looked again, there was no one there. Heading into the grocery store, Jay decided against doing anything else in town that day. His imagination was doing weird things to him, so perhaps this was not a good day to be asking about people.

However, he would be back. In the meantime, maybe Melvin would be the person to ask about the history of Doveland.

Hannah looked up at Eric and Grace and smiled. Eric had brought her to the coffee shop to get a book for Ava, and because Grace had promised her a treat if she got an "A" on her spelling test.

Hannah had chosen a treat of two chocolate chip cookies, but she was saving one for her mom. *How lucky I am to have two moms,* she thought, *and now two dads.* Of course, she couldn't let Evan know because that would bring danger to someone else she loved.

So when she realized the man was looking at her, she automatically shielded the three of them from his sight.

Sometimes she surprised herself at what she could do. It wasn't much, but compared to what everyone else thought was possible, it was a lot.

Hannah knew that she should tell someone about the man, but everyone was so happy she didn't want to spoil it. *It can wait,* she told herself. *Maybe tomorrow.* Then being just nine years old, Hannah returned to her cookie and promptly forgot the promise she made to herself.

Sitting on a park bench in the town square, taking up no space at all, Suzanne watched both Hannah and Jay. *Not long now,* she thought.

Fifteen

Grace didn't miss the interaction between Hannah and the man who got out of the old truck. She had watched the truck make its way around the square a few times before pulling into the grocery store. Unless you had been to Doveland before, the entrance was easy to miss, so his tour around the square had already alerted her to a new arrival in town.

One of the carpenters working on the gazebo had told her Melvin had a new helper. *So that must be him,* she thought. But what did that have to do with Hannah, she wondered. Of course, she may have imagined the interaction. Both seemed to have turned away from it, and besides, how could a newcomer to town know Hannah?

Grace watched until she saw the man climb back into the truck, stop at the gas station, and head back out of town towards Melvin's place. Yep, new helper. She noticed that Eric was also tracking what the man was doing.

Eric. Who knew she would find someone like him so late in life? And it was late in life. Once they both realized that there was a mutual attraction, they didn't waste time talking about it. Eric would drop Hannah off at school, and they would meet.

Sometimes Grace walked over to his tiny house a few blocks away, and other times he came to her apartment over her store. They were keeping it secret for now, although Mandy had already started looking at them differently as if she suspected.

When Eric told her he hadn't been feeling well, she made him see a doctor. Grace, always practical, said they might as well find out what was happening, and how much time they had together. It wasn't long it turned out, or at least that was the medical view. Grace wasn't so sure she was ready to believe that the medical opinion was the one they needed to accept. Instead, she had changed Eric's diet, made him get more sleep, and started praying in every form she knew how to pray.

No matter what, they were going to enjoy their time together. If Eric were getting ready to walk through the door to the next lifetime, she would enjoy him as much as possible in this one.

As if he knew what she was thinking, Eric reached across the table, held her hand, and winked at her. Hannah looked at them both and asked, "Can I be at the wedding?"

"Told you," Eric said to Grace.

"Told her what?" asked Hannah.

"That you know things."

"I do," Hannah said with a giggle. "So, can I be? I know it's a secret. I can keep a secret. I do it all the time."

"I bet you do," said Grace. "And, we'll see."

"Well, I see that I will be there, so you might as well say yes now and make it easy for yourself."

Eric and Grace burst out laughing. "Okay, young lady, we'll take you for a drive with us next Saturday morning."

Hannah reached across the table and held both their hands. "That is the best news ever. Then I will have a grandmother, too."

Grace's eyes filled with tears as she looked at the two loves of her life—Eric smiling at her with his kind eyes, and Hannah with a touch of chocolate chip cookie on the corner of her mouth.

Who knew this would happen, Grace thought. *Oh, well, it appeared that Hannah did.* She wondered what else Hannah knew, and as a soon to be grandmother she was definitely going to be paying more attention to the child. And the man who had just left town.

****

Pete had also watched the man in the rickety truck make his way around the square a few times before heading to the grocery store, and wondered who he was. He saw him check out the Diner and figured, if they were open, he might have come in for lunch.

Soon, he thought. Evan had lived up to his promises, as Pete knew he would. Evan had paid for the help to clean and paint and replace old fixtures with new ones that looked old. However, the kitchen was brand spanking new. The cook Evan had hired to teach Pete to cook was both patient and skilled. At first, Pete thought he would never get the hang of it, but the menu was simple, and after many burned or tasteless trials, he was beginning to turn out some decent food.

He was not ready for the catering business that Sam ran, though. That would have to wait, or they would need to hire someone. There was no way he would ever be that kind of cook. Besides, he didn't want to work that hard. He and Barbara had chosen this life and town so they could spend more time together.

Once they got the Diner up and running, Pete was planning to find some skilled people looking for work, and get them involved. He and Barbara would have time to spend long days together and even nights. The fact that he was sleeping in his own bed every night with his wife was a dream come true.

Yes, he had loved trucking. But now he loved this life. Before moving, they had sold almost everything, including his rig. They bought a new pickup truck that even Barbara could drive, and put the rest in the bank. It gave them a cushion of safety, and if things went well, they might buy a house near the center of town. For now, they liked living above their diner.

Pete looked up from cooking hamburgers for the guys doing the last of the painting to see Barbara coming through the door with her arms filled with flowers, beaming ear to ear. He had never seen her that happy.

"Look at these," she said. "I was out walking, and a lady a few blocks away was working in her garden and then she cut all these flowers for me. I can't believe how wonderful everyone is here."

Pete took the flowers from her and put them in a mason jar on the counter, and then hugged his wife. Yes, everything is wonderful here, but then why the long faces of his new friends when they thought no one was watching? Something else was going on. Also, there was something he knew he wanted to tell everyone, but he kept forgetting what it was. *It will come back to me,* he thought.

"French fries, anyone?" he asked. A resounding "yes" was the answer from both the painters and his wife. Pete lifted the basket filled with golden crispy fries and breathed in deep. *Yep, heaven. He was in heaven.*

Now if he could just remember what it was that was bothering him, he could rest easy.

His phone beeped. It was Mandy inviting him to a small gathering at the store on Saturday at 3:00 p.m.. That was easy, right next door. Yep, we'll be there, he texted back.

Pete had a suspicion what the gathering was all about, but if Mandy wanted to keep it a secret, he would keep his suspicions to himself. However, he would be sure to wear a nice new shirt to celebrate the occasion.

Out on the green, the Gazebo was almost done; workers were sprawled out on the lawn and the park benches eating their lunches. Most of the workers had stopped in to chat and help with the Diner, saying the faster it was finished, the sooner they could get back to eating breakfast in town.

Pete recognized some of the workers from last year when they were in town, which made him wonder if they were Sam's people, and why that would be.

It was amazing how much building was going on in preparation for the summer solstice. The village was going all out this year, spurred on by the new people in town. Almost everyone was happy about that. Those who weren't were keeping it mostly to themselves, for now anyway. Pete wasn't worried. He had proof in his life that good always wins in the end, and there was plenty of good in Doveland. Pete planned to add as much to the stockpile as possible.

Sixteen

Jay's original plan was to stay in town for a while, but the little girl's stare freaked him out. When she looked at him, his peripheral vision had shut down leaving him with a narrow sliver of the world that directed his focus straight into her eyes. That was impossible considering how far away she was. He should only have been able to see a form in the window, not eyes.

When it was happening his heart raced, his breath shortened, and he wondered if he would faint. Jay had the fleeting thought of how embarrassed he would feel. Then his vision cleared, and he felt fine. Except for the fact that he thought he was losing his mind, since the little girl wasn't in the window anymore. No one was.

Once he got the truck on the road heading out of town, he tried to think it through. Did he really see her, or didn't he? That kind of vision had never happened to him before, why was it happening now?

Just thinking about it made his heart race again, and he found himself rubbing his thumb on the palm of his hand. He thought he had broken himself of that habit because it broadcast that he was nervous and confused.

Nevertheless, here he was doing it again, just as he had in the last lifetime. Realizing that no amount of thinking was going to help him figure out if what he saw was an illusion or not, he settled back into driving and making sure the old truck kept its wheels on the road. His only mission was getting back to the farm safely.

A few miles out of town, he came to where he had felt the first jolt of the day. There was a car at the entrance of what he could see now was a driveway. It was waiting for him to go by before pulling out. As he passed the car, he glanced at the occupants and saw a man and a woman and what looked like a baby in a car seat in the back.

A stab of pain hit him between the eyes, and Jay struggled to keep the truck from rolling into the ditch on the far side of the road. As he righted the truck, he glanced in the rear view mirror and saw the car head into town. As quickly as the pain appeared, it disappeared. *Maybe I imagined it,* he thought. However, he knew he didn't.

A calm feeling settled over him. He didn't know what was going on, but he knew none of it would be happening if he weren't in the right place. His revenge was closer. He could almost see it happening. He would never have his wife and daughter again, so retribution would have to take their place. That was all he wanted. Then he could be at peace.

****

"Wasn't that Melvin's old truck?" Ava asked Evan, as she looked back to see it swerve across the road before righting itself. "But that wasn't Melvin driving it. Hope that driver isn't drunk or something. That was a weird swerve."

"Could be the truck. Last time I saw Mel, he said it pulled to the left. Guess he hasn't fixed it yet."

Ava nodded, but something felt off. She just couldn't put her finger on it. Then Ben cooed and everything was forgotten as she looked back at him, and then at Evan and thought about how lucky she was to have them and Hannah in her life.

A few minutes later, they pulled into an empty parking space in front of Your Second Home. Inside, Grace, Hannah, and Eric were back in the kitchen making cookies. Evan had gone to the Diner to check on Pete and Barbara. Ava stood silently in the kitchen door, holding a sleeping Ben, watching the domestic scene spread before her.

"It's sweet, isn't it?" Mandy whispered. Somehow, she had managed to slip in beside Ava.

"You were always sneaky," Ava said to her, "I have no idea how you can be so quiet. But, you are right, it is sweet."

"I had lots of practice. In my house growing up, it was best not to be noticed."

Ava reached out and pulled Mandy in close. She had long ago forgiven her for lying to her in the beginning. Mandy had protected Hannah as she promised she would, and now she was even a better friend than before.

They had gone through something together, and that had strengthened their bond.

Hannah looked up from the baking. Her face had splotches of white flour on it, and her hands were sticky with dough. "Can I finish helping bake this batch of cookies?" she asked Ava.

"Help yourself to coffee while you wait," Grace said, and Eric winked at Ava, letting her know it was fine with him.

As Ava headed for the coffee, Mandy reached for Ben and stuck her nose into his neck, breathing deeply.

"If there were only a way we could keep on smelling like this, I would be sniffing strangers' necks."

"Well, that's probably why we don't," Ava laughed.

Settling Ben in the curve of her arm, Mandy flicked her gaze into the kitchen where Grace and Eric stood side by side. "Did you see that coming? she asked.

"No. But, then I don't think they did either. They aren't wasting any time enjoying each other, though."

"The wisdom of getting older," Ava said. "Or the wisdom of seeing what can happen in the world, so grab love any chance you can. That is definitely something I learned last year, and I am still learning. And speaking of grabbing love, what about you and Tom?"

Mandy's face turned a bright red, and Ava laughed, "Wow, that good."

"That good, and not."

"What do you mean?"

"Well, do you see him here in town? He has a place, but he is almost never here, and even when he is, he holds himself back for some reason. So, yes, that good, but not that good. I worry if he just doesn't want me because of my awful past."

Ava reached over and held Mandy's hand. She didn't know what was going on with Tom, but she was going to find out. If he wasn't going to commit to her friend because of what she had to do to survive, well, then he was going to get a good talking to from her. He was due back in town in a week. He better have a good reason for staying away.

Besides, Ava thought, *there is the danger they are in, now that Grant had escaped. Yes, it was time for Tom to come home, ready or not.*

Her phone beeped with a text from Evan. Just across the street and he has to text?

But after reading the message, she understood. He was asking if everyone would like to meet him, Pete, and Barbara on the other side of the town square for dinner at the Thai Place. It used to be Laura's, but the new owners had changed the name. It made more sense really. Now visitors knew precisely what kind of food they would be eating there.

Ava held up the phone to Mandy who nodded yes and then walked over to Grace and Eric who also nodded yes. Perhaps even more enthusiastically than Mandy, if that was possible.

"Yes," was Ava's answer to Evan. "Grace is closing shop, so we'll be over in five minutes." Then she texted Mira to see if she wanted to come too. "I'll be there in ten minutes," was the answer.

Mandy asked, "What's with a town that names everything for what it is? You know, the Diner, the Bed and Breakfast Inn, the Thai Place…"

"And Your Second Home," chimed in Grace.

"I don't get that one," Hannah said.

"Doesn't this feel like your second home?" Eric asked.

Hannah paused, looked down, and nodded. Inside she was thinking how many places felt like a second home to her, but how would she ever explain that to anyone? She barely understood it herself.

Grace and Eric exchanged looks. There it was again. Something more was going on with Hannah.

As if sensing their worries, Hannah glanced up, smiled, and reached for both of their hands with her sticky cookie hands. Neither cared about the sticky hands as she said, "What I mean is, I love so many people that when I am with them, it feels like home."

"What a good answer," Ava said, hugging Hannah.

What a good save, Grace thought.

The next few minutes everyone rushed around cleaning up the cookie mess, leaving the fresh cookies inside the case to cool down and be ready for the next day. Grace flipped the "open" sign in the window to say, "closed" and then, as if her whole life wasn't going to change in a few days, she casually asked Ava if she and Eric could take Hannah for a drive with them on Saturday morning.

Ava caught an undertone of something, but seeing the smiles on their three faces, she responded with a nod. Arrangements were made, and after locking the door behind them, they linked arms and strolled across the green lawn to meet their other friends for dinner. Mandy, walking slightly ahead holding Ben in her arms, looked behind at her friends and felt the warmth of having such good friends. But along with the warmth was a stab of fear. Grant was still out there, and he hated them.

Also, something else was happening. Was Lenny coming to town, too? Or was there something else that no one knew about? Or maybe someone does, she thought, as she looked at Hannah who smiled at her as if to assure her that all was well.

Looking around at the people sitting on park benches in the square, Mandy only saw friendly faces, some she knew, some she didn't. But she, of all people, knew that friendly faces sometimes hid evil hearts.

She clutched Ben closer to her heart. He was the second child belonging to Ava that she loved as much as if she was their mother. Perhaps, someday she would have her own children to love, but if not, it didn't matter. She would cherish these two and protect them with every cell of her being.

A bluebird flew by, heading for one of the bluebird houses the town had installed in the green. She took it as a sign and gathered strength from it and from the baby who looked up at her and cooed.

Seventeen

Early Saturday morning, Grace and Eric pulled up outside of Ava and Evan's house. There was no need to honk the horn because Hannah was already sitting on the front steps waiting for them. Ava waved at them from the window, holding Ben and making him wave too. Hannah got into the car and said, "Pretend that you are driving away."

Grace looked at Hannah in the back seat with a puzzled glance. "Please? Just start moving a little and then stop after mom leaves."

Grace did as Hannah asked and after Ava stepped away from the window, she brought the car to a stop. Hannah quietly opened the door and dashed to the side of the house, reached under a bush and brought out a canvas bag. Within seconds, she was back in the car, buckling up as if nothing had happened.

"Okay, we can go now. This is so exciting!"

Once they were on the road, Eric angled his body so he could look directly at Hannah. "And what was that about, young lady?"

"Well, look at me," Hannah said pointing to her outfit. She was wearing jeans and a T-shirt with a doggy on the front. "This is cute, but not suitable for a wedding."

Unzipping her bag, she pulled out a simple blue dress with a white bow. "But, this is!"

Grace and Eric laughed. Then Eric reached down to the bag at his feet and pulled out a beautiful off white dress for Grace. "My jacket is in the trunk," he said.

Laughing with joy, Hannah and Eric high-fived and then carefully included Grace who was keeping her eyes on the road.

"Well, aren't we the tricky ones," Grace said. In the rear view mirror, Hannah could see that Grace's eyes were full of tears. They smiled at each other, and as Eric reached across the seat to hold hands with Grace, they all sighed with happiness. Then Eric and Hannah sat back and watched the spring scenery go by, leaving Grace to driving.

However, Hannah couldn't be still for long, so within minutes she had questions. "Did you write vows? Do you have a special song? Is there going to be a party so everyone will find out?"

Eric answered for the two of them. "Yes, we wrote a few words to say. However, we already made a vow to each other in private, and that is how those words are going to stay. Yes, we have a special song. And, yes, there will be a party someday."

What Eric didn't know was that the party would be that day. Because as the three of them headed to the private wedding, Mandy was preparing Your Second Home for a gathering of their family and friends.

Mandy waited until Eric and Grace had gone and then sent a text to everyone and asked them to stop by at 3:00 p.m.. She had a surprise. Pete already knew about the party because he was bringing some of the food. For almost everyone else, it was a surprise party.

Mandy knew that they would all say yes. The promise of a surprise would bring them.

But they didn't even need that reason. Just the idea that there would be a gathering where everyone would be in one place at one time would be enough.

"Should I ask Sarah and Leif to be there when we have the party?" Hannah asked, and then bit her lip. "Whoops."

"Ha. So you do know how to reach them, don't you? You don't mean calling them on the phone do you?" Eric said.

Hannah nodded, looking downcast.

"Hannah. We know you have some gifts that you are not sharing. It's not something to be embarrassed about, or need to hide. If you don't want us to tell anyone, we won't. But sooner or later, everyone will figure it out, and they will wonder why you haven't said anything," Grace said while glancing up in the rear view mirror to see Hannah.

"Okay. I will tell people. But not now. Maybe I could talk to you two about something first? Later? After the wedding? Maybe next week or the week after or…"

"We get the idea, Hannah. Tell them when you are ready, but remember that we have been around. We see and know things. We can help. And of course, all of the Circle and our friends are always prepared to help."

Hannah nodded. She knew they would want to help. But could they? Besides, it was kinda scary, like pretend monsters under the bed. Except this wasn't make-believe. Making up her mind, she decided to talk to Sarah about it first. She would know what to do. In the meantime, she was going to a wedding. She loved weddings. Hannah even understood why she loved weddings. But that was something she couldn't tell either. Not yet.

****

The wedding happened just as they planned. It was a small, simple, and profoundly beautiful ceremony between two people who knew the value of time, witnessed by a young girl who loved them with all her heart.

As Mandy expected, a text inviting everyone to a surprise party brought them all. As soon as they walked in the door, they each knew why they were there. Mandy had hung white streamers and balloons everywhere she could and added white sparkle tablecloths, and set a bowl of flowers on every table. A beautiful white layered cake with two doves on top sat on the pastry counter.

When Grace, Eric, and Hannah came in the door, everyone cheered and Grace burst into tears. "How did you know to do this?" she asked Mandy as she hugged her.

"You are not the only one who can keep a secret," she said. "Mira and I had an idea this was going to happen, so we laid up supplies waiting for the day."

"But the cake? There was no time for that."

"Oh, but I didn't make it," she said stepping aside so that Grace could see the man standing behind her.

"Sam! You came, and you baked!"

"I did. I was already planning to visit, and Mira told me what she thought was happening today, so I started baking. Hope you like it."

Grace just shook her head. Last year when she had asked Sarah and Leif to include her in their plans and let her help, she never thought so much love would result from that choice.

As everyone crowded around the happy couple to hug them, Grace sighed and said, "We are almost all here. Too bad Hank and Tom couldn't come."

"Oh, but we did," Tom said as he and Hank stepped out of the shadows.

Tom headed to Mandy and hugged her as Hank went to Ava's family and gathered them up in his arms.

Once everyone was settled into their seats at the tables, and coffee and cake were served, Eric tapped his water glass to get their attention.

"Over fifty years ago I was given a gift. A little girl, about your age, Hannah, was lying in a pile of blankets in the waiting room of the clinic where I worked. I fell in love with her the minute I saw her. I chose to take her home and become her family. It changed everything in my life. I had to move, get a new job, and take care of a child. But it was the best thing I ever did. Abbie was a gift from heaven for me. I can never thank you enough, Hank, for choosing me to care for her.

"That was the best day of my life—until now. From that one choice, all this has sprung. You have all become my family. Now I have grandchildren and great grandchildren, and the best friends anyone could ever want.

"But today, I have married the love of my life. I expected the woman would arrive so much sooner, but she is here now. I do believe we promised to meet again in this lifetime.

"I believe that she has always been my wife and she will continue to be my wife when we leave here and go to the next life. However, today we are all here and now. Together. It is a day of celebration. Thank you for being here. I love you all with my whole heart."

As tears of happiness freely flowed, water glasses and coffee cups were raised high in salute. Eric remained standing, and the room settled down as he spoke again.

"Yes, it is a day of celebration, but Grace and I know that some of you are here for another reason, too.

"We know you are also here because there is danger and after this party, it will be time to talk about it. Count me in to whatever needs to be done."

Once again, they raised their glasses and cups. This time in a silent salute to solidarity.

Eighteen

Grant laughed. Lenny was in the fish bowl room at Panera's with his new crew. *What an idiot.* He chose the same place to meet that the FBI already knew existed. Besides, this wasn't the old geezer crowd. Lenny's group was a bunch of young punks. Granted, he had them dressing in slacks and sports shirts so it could have been a company meeting, but still, stupid.

Grant didn't see Hank. He was probably visiting the do-gooders in Pennsylvania. After Grant took care of Lenny, Hank would see him next. Right now, this was like watching a bad movie. Lenny was acting as if he knew what he was doing while running drugs.

Grant laughed again. Looking around the room, he spotted at least one person watching Lenny.

Grant was aware they would also be looking for him, and although he was here in plain sight, he wasn't worried. Grant felt secure that with his new face and new weight he was invisible. Lenny had glanced right at him when he came in the door and didn't register a thing.

If anyone did look, all they would see was a man sitting in front of a computer, nursing a coffee. He had been there every day that week, waiting for Lenny to show up.

Grant always knew Lenny was stupid, so he figured it would happen sooner or later. What he had wanted to find out was if Lenny was being watched by the FBI. Seeing the FBI at Panera's made Grant giddy with happiness.

Still, Grant had no plans to let the FBI arrest Lenny so he could get out in a few years, or escape somehow the way that Grant had.

No, he needed Lenny gone forever. Later, he would take care of him. For now, he was going to take the four-hour drive to Doveland and see what was happening there.

If all went according to his plan, he would get Lenny and Hank in the same place at the same time, and take care of them right there in Doveland. It would be a perfect payback. If he were able to include all of Hank's friends and family at the same time, it would be even more satisfying.

Grant tapped his untraceable burner phone and placed a call. Four hours away, his latest recruit answered.

Grant laughed again. Another wedding? How stupid was that? Two old people a few feet from the grave got married. Priceless. Well, perhaps he could speed up their journey.

He packed up his computer, and like a good customer bussed his table and tossed his coffee cup in the trash before heading out the door to his latest ride.

He had chosen a car that fit right into the surroundings, a white Chevrolet Cruze. *It's fun not hiding my face,* he thought. *Being a new me is very satisfying.*

Back in Panera's a man waited until he was sure that Grant was gone, and then casually threw his cup in the same trash, while quietly pocketing the cup that Grant had tossed.

Maybe he was crazy, but the way that man moved reminded him of someone. And if it was the someone he thought it was, well, he had just scored big time with his bosses.

****

The party lasted all afternoon. They didn't just eat cake. Pete had brought plates and plates of burgers and a few over-sized bowls of salad from the Diner.

Seeing the party going on inside, a few residents of Doveland stopped in and joined in the celebration. By 5:00, Grace and Eric were bushed and after hugging everyone headed up to Grace's apartment, promising they would be at Ava's house the next morning for breakfast.

One by one, the guests said good night, wishing everyone happiness. Finally, Tom shooed Mira and Sam out the door with the rest of them, saying he and Mandy could handle the dishes and clean up.

"Sure, that's what you are going to be doing," Sam laughed.

Tom gave him a friendly push towards the door, hugged his sister, and locked the door behind them. Across the town square, he caught a glimpse of Mr. Jacks standing at the gas pumps. Tom gave him a friendly wave as he closed the blinds.

"I don't know why, but that guy gives me the creeps," he said.

"Mr. Jacks? I think he is harmless enough, but he is a bit of a letch. Always winking and making eyes at me during town hall meetings."

"Well, who could blame him," Tom said, trying to pull Mandy close to him. She pulled back to an arm's length away.

"You know, Tom, I am happy to see you, and I am happy to be spending time with you, but sooner or later, you are going to have to decide if you want us to be a couple. I don't have the capacity anymore to play male-female games."

"Why do you think I don't think of us as a couple?"

Mandy stepped back from Tom and studied his face.

"Perhaps, it would be because you haven't asked me, and you have barely been here the past few months. Always traveling, and rarely getting in touch with me. That's not what couples do, Tom."

Tom stood silent, his full attention on the beautiful woman in front of him. The time in Doveland had been kind to her, she was no longer too thin and stressed. For him, meeting her had been a door opening into a future that he had always wanted. So he wasn't sure why he hesitated. Mandy was right. He stayed away too much and said too little.

"You're right, Mandy. I haven't asked. I assumed you knew, and that's wrong. Help me learn how to be the man in your life that you deserve."

This time, Mandy stepped forward into his embrace. "I have a lot to learn about this too, Tom. I have many things to forgive myself for, and guilt to overcome, but I believe we can find our path together.

"Let's finish the dishes and go to your house. Leave this place for the two lovebirds."

"Your wish is my command," Tom said as he rolled up his sleeves and headed to the sink, Mandy right behind him, both of them thinking about the possibility that they could make their budding romance work.

Across the street Frank Jacks took out a tattered notebook with the words Electricians Do It In The Dark on it, spit on his fingers to flip to a clean page, and made a note of the date and time. Behind him, the gas station light pulsed on and off. Soon he would have enough money to get them fixed if he felt like wasting his money on it.

Kicking an empty soda can, he wondered why anyone would want to run a gas station in a small hick town like this anyway. Buying it was the biggest mistake of his life. He thought it would make Tina happy to stay in Doveland. It did, for a year.

Perhaps there would be enough money to track her down. Then she would see who the smart one was. Frank was sure it wasn't Tina.

Nineteen

"We don't have many people staying at the bunkhouse anymore, do we?" Ava said as she handed Evan his morning coffee. They were in the kitchen making up plates of crepes and scrambled eggs.

Ben had already nursed and was taking his morning nap. They hadn't heard a peep out of Hannah. When they had looked in her room, she was still sound asleep. The day before had been a long and exciting time for her; they would let her sleep as long as she wanted.

"No, our Circle appears to be widening and bonding, though.

"Now we have Pete and Barbara in town, and Mandy has her own apartment even though she sometimes stays at Tom's house. Then there are Eric and Grace in Grace's apartment, and Sam and Mira at Mira's."

"I wish Hank could have stayed, but guess he has work to do. I can't wait until this is all over, and I can have my Uncle Hank in my life all the time," Ava said.

As Evan hugged her, he added, "Besides Hank, the only part of our Circle that is not here is Craig and his wife, Jo Anne, and of course Sarah and Leif.

"Oh, but we are here," Leif said as he and Sarah appeared in the kitchen. At the same time, Hannah stumbled in the door wearing rumpled pajamas.

"Sarah," she called and ran to her, putting her arms around her and failing. "Oh, phooey, I keep forgetting you're not really here."

"No, not now. But we are coming for Ben's christening. We already booked the tickets. So if your bunkhouse is open, we will be happy to occupy it," Sarah replied.

"It is always open to you. I am so excited that you are coming. We have missed you so much," Ava said.

"And, we have missed you too," Sarah said glancing at Hannah who had retreated to her seat at the table and was staring at the plate of eggs her mom had put in front of her.

"Hannah," she said. "May we speak with you for a second in your room? If that's okay with your parents?"

Ava and Evan nodded "yes" and then stared at each other. What was going on? Why bother to come to them first? Sarah and Leif could have just gone straight to Hannah.

Multiple beeps from the alarm system sounded as cars pulled up the driveway. "I guess we'll have to find out later," Evan said to Ava as Hannah, Sarah and Leif left the room.

Eric and Grace came in the door first, looking ten years younger.

"Wow, love sure makes you guys glow," Evan said.

The response was a big hug from both of them, and Eric's whisper in Evan's ear, "You should know!"

Within minutes, everyone had piled through the door. But first they left their shoes, purses, and jackets in the front mud room.

"Where's Hannah?" Mandy asked as she looked around the living room.

"With Sarah and Leif in her bedroom," Ava answered.

Grace and Eric exchanged glances.

"Okay, are we the last to know about something? What's going on?"

"Nothing bad," Leif said entering the room with Sarah and Hannah trailing behind him. "But, I think it is something Hannah needs to tell you herself. Perhaps after everyone has breakfast and settles down?

As he and Sarah started to fade away, Tom called after him, "Wait, what's happening with Craig? We haven't heard from him for a while?"

"Did you ever hear of a phone?" Leif laughed, and they were gone.

After a moment of silence, everyone laughed too and headed into the kitchen to fill up their plates. As Leif said, first things first—food, coffee, some good conversation, and then they could deal with the unknowns.

****

Jay stood on the edge of the field and admired his work. *Not bad for never having done it before, in this life time anyway.* He had used Melvin's ancient tractor with his old plow, harrow, and corn planter. There was no new equipment on this farm. But, it was only one hundred acres. Not that hard, just time consuming.

However, now that he had finished the planting, Jay was restless. Four weeks had gone by since he had heard about Doveland from the truck driver and almost three weeks since he had moved to Concourse. The problem was, Jay still wasn't positive he had found the right place. He needed to explore the other roads.

To do that he would need Melvin's truck and some time off. *How would he explain that to Melvin?*

Without warning, Melvin came up behind him and clapped him on the back. Together they admired the field that Jay had just finished plowing and planting. They had waited until the threat of frost was over, and now it was promising to rain during the next week, so it was the perfect time to have finished.

"If I didn't know better, Jay, I would think you have done this for more years than me. Those rows are perfect."

It was those kind words that got Jay every time. Keeping his eyes on the rows, he grunted a thank-you.

"I need some more supplies in town, but I don't need them until tomorrow, so if you would like to take the truck and a day off, this would be the day."

This time Jay couldn't help himself. He turned to look at Melvin. *How does he know?* Jay wondered.

"Yes, if you don't mind, I could use a day off. Maybe stop in the bar in town on the way back and have a beer."

"As long as it is just one beer," Melvin huffed as he walked back to the house, yelling over his shoulder, "Time is a-wastin, boy. Get going!"

Jay didn't need another invitation. Following Melvin back to the house, he ran up the stairs two at a time, grabbed his wallet, with his new driver's license, some cash from the envelope in his dresser, and flew down the stairs and out to the truck.

Melvin watched him drive away, shaking his head. *It isn't possible,* he thought. And then being the practical farmer that he had been his entire life, he headed out to his small garden patch to do some serious weeding.

As Jay drove, he made a plan.

To get from Concourse to Doveland he had to take the same road as before, but this time he would slow down at that driveway that creeped him out the last time. If possible, he would park and walk back to see who lived there. After that, he would explore the other three roads that led out of town.

He only needed to drive a few miles down each of the roads to see if he could find his old place. When he finished, he would come back to town for a bite to eat, pick up what Melvin needed, maybe eat at the Diner if it was open, and then a beer at the bar.

Perhaps bring one home for Melvin. It was promising to be a good day.

Twenty

Hannah didn't want to tell, so after saying hello to everyone, she had gone back to her bedroom and sat on the bed. Finally, hunger drove her back to the kitchen. Even though no one was there, her mom had left her a plate of crepes and scrambled eggs on the warmer.

She could hear them all talking in the living room, so there was no point in putting it off any longer. Besides, she wouldn't be able to eat until she told them. At that moment, as if knowing what she was thinking, Grace came into the kitchen and asked if she was ready.

Hannah nodded yes, grateful that someone could read her mind, and that it was Grace. Holding her new grandmother's hand, she went in to face the others.

"I don't know how to explain it to you," Hannah said as everyone turned to look at her, "I just know things."

"Does it worry you that you do, Hannah?" Evan asked her.

"Sorta. I am not sure if I should tell, or pretend I don't know, or forget that I do so I will be like other people."

Grace led Hannah over to the couch where her mom and Evan were sitting. Sandwiched between them Hannah felt much more secure.

Ava turned to look at her, cupping her face softly in her hands. "Hannah, don't you know that most people in this room do things that some people can't do?"

"That's different," she said.

"How is it different?"

"I'm a little kid."

"True words," Mandy said as she reached up from where she was sitting on the floor to hold Hannah's hand. "I don't have the gifts that some of your family has, Hannah, so I can only speak as one of the 'other people,' but if I could know things I think I would be both happy about it and afraid of it too, even though I am a grownup."

"Really?"

"Yes, really. All gifts carry a responsibility with them. It doesn't matter if it's a gift to play music, write books, speak many languages, or throw a fastball. They all require us to acknowledge that we have a gift and then practice at making the gift better. It takes work and patience. But, Hannah, I know you can do both, even as a little kid."

Hannah leapt off the couch and into Mandy's lap. "Thank you, Auntie Mandy. And since I do know things, I think it's time that you include me in these kinds of meetings, because I can tell you things you might want to know."

Ava felt her heart thump. Hannah was only nine years old, and now she would have to learn about people who do evil things on purpose. Ava wanted her daughter to stay innocent. She longed to protect her forever.

"But mommy, I already know about those people, and that's why you need me to be here. Because not only do I know things, I remember things too."

"So you heard what I was thinking?"

"Yes, but I promise I don't listen in all the time. It's just that it's important right now for you to believe me. Because I have to tell you something else too."

Everyone sighed and then paused to appreciate the moment. Once Hannah told them what she knew, things would be different. It was one of those pivotal moments. Only a few minutes before they treated Hannah as a child, and now, she, although still a child, was going to participate as a young woman.

"Okay, Hannah. Sarah and Leif told us not to worry. I think we can handle it, and for sure we want you to know that we are always going to support and encourage you in every way possible. What do you want to tell us?" Evan asked.

"I remember myself from before."

"From before what?"

"From before I lived in this lifetime."

Ava blew her bangs out of her eyes and sank back into the couch. Her baby girl knew herself from before. Ava had no idea what that meant, but she was reasonably sure that life was going to be different again for all of them. A million questions rose up. Was I her mother before? Where did she live?

"No, mom. You weren't. But you are this time, and that is something you have to remember because my dad is coming to find me."

"Your dad? Your dad died. Evan's your dad now."

"No, not that dad. The other one. The before one."

No one spoke.

Hannah looked down at her hands resting on her lap afraid to look at their faces. She could feel hot tears trickling down her face but didn't want to move to brush them away. What would they think of her now?

It felt like hours before anyone moved or spoke, but it was only a moment until everyone rose from their seats and moved to the floor, forming a circle around her where she rested on Mandy's lap.

"Since you know things, Hannah, can you feel how much we all love you? We want to learn about what you know, and what you mean, but it doesn't change the fact that we are a family," Eric said.

Hannah's tear-stained face lifted to look at each of them, "A circle?"

"Yes, our Circle. Stronger because all of us are here, and stronger because you are here, Hannah. We are a Circle—we are a Karass."

A bright smile broke out on Hannah's face as she said, "Oh goodie, now I feel like eating," and jumped up to go get her crepes from the kitchen.

Ava smiled, and as Hannah darted out into the kitchen, she whispered, "And still my little girl."

****

A few hours later, and a few hundred yards away, Jay parked Melvin's truck by the side of the road and walked back towards that driveway he had noticed the last time he came to town.

He had hoped that it would be straight so he could see where it went, but it curved around. Jay was tempted to start walking up the driveway to see where it went but stopped himself when he noticed cameras aimed at the entrance.

They might have already seen him, but he didn't think he had triggered any alarms since he was still standing on the road. Instead of going forward, he pretended to look for something and then casually strolled back towards the truck.

Nothing to see here, he thought. Just like the Star Wars movie with that line, it really meant there *was everything* to see here. He'd have to go about getting more information in town.

To do that, he had to be on his best behavior all the time. It was going to be hard. The acute discomfort he had always felt, was getting worse.

He barely slept at night. If he fell asleep, he kept reliving the nightmare of the fire. Over and over again he wanted to run inside the house to save them. Over and over again he failed. Over and over again he saw that man, kneeling on the ground with his head in his hands.

Every morning, he woke up to where nothing had changed. He was haunted because he remembered two lifetimes. He often got confused which one was which, and he still didn't have the two people he loved the most.

The only good that Jay could find was the hope that his anxiety was increasing because he was closer to finding that man and punishing him.

First things first though. He needed to confirm that he was in the right town.

That meant driving those back roads. Best to start now, and then get food and information he needed in Doveland. He had all day to do what he wanted to do, and he was going to make use of every minute of it.

Twenty-One

Pete scrubbed the counter again. He had already rubbed it until it shone, but it gave him something to do. After the breakfast at Ava and Evan's, he and Barbara had come back to the Diner. Barbara was exhausted, so he sent her straight up to their apartment to get some rest. He worried about her. She had beat cancer this time, perhaps forever. But any time she looked tired, it felt as if a hand was squeezing his chest.

What was he doing? The lunch crowd was gone. She had been up there for hours, alone. He wanted to be with her.

Alex Bender, the new man they hired, was a decent cook, and Sunday afternoons were slow, so Pete didn't need to be in the Diner leaving Barbara by herself. A short conversation with Alex who told him he could handle the Diner and would call Pete if he needed help, assured him that it was the right decision.

As Pete headed up the back stairs, the bell on the door of the Diner dinged. He didn't turn to look. Alex would let him know if he needed him.

Nevertheless, he still had that nagging feeling that he forgot to tell the Circle something. Heck, if he couldn't remember soon, he could ask Hannah if she knew—since she knew things.

******

Jay heard the bell ding as he entered the Diner. He was expecting it to be full of people; instead, there were only two men in the corner nursing their coffees.

"Go ahead, sit anywhere," he heard someone call out, and turned to see a young man with one of those trendy short beards standing behind the counter.

He chose a booth looking out over the town square. He could see the gas station and grocery store; both places he would need to stop at before he went back to the farm. Now that he had driven the roads out of town, he also knew where to find the bar. It was just where he remembered it. It was thirty years rattier than before, but the same bar.

When he had climbed that last rise and saw the hill where his house used to be, Jay almost drove off the road. Instead, he managed to pull off onto a dirt logging trail. He barely managed to park and open the door before everything in his stomach came up. Then he passed out.

When he came to, he checked his watch and realized that an hour had passed. Still shaking, he pulled the truck even further onto the path, and then Jay stepped out and looked at the view he had once known like the back of his hand.

Yes, the trees were more mature. However, it was the place. Except there wasn't a house anymore. It was a meadow with a few trees scattered where he and his family had once played in the yard. Then something struck him that he had forgotten entirely.

Unbelievable, he thought. *I could have looked for them in the graveyard.* After beating himself up for a few minutes, he realized why he had not thought of it before.

If he saw their graves, he would have to admit that he wasn't crazy, that he had a life before this one—a life where he had lost everything.

"You okay?" the young man with the beard and a name tag that read, Alex, asked him.

"Sure. Just haven't eaten yet today," Jay said.

"Well, I'm both the cook and waiter today, so I can get you whatever you want, but I make a perfect omelet. The owner is teaching me other things, but omelets are my specialty."

"Sounds good," Jay said. "And coffee?"

Before Alex walked away. "Hey, could you tell me if this diner was here before?"

"Well, it's been here as long as I can remember, and my parents said they used to come to it when they were young. Changed owners a bunch of times. The new owner just opened it a week or so ago."

"Okay, thanks," Jay said looking around. Yes, he was right. He'd been here before too. Now that he knew that he was in the right town, would the pain stop, or get worse?

He was reasonably sure it would get worse because it already had. This was the town he used to live in with his family, but this time he was alone.

Twenty-Two

After Hannah's announcement, Ava wanted an immediate meeting of the Stone Circle but needed to wait until the next day when Hannah was in school.

There was a reason she called their circle the Stone Circle. She and Evan, Tom, Mira, Sarah, Leif, and Craig had all received stones when they first met at Earl Wieland's house before he left for the Forest Circle to be with his wife, Ariel.

The stones had tumbled out of the bag and started glowing. Earl had said that there was a stone for each of them, and without thinking, they each had picked one, although it had felt more like the stones had chosen them instead. Ava kept hers in the office on her desk. It hadn't glowed since then, and she had no idea why they had them. However, right now, that wasn't what concerned her. She was worried about Hannah.

She needed the Stone Circle to help her figure out what to do. Sarah and Leif would drop in remotely and they would video-call Craig. Everyone else lived in town. Ava had talked to Craig earlier and caught him up with what Hannah had told them the day before.

Craig hadn't said much; just that she shouldn't worry, and he would do some research on the subject before the call.

They met Monday morning after Eric picked up Hannah for school, and the house had been swept of listening devices and cameras as it was every morning. Hank had taught them the value of caution. Even though they were focused on Hannah, none of them had forgotten the ever-present danger of Grant.

They met in the kitchen with Ava's laptop on the counter so everyone could see the screen. Each of them had their favorite drink in front of them. Ava had baked blueberry scones to distract herself, so the members of the Stone Circle that were present were busy munching away.

After a few failed attempts, Craig's happy face appeared. He looked around at his friends and asked, "Where's Ben? I wanted to look at the big guy. How old is he now?"

Ava smiled. "He's sleeping. He's over a month old now. You'll be here for the christening, won't you? As always, we have a room in the bunkhouse for you."

"Wouldn't miss it for the world," he answered. "But, I can see from all of your faces you really want some answers."

Evan broke in, "What we first need to know is if it is possible. Is it possible that Hannah remembers her dad from a past life? Once we know the answer to that, we can talk about whether what she sees happening is dangerous or not."

"There are opinions on both sides. If you believe that we are our bodies and all the chemical reactions and biological actions and reactions within it, then it is unlikely that you would think reincarnation is possible.

"However, we all know that we are not our bodies. So the next question is: would and could the soul come back to earth again in another form? I think we all believe that our souls are eternal. John Lennon said, 'I'm not afraid of death because it's just getting out of one car, and into another.'

"Therefore, the remaining question is, can we remember who we used to be in another lifetime.

"Does that about sum up your questions?" Craig asked.

After seeing everyone nod yes, Craig continued, "So, assuming that we agree it's possible to return to this life, we could also agree that Hannah might be one of those people who has done it.

As for remembering past lives, there is a name for someone who remembers-----even though surprisingly few people know the word.

It makes sense that it's a Hindu word because Hindus believe in rebirth. They call a person who can vividly recall incidents of their past life a Jatismar."

"So, Hannah is a Jatismar?" Ava said.

"Sounds like it," answered Craig.

"So the next question is, who is this man that she says is her dad? Is he a Jatismar, too? Does he remember her? Will he try to take her away if he does?"

****

Sam put down the phone and pumped his fist in the air. Watching Lenny had paid off, and Grant's huge ego helped.

They found Grant in plain sight, watching Lenny running his crew right there in the fish bowl at Panera's. Sam couldn't figure out who was stupider. Was it Lenny for holding his meeting in the same place that Grant had held his meetings? Or, was it, Grant, assuming that because his face no longer looked the same, he would never be recognized?

People often forgot that the way they move identifies them too. When Sam was in college, his girlfriend had explained to him how she recognized people. Before she got glasses, she couldn't see people's faces. So she learned how to identify them from the way they walked. Later, Sam had taken a class in kinesthetic recognition and learned even more subtle ways to recognize people. He had made sure everyone working for him did the same, and it had paid off.

His operative had tailed Grant for a few miles, but then lost him when his car was stopped in a construction zone, and Grant's car had gone through.

It didn't matter. They knew what he looked like, and Sam had a pretty good idea of where Grant was heading. They would be waiting for him.

Twenty-Three

Jay had returned to the farm without a single idea of what to do next. Yes, he had found his old home. But what good did it do him? Jay had harbored a hope that when he discovered the place where he had lived before, he would feel better. Instead, he felt worse.

For days, he moped around the farm, doing his best to keep up with the work that Melvin gave him. But as soon as dinner was over, he would go to his room and lie on the bed trying to think about nothing.

One morning, Melvin was waiting at the bottom of the stairs for him when he came down to breakfast. "We gotta talk, boy," he said.

Jay's heart sunk. On top of everything else, he was going to lose his job. There was nowhere to go. He might as well just end it now.

"Stop your moping. No, you're not fired. Not yet anyways, but we do gotta talk. What you tell me is going to make all the difference.

"Get your coffee and biscuit and meet me in the living room in ten minutes. And try to get some gumption in you before you get there."

Jay nodded and headed into the kitchen where Melvin had laid out a fresh biscuit, butter they had made together, and the jelly that Melvin had preserved in the fall. A tiny ray of hope entered Jay's heart. *What if it was something good Melvin wanted to talk about?*

Ten minutes later Jay found Melvin in what Melvin called the living room. It was small and dark, but it was evident that at one time a woman had taken pains to make it comfortable. That time was long past. Jay had seen a picture of Melvin and his wife on the fireplace mantle, but all he could get out of Melvin was that she had passed years before. The living room was evidence that it had been a long time.

Still, it was comfortable and clean. Every Friday Jay heard Melvin running a vacuum that sounded like a small pickup truck. "Getting ready for the weekend," Melvin would say.

However, Saturday was no different from any other day. Up as soon as the sun rose, and back in for dinner when it set.

Sunday morning Melvin did something different. Melvin went to church in town. Said he wanted to make sure he saw his wife again in heaven, so if that meant going to church, then that was what he would do. The no-work Sunday morning was the only thing to mark the turn of the week.

Melvin was sitting in his chair by the window. He gestured to Jay to sit on the couch opposite him.

Neither of them spoke. Melvin, clearly uncomfortable about what he was going to say, kept glancing at Jay and then out the window.

Jay, unable to take any more, burst out, "Look, I know I haven't been doing a good job this past week. But, if you'll give me a chance…"

Melvin stopped him with a raised hand. "No."

"No, what?" Jay asked.

"It's not that, Jay. What I need from you is the truth. I've been thinking about this since the moment I seen you. But, my religion says it's not possible, so I haven't been able to reconcile what I thought was true, and what I see."

While Melvin talked, Jay could feel his face flush red. Fear gripped his heart. He had to keep his hands clasped in his lap so they wouldn't shake. Without raising his head, he mumbled, "What do you see?"

It was a long moment before Melvin answered. "I see a man I've seen before. He used to live in Doveland, had a pretty wife and a little girl. Probably going on thirty years ago. Heard his farm burned down, and he done drunk himself to death.

"Now, I don't believe in ghosts. Plus I seen you work, and eat, which means you can't be a ghost. So I went and talked to the old biddy in town that I done known since we were kids. She is always telling me that there is more going on than meets the eye. She told me it's possible. She says people do come back to their lives, and some of them remember them, too.

"She even knew this fancy Hindu name for that kind of person. Jatismar, I think is what she said. Anyways, I told her about you, and she says it's possible you are one of those people.

"So help me out, Jay. Tell me the truth. Are you? Cause you ain't no good to me the way you're acting."

As Melvin spoke, Jay's head dropped lower and lower. He couldn't believe what he was hearing. He felt torn between elation that someone knew him, and maybe could help, and fear of what would happen because someone found out the truth.

Melvin waited him out. Minutes later Jay lifted a pale, tear stained face and stared at the man who could either save him or ruin him. Remembering his kind eyes, he decided to go for hope.

"Yes, it's true."

"Well," humphed Melvin as he pushed himself out of his chair. I think it's time you told me all about it. Come on, let's walk, and talk. The farm can wait. If I have this figured out correctly, you have thirty years of telling to do, so we best get the talking going. You talk; I'll listen to your tale. Perhaps after telling me, you will feel better. If not. At least we will understand each other.

"Come on. Times a-wasting."

Jay rose from the couch and followed the old man out the door. They both slapped hats on their heads and stopped to look at the newly planted kitchen garden before heading out across the front yard toward the fields.

If I had been lucky, thought Jay, *this is the man I would have chosen to be my dad.* Looking at Melvin as he strode across the lawn, Jay had another thought. *Maybe I am lucky; perhaps this is the beginning of a better life.*

Hurrying to catch up, Jay let himself see the future as something with a bit of joy in it. And then he shut it down. He hadn't yet told Melvin everything, and once he did, there was a possibility that he would not still want him around.

It was almost sunset before the two of them returned to the kitchen. Both were talked out. Jay hadn't kept anything back. Melvin hadn't given any opinions. As he promised, he had listened.

In the kitchen, Melvin scrambled some eggs while Jay made toast. They ate in silence, and then they both went to their rooms. Nothing had been decided.

Jay was fully aware that Melvin held his future in his hands, but he was too tired to worry about it. He fell asleep the moment his head hit the pillow, and for the first time in his adult life, he slept without waking up to the nightmare.

It was Melvin's turn to stay awake.

As he always did when he was troubled, he spoke to his wife and asked her what he should do. And as always, he got the same answer. "Melvin, do what your heart tells you to do. And be kind about it."

Twenty-Four

For the next few days, neither Jay nor Melvin talked about Jay's revelation. There was plenty of work to do on the farm to keep them both busy.

One day, instead of sending Jay into Doveland to pick up supplies, Melvin drove himself. Melvin rarely visited Doveland. Everything he needed was right there in his town—most of the time.

He had lived in Concourse his whole life. He had met his wife, Sally, in grade school. From the moment he saw her, he knew she was the one. He didn't think of it that way then. Instead, he teased her and pulled her ponytail. By junior high, he was walking her home from school. By the time they were seniors in high school, they had planned their wedding day. Neither of them ever dated anyone else.

Melvin knew that was old-fashioned, but he didn't care. She was all he ever wanted. He also knew that they had been lucky. Melvin had friends whose marriages ended because they grew apart. He and Sally grew together.

It seemed like a flash of time before his son had grown up and gone. He only came home for his mother's funeral, and then left again.

Melvin couldn't blame him. His son wanted more from life than the hard work of farming. Still, Melvin had been lonely for a long time. Until Jay showed up and started helping.

The farm hasn't looked this good in years, Melvin mused. Jay was a troubled young man, but Melvin was trusting that he was a good man. Melvin was sure that if he asked Jay, he would say that he wasn't. But pain and loneliness can do that to you, Melvin knew about that.

Yes, he remembered the man Jay from before when he had a different name and a different life. Thirty years ago, he had read his obituary in the paper. However, Melvin was choosing to put that thought into a box for now since he had no idea how that could be true, except it was. Instead of trying to figure it out, he was going to focus on helping Jay in this lifetime.

And that meant getting him away from the farm so he could make some friends. To make that happen, he too would have to come out of hiding. Melvin wasn't concerned too much about that. It was time for him to do a good deed or two.

Truth be told, he was being selfish. He wanted to make sure that when he died, he was good enough to join Sally. Therefore, he was going to have to do more than just go to church once a week and say a few prayers. It was time to take action.

Melvin didn't really need anything in Doveland. What he was looking for was information. What kind of community had it grown into? Could Jay be happy here, and how could he help make that happen for Jay?

Driving around the town square on his way to a parking spot at the grocery store, he was amazed at the changes that had taken place since the last time he was in town.

The first stop would have to be the Diner. He was hungry for a piece of apple pie. In addition, it used to be an excellent place to catch up with the news. Perhaps it still was.

****

Pete had watched the old truck circle the square and park at the grocery store. He was happy to see the man who got out head towards the Diner. Pete loved meeting people. This discovery came as a small shock to him. After all, he had spent most of his adult life by himself, driving trucks.

Now in this phase of life, he was rarely by himself. Pete had learned the names of everyone who came into the Diner and got a thrill seeing people's faces light up when he called them by their name as they walked through the door.

It reminded him of that old TV show, "Cheers." The theme song said it was a place where everyone knows your name. Well, that is what he wanted for the Diner. And if you wanted to know what was going on in town, this was the place to be.

But although he had seen the truck before, Pete had never seen the driver. *This guy looks like he has been around, and knows a lot,* thought Pete.

It didn't take long for Pete and Melvin to strike up a conversation over Melvin's coffee and pancakes. However, they didn't have much time together before the rest of the morning regulars started coming in.

Pete clapped Melvin on the back and said. "It was good to meet you. Come back, and we'll talk some more," and then headed off to cook. Pete's wife Barbara took over the coffee filling and taking orders.

Before long patrons talking to each other filled the Diner. It was just what Melvin was hoping would happen. He sipped his coffee, and ate his pancakes, reveling in the swirl of gossip and information that filled the restaurant.

Forty-five minutes later, Melvin left a tip for Barbara under his coffee cup, waved to Pete, and headed to the grocery store for the few things he could get in Doveland that he couldn't find in Concourse.

After that, he would fill the truck with gas and head home. Melvin had some ideas for Jay. It would probably take some fancy talking to convince him, but he had lots of practice waiting people out. Plus, he had a good idea on his side, and nothing can stop a good idea from happening. At least, that's what Sally used to say, and she was always right.

He thought he heard Sally giggle, so he said to her, "I know, you always said you were always right; now I'm agreeing." Melvin drove back to the farm a happier man than he had been in a long time. He had a project, and it was a good one. It would be interesting to see how it turned out.

****

Melvin told Jay about the solstice celebration. "It is all the talk in town. Everyone will be there. If the man you are looking for is in town, he will probably be there. Otherwise, you could meet some new people, and that could lead to finding the man."

Jay said, "No."

He had seen the signs when he went to Doveland. But then he found out what it was and there was no way he was going to some fancy celebration with people laughing, and doing all that artsy crafty thing. No way at all.

Melvin wasn't concerned.

He remembered when his son was growing up how often he would say no to ideas. New people and doing new things scared him. Melvin always had a solution.

He would say to him, "If you go, and you don't like it, you never have to go again. But since I am the head of the house I say you are going at least once."

That's what he would say to his son. Almost always his son would find that his dad was right. But if he didn't like it after giving it a try, Melvin had no problem telling him he didn't have to go again.

He used the same tactic on Jay. He reminded him why he had come to Concourse—to find closure and hopefully some peace around his family's death. If it was revenge that would bring him peace, Melvin would support him.

But hanging out at the farm afraid to meet up with the guy would never get him what he wanted. Then Melvin threw in the most important question, "You're not afraid of finding him are you?"

Melvin sweetened the offer by saying he would go with Jay, even though it was the last place Melvin wanted to go. To seal the deal, Melvin asked Jay to show him where his farm used to be.

Melvin could see that Jay was weakening, so he stopped talking and stood in front of him without moving. His son called him a stone when he did that. It was pretty accurate. He was unmoving.

Finally, Jay sighed and said, "Okay."

Secretly Jay was happy. Melvin was making him take action. For the last few weeks, he could feel himself sinking into a pit of depression. It reminded him of what happened to him the last time around.

There was no way he was going back to drugs and booze. Melvin was right, he had to find the man, and get his revenge. Only then could he consider being happy.

Twenty-Five

Grant inserted his passkey into the door, stepped into his motel room, and gave it a silent seal of approval. Not fancy, but clean. Perfect for the man he was pretending to be—a traveling salesman checking out a new territory.

He paid cash out of habit. There was no need to do so because no one was tracking his new identity. But it was a good habit. One he intended to keep.

Grant wasn't planning to stay for more than a few days; not long enough for anyone to pay attention to him. All he needed to do was confirm that his plans for Hank and his family would work.

This time Grant wasn't staying in Doveland. That would be taking too many chances. Instead, he was in a larger town where it was easier to hide. It was wasn't that far away from Doveland.

However, on the way to the motel, Grant had passed through Doveland just to prove that he could. It was taking a chance because everyone had to drive around the town square to get anywhere, so it was possible someone could have seen him.

However, he wasn't worried. There was no way anyone would recognize him. It gave him a perverse thrill that just like him, Doveland had a new look. Grant liked it.

He would have to give them that. Since last summer many of the main buildings had been spruced up, and the gazebo in Doveland's town square was very charming—that is, if you liked that kind of thing.

He didn't. At least he hadn't before.

Now he was trying to build a new persona, one that would fit in where he was planning to retire.

He would be a gentleman with refined tastes and quiet money. *What a life that was going to be.* However, for now, the motel fit his simple salesman image.

Grant just needed a few days to check out the area. He wanted to see for himself what that Circle was doing. It was growing. More of them were moving to Doveland. That was not a good thing. Grant knew there was strength in numbers.

But since he didn't have a desire to run the world anymore—it wasn't worth it—if some of them survived what he was going to do, he could live with it.

All of the people who lived in Doveland didn't need to die. But, everyone who conspired to put him in jail had to be punished.

Grant had hated that damn Circle before because they knew things they shouldn't. Now he despised them even more because they had helped put him in jail.

No matter what happened, he was going to get rid of Hank. His actions were a betrayal. Grant wanted revenge. This time he was doing it all himself. That way, he would be sure to succeed.

****

While Grant was making his way around the town square, the solstice committee was wrapping up a meeting.

Valerie had spent the last few minutes admonishing each of the committee members that they might not realize how little time they had left to finish preparing for the event. It was only nine days away.

The plans weren't elaborate. It was a small town after all. However, there were many moving parts, and to Valerie, there didn't appear to be much moving going on.

In desperation, Valerie turned to Grace, who in a short time had become her most trusted committee member. If Grace said she would do something, she would, and Grace somehow motivated other people to do their part too.

But this time, Grace wasn't paying any attention at all to the meeting. "Grace?" Valerie said, tapping her on the shoulder.

When Grace turned to look at her, Valerie was surprised at Grace's distressed face. She had never seen Grace distressed before. However, she didn't have a chance to ask her about it because within moments it was gone and her good friend Grace was back, ready to help.

They had to make sure that the elementary school choir was prepared to perform. The music teacher was rehearsing the song, "Walking On Sunshine," for the little ones to sing. Dancing maidens would surround them wearing flower wreaths in their hair.

There was a new dance instructor in town, and the rumor was that the music and dance teachers were more than friends. Valerie didn't care about that. She just wanted their combined performance to work.

There would be yoga on the grass since it was also national yoga day; crafts in the new gazebo and for those that were still awake, a bonfire to finish off the evening.

Everyone on the committee would bring food, like one big block party. But it needed coordination, so they didn't end up with all potato salad. That was Grace's job.

Satisfied that everyone knew what had to be done by the next meeting, Valerie dismissed them with a wave of her hand and turned to her friend.

"Grace, is there something wrong?"

"I don't know. For a minute, it felt as if something terrible was going to happen. Silly, I know," Grace said, patting her friend's hand to assure her that all was well.

But Grace knew it wasn't silly. She knew that something evil was coming to town; not because she had been told about Grant's escape, but because she felt it. The feeling was gone now, though, and Mandy needed help at the coffee shop, so she put it out of her mind.

Still, Grace was too wise to hope that putting it out of her mind meant making it go away. She had learned more than enough about evil in her lifetime. At the same time, since moving to Doveland, she had also strengthened her belief in the power of good.

Just a year ago, she was going crazy with boredom, and now she was surrounded by friends and adopted family. She had a new husband and a new business.

In all her wildest dreams, Grace had never thought she would be this happy this late in life. Nevertheless, she knew that happiness could ebb and flow. Eric hadn't been feeling well for a long time. He had hinted at it the past year, trying to prepare everyone.

Well, I am not prepared to lose him now that I have just found him. She would do everything she could to keep him happy and healthy for as long as possible. She had even searched out alternative healing methods, and they looked promising.

Last weekend, Evan and his friends had moved Eric to Grace's simply furnished apartment above the store. Once she knew she was staying in Doveland, she arranged to have her belongings moved from storage in Sandpoint.

There weren't many things, but they were precious to her. Eric had moved to Doveland with even less. He had only a suitcase. Having traveled for years with Doctors Without Borders, Eric had learned not to keep anything. Eric said he had one precious thing, a picture of him with Abbie and Ava.

As Grace walked across the town square, she began listing all the wonderful things coming. Ben would be christened on the morning of the solstice at the chapel where his parents were married.

Everyone would be there, including Hank, and that is what scared Grace. Everyone would be in town at one time. It was a perfect scenario for Grant to do something.

Last year, he first tried to blow them all up, and then poison them with gas dropped from a drone. What would he try to do this year? It was Hank and Sam that stopped him last year, would they be able to repeat that?

I need to talk to Sam, she thought. *And Sarah and Leif. I think they need my help again.*

When Grace opened the door of Your Second Home, the delicious smell of coffee and cookies floated towards her. Everything about her store looked warm and comfortable. Mandy and Eric were waiting on customers.

Some were reading books, and some were typing. A few people were talking together, and a man was reading the newspaper in one of the chairs by the window. It was precisely how she had envisioned it would be.

As she opened the door, Eric looked up and smiled. Nothing ever looked as beautiful to Grace as that smile.

No one is going to take this from us, she declared to herself.

But just thirty minutes away, Grant was making plans to do just that.

Twenty-Six

Ava finished sewing the last button on the dress that Hannah wanted to wear to the solstice and stuck the needle into the pincushion with a sigh.

The subject of Hannah's past had not come up again. Every time she tried to bring it up, Hannah would tell her it wasn't the time. What was she supposed to do? She couldn't force Hannah into revealing what she wasn't ready to share. She would have to trust that Hannah knew what she was talking about when she said it would all be alright in the end.

But Hannah seemed particularly interested in what she was going to wear to the solstice celebration. She had described the dress in detail. Frustrated that her mom couldn't figure out what she meant, she sat beside Ava as they searched the internet for a pattern for the dress that she wanted.

Ava had learned to sew when her mom insisted she take the sewing badge as a girl scout. Not having sewn for years, Ava was worried she couldn't pull it off. But she took it slow and eventually made Hannah's dress, just the way she wanted it to look, because Hannah also picked the color and the fabric. This from a child who wore whatever happened to be lying around clean or not.

The entire time Ava was making the dress, she was afraid that Hannah wanted it because it reminded her of her past life. But when asked, Hannah managed to divert her attention away from the question. Eventually, Ava gave in to letting things flow. Besides, Ben took up most of her time and sleep, so she had very little energy to fight where this was taking her.

Ava laid the dress aside so she could show Hannah when she came home from school. The house was quiet for once. Evan was in town at the last meeting of the solstice committee before the event. Grace had roped him in to designing and managing the traffic flow and parking plan. Grace had also designated Mandy in charge of the food tables. They were using the Diner as the central food hub. They could use Pete's updated kitchen for last minute preparation and his refrigerators and walk-in freezer as storage.

It was going to be a beautiful day, but Ava wondered if it had been wise to schedule Ben's christening on the same day as the solstice. It had seemed a good idea when they planned it. However, that was before Grant had escaped. With another deep sign Ava leaned back on the couch and closed her eyes, trying to grab a few minutes of sleep before Hannah came home or Ben woke up.

With only two more days to the festival, and with guests arriving in town, she needed all the rest that she could get.

****

Hank told Lenny that he would be away for a few days. He needed to go to Doveland to be at his great-nephews' christening.

While he was there, he would watch for Grant. Hank didn't have to hide where he was going or why he was going.

Lenny had learned all about that the year before. Lenny didn't care about the do-gooders, as Grant called them. He only cared about making money, and now he cared about Grant.

Lenny figured that Grant knew that Lenny had been tipped off about the raid the year before, and that's how he escaped. It was true. Someone in town had warned him, and he had rewarded the man who told him what was going to happen.

Lenny hadn't minded too much about being the one who was supposed to carry out Grant's plans of killing Hank's entire family in Doveland, but he certainly didn't want to be caught doing it. So, he saved himself.

He was promised that Grant would be captured, which he was, and Lenny figured he was home free. When Hank told him about Grant's escape from prison, Lenny knew that Grant would come after him.

Lenny didn't trust Hank, but on the subject of Grant, they were on the same side. Except Hank wanted Grant captured, and Lenny wanted him dead.

Therefore, when Hank said he was heading to Doveland, he had Lenny's blessing. Lenny also figured that if Grant killed Hank, it wouldn't be such a bad thing. He knew Hank was the snitch to the FBI, and he didn't think anything had changed. He still was a snitch. One way or another, Hank would have to be eliminated, and if Grant wanted to do that for him, it would save him the trouble. Otherwise, once Grant was caught, he would kill Hank himself.

Sam was also heading to Doveland, and he wasn't hiding the reason either. He had fallen in love with a woman who lived there. Everyone understood that.

However, he was also going for another reason. He knew Grant would be there. What Sam didn't know was what Grant was planning to do.

Last year, they had Hank keeping them up to date with what Grant was planning. This year, they could only guess at his plans because as far as they could tell, he was working alone. At least they knew what he looked like now. The DNA test on the coffee cup confirmed that it had been Grant in Panera's.

In town, Grant's spy answered his phone. "Yep," was all that he said.

Let the fun begin, Grant's spy thought. He was a little worried about what was coming, but not much. No one was going to figure that he was the one who tipped Lenny off last year and was still on his payroll.

Now he was working with Grant too. Both of them had promised him a big payoff. He knew that playing them both was a dangerous game, but this way at least one of them would pay him. If it all went well, both of them would pay. Then he would leave Doveland and never return.

Watching the solstice celebration, he wished he had the guts to blow the place up himself. I hate these people, he thought, but they aren't worth the trouble that would be. Instead, he would let Grant or Lenny do the dirty work, and he would reap all the benefits.

Twenty-Seven

It felt weird to Hank not to sneak into town. He still owned the beat up old truck he drove in Doveland the year before, but this time he didn't stop in Concourse to see his father's grave. That part of him was beginning to heal, and he saw no reason to bring up that pain again. He had done what a fourteen-year-old boy thought he needed to do to protect his sister. Now, he was doing what he knew had to be done to protect his sister's daughter and all her friends—now his friends.

This time he drove straight to Ava's house, hugged Hannah, kissed a sleeping Ben, dumped his backpack in his room in the bunkhouse, and headed into Doveland and the Diner to see Pete and Eric.

Just as an average person would do, he thought. *I can talk to my friends openly over a burger.* In some ways, he was beginning to feel like a regular guy, but on the other hand, most people don't meet up with their friends to discuss how to keep their families safe.

As Hank pushed open the Diner door, he reminded himself how lucky he was. Now he had friends, and they liked and trusted him. Pete's big hug as he greeted Hank and dragged him to a booth in the corner was proof enough of that.

When Alex asked Hank what he wanted to drink, Pete introduced him to Hank as his new cook. Alex said he was also a waiter when Barbara was busy doing something else. As Hank shook hands with Alex, Hank could see why Pete hired him. Alex was young, but he had a quiet confidence and maturity about him.

As soon as Eric opened the door to the Diner, he saw Hank and Pete in the booth and made his way over to see them. Hank stood and gave Eric a bear hug. "You've lost weight, my friend," he said.

"Appreciate that you're not beating around the bush," Eric answered. "Grace has me on a crazy plant-based diet. It's a regime. Not just some vegetables here and there. I drink these weird smoothies four times a day and pop enough herbal remedies to make your head spin. That's why I'm losing weight, and I do feel better. I would rather go out feeling better than medicating myself into a stupor. I want to live fully until the end."

Hank looked closely at Eric, "If it is the end."

Eric smiled at them both, "That's what Grace says."

"You know that every one of us is praying for you in our own way. And with what Grace says your powerful friends are doing, who knows? We may be stuck with you for years!" Pete added.

"Amen to that," Eric answered. Turning to Hank, he asked, "Did you ever in your wildest dreams think that the two of us would end up like this? We lived just thirty miles from here, then we both left Concourse, and now we're here together in Doveland. There must be some kind of plan at work, don't you think?"

"What ever plan it is, I love it," Pete said. "This life is what I wished for so long ago, I forgot I wanted it."

Hank paused as Alex deposited the Diner's special burger in front of each of them and a heaping plate of french fries in the center of the table.

"You two have always been good men. I have done things that I would give anything to undo," Hank said.

"I think that is exactly what you are doing now," Eric replied.

Hank smiled and said, "Thank you," but couldn't stop thinking about something that happened thirty-five years before in Doveland. It was a time when he didn't have any friends except Grant. It was a time when he would do anything Grant asked him to do.

I wonder if Grant remembers it, Hank thought. I will never forget it.

******

Grant watched the three men laughing and having fun in the Diner. It was so different from the last time he had been in Doveland.

This year Grant sat on a bench in the town square without a care in the world. Last year he had to sneak around waiting for the moment when they all gathered at Ava's and Evan's wedding reception.

It was different for Hank too. Last year Hank didn't have any friends. This year he has friends and a family.

I was played for a fool last year, Grant thought. *I missed the fact they had moved the reception to another venue. I had missed the fact that Hank had betrayed me; Hank, the man I trusted for so many years.*

As Grant watched, he allowed himself to think back to when he had first found Hank as a boy living on the streets, doing petty crimes to survive. Grant had taught Hank the ways of hidden crime. Hank was good at it too. But what Hank didn't know was that Grant often set him up to fail and make him think it was his own fault.

It was a stroke of genius on my part, Grant mused. If Hank made a mistake, he would feel guilty about it and become even more vulnerable to Grant's control.

Grant chuckled to himself, thinking about the first time he had played that trick on Hank. It was right here in this town. A mistake so big, Hank cried at night over it for years. Yes, it was a masterful stroke of manipulation.

Grant loved synchronicity. He took it as a sign that Hank's family had moved to the same town where Grant had truly begun to own Hank. And then, last year, Hank had betrayed him right here in Doveland.

What a perfect circle of harmony that Hank would also die in Doveland. But not before he suffered. Because, if all goes well, Hank's friends and family will die right before his eyes, and it will be his fault.

Grant, fingered the vial in his pocket. When he was sure no one was looking, he put it under the bench between the iron legs and the bottom slat.

Later tonight, his man in town would retrieve it. Tomorrow, Grant would attend the solstice, but not eat the potato salad that Pete was making. More synchronicity, Grant mused. Pete will unwittingly poison every person in town who likes his potato salad, and I will get to watch what happens.

Twenty-Eight

Frank Jacks scratched his nose, frowned, and went back into the gas station's waiting room. Tomorrow would be a zoo with everyone coming to town to celebrate the solstice. They would use up every available parking space.

Pete gave him some orange cones so he could block the driveway into his gas station. But that meant he would have to stand outside all day to let in the people who wanted to buy gas.

I was an idiot to buy this place, he thought. Once I get that money, I am outta here. I'm not going to lock the doors or turn off the pumps. I'm just leaving. Let the town deal with the mess. First, I find Tina, then I am gone forever. It's a few more weeks at the most, and I will have finished my job one way or another.

Jacks turned as the bell dinged on a pump. Ava Anders' Uncle Hank was filling his car. They had met briefly the last time Hank was in town.

Seeing Frank looking at him, Hank waved. Frank decided he might as well act like a friendly neighbor and go out and talk to him.

Hank was a crucial player in the game that was going on. Finding out more about him might be wise.

"Ready for the big day tomorrow?" Frank asked.

"Not much for me to do," answered Hank. "Ava and Evan are handling the christening, and Pete is taking care of the food."

"Yea, I hear he is making a huge batch of his famous potato salad."

"That he is. Too bad, I don't like that stuff, but there will be plenty more for me to eat with everyone bringing food for the event. By the way, I know you will be stuck here at the station, so if you need help, just give me a holler. I'll be happy to spell you for a bit."

"Mighty nice of you," Frank responded. "Don't much care for potato salad myself. However, as you said, there will be a lot more to eat. Maybe I will have you come over so I can grab a plate of food."

Hank turned to Frank and shook his hand. "Great, it's a plan. See you tomorrow."

Frank watched Hank pull out and headed back towards the Anders' place. Hum, not a bad guy. It's a good thing Hank doesn't like potato salad.

Frank scratched his nose again before heading back into his office wondering if his anonymous boss knew that Hank doesn't eat potato salad, or was that the point? *I'll find out tomorrow.*

****

Sarah and Leif had decided to drive their car to the Spokane, Washington, airport rather than take the shuttle. It gave them a chance to talk and have no one hear what they were saying.

Both of them had disabled their phones, and they had the car checked for listening devices. No need to look for a tracker on the car. Everyone knew that they were heading to Pennsylvania.

Even though neither Leif nor Sarah thought they needed to be so careful about listening and tracking devices anymore, they still did the checks out of habit. Things had changed when Grant was captured. They knew they weren't the center of his rage anymore. Grant now directed his anger at the group in Doveland, and principally, Hank.

Even though they both put on a brave front, they were afraid. Sam had told them that Grant was in Doveland. "I don't know why they just don't arrest him," Sarah said. "Isn't it dangerous to leave him out there doing things? What if he's able to carry off whatever he is planning to do?"

"I asked Sam the same thing," Leif said. "His answer was they wanted to catch anyone else that is helping him. Sam asked us to trust him the same way we did last year."

"Alright. It's true that Sam was successful last year and I suppose there is nothing we can do about his plans anyway. But, I am glad that Suzanne and Gillian will also be there," Sarah said as she squeezed Leif's free hand.

The last time I spoke to Gillian, he said he was looking forward to seeing his friends. The ones that can see him will be delighted to see him again. Of course, they might call him Andy instead of Gillian.

"Do you think he is happy to have joined the Forest Circle? I know he and Suzanne are the only two that have remained behind. I wonder if the others can shift between dimensions the way that they do."

"That would be a good question to ask him," Leif said.

"I have many questions. Perhaps there will be time to get some of them answered," Sarah said. "One thing is for sure. I'm going to enjoy that solstice party. Besides all the entertainment, there will be a multitude of delicious things to eat.

Pete told me he was making his potato salad just for you. He heard you like mine, so you are going to get to choose which one is best."

Leif nodded and smiled at Sarah. He was wise enough not to say anything. It would always have to be Sarah's that he loved the most, but he was looking forward to Pete's.

It was going to be a good day.

****

Before heading back to Ben's room, Evan grabbed his car keys off the key holder in the kitchen and checked to make sure his wallet was in his jacket.

Pausing in the doorway of Ben's room, Evan took in the sight of Ava sitting in the glider nursing Ben. He loved collecting mental pictures of the precious times in his life, and this was one of them.

Ben's closet door stood open to reveal the christening gown hanging inside. He was sure Ava had left the door open on purpose so she could see it while she was feeding Ben.

The same seamstress that had sown Ava's wedding dress last year had made the gown for Ben. It was beautiful. Ava was beautiful. Ben was beautiful.

"Hon, are you lost?" Ava asked, laughing.

"I guess I am—lost in the loveliness of what I see," he said coming into the room and kissing them both on the top of their heads.

"I am off to Pittsburgh to pick up Sarah, Leif, and Craig."

"It's weird that they are all arriving together considering they are coming from different places."

"They aren't, but it's close enough. Craig will get there first and wait for them."

"I wonder why Jo Ann isn't coming with Craig. Do you think we should ask him about it?"

"Let's let him decide what he wants to share. I guess that he will. We are his Circle after all. It's a safe place to talk."

Noticing his keys in his hand, Ava said, "Oh, you're driving this time instead of using a car service?"

"Yep. I wanted to stop off in Concourse to see the graveyard. Hank told me that's where the town buried his father, and it's on the way. I find it interesting that both Hank and Eric, and your mom come to think about it, lived there.

"Plus, it is a beautiful day, and I have the time. Everything is being handled by Grace and her crew in Doveland for the solstice, and Mira and Tom are confirming the details with the church for the christening tomorrow.

"We'll pick up something for dinner on the way home. Do you have a preference?"

"Something light. We'll be stuffing ourselves tomorrow," Ava answered.

Evan gave Ben and Ava another kiss and headed to the garage. Lost in thought, he didn't notice that Suzanne and Gillian were waiting for him in the car. "Good grief, you two. You scared the crap out of me!"

When they both started laughing, Evan couldn't help himself and joined in. "Okay, I should have been expecting you, but geez. Could have at least waited outside the car?"

"Sure," Gillian said crossing his fingers in front of his face, "Next time."

"Are you two riding with me? Not that you need a car to go anywhere, but still."

"No," Suzanne answered. "We'll wait here for everyone to arrive. Keeping track of things going on in the village is our primary focus. So we will be floating in and out."

Evan laughed. "Figuratively speaking, of course."

"Of course," they both said at the same time.

"Any reason why you are waiting in the car then? I mean, other than giving me a good scare?"

"Well, that was the primary reason," Gillian answered laughing, "And of course to let you know we are here."

"And to remind you to be careful, and let you know what we will be doing" Suzanne added. "Gillian will be spending most of his time in town. I'll be here with Ava and the kids."

"Thank you," Evan began but didn't quite finish before they both faded away.

Shaking his head, Evan pulled out of the garage, made sure the garage door was closed, and headed down the long driveway to the road. He was looking forward to the drive. It would give him plenty of quiet time to think.

As Evan waited to turn right towards the airport, a white Cruze passed by heading into town. Something felt off about the car and driver, but it went by too fast for him to see who was driving. He would have to trust that Sam and his team were paying attention. Besides, he saw Gillian standing beside the road watching the car.

We are in good hands, Evan thought as he waved at Gillian and headed to the airport. *I trust all will be well.*

Twenty-Nine

Mira and Tom sat in one of the booths in the back of Your Second Home. They sat facing the door. They did this for two reasons. Sam had told them to never have their back to the door. But being able to observe the whole room also gave them a chance to practice one of their favorite activities—watching people, and if possible, listening in on conversations.

They justified their behavior saying that it helped the Circle feel safe knowing that they were paying attention, but actually Mira and Tom did it because they loved doing it. Sometimes when someone they didn't know came in, they would pretend that they had detective skills like Sherlock Holmes. They would search for clues to find out more about them.

Then, one of them would attempt to confirm their guesses by becoming friendly with the stranger. That was another part of the game that they loved, meeting new people.

Today, they were watching two men who appeared extremely uncomfortable about being in the cafe. They were hunched over a small table in the corner and whispering so neither Tom nor Mira could hear a single word they said.

"Stop it!" Grace said as she came to the table holding two steaming cups of coffee and two freshly baked scones.

"Don't you two have something better to do then be snoops? It's going to be a busy day today."

Mira and Tom smirked at the word snoops and then pointed to Grace. All three started laughing. "Okay, you're right. I'm a snoop too, but seriously, don't you two have something better to do today? Besides, I know who they are. Well, at least one of them."

Mira gestured at the empty seat opposite her and said, "Sit, tell us who they are, and then we'll talk about what you need us to do today."

"Okay, I've got a minute. Then I want to change into something pretty for the christening, and after it will be a big rush-rush until the end of the day."

Grace glanced at the two men and confirmed that they were busy paying attention to Mandy filling their coffee cups.

"Well, the old guy is Melvin who lives in Concourse. He rarely comes into town, especially since his wife died years ago. I'm sure you've seen his truck. The young guy—I don't know who he is, but my guess is he is his new hired hand."

"That's right," Mandy said as she sat down beside Grace. "They're coming back for the solstice, but right now they're heading out of town to look at some property. Don't know why. They just kinda mumbled.

"Melvin seems like a nice man. The young guy wouldn't even look up at me. Melvin introduced him as Jay. I think they are only here because the Diner is closed because it is full of food for the celebration."

"Did you let them know that we will be closing in an hour or so?"

"Yep. Told them about the christening and of course, they know about the solstice."

"Speaking of the christening, is there anything else we need to do? I gave Pete the flowers for the church, and he and Barbara are probably already there setting it up," Mandy asked.

"As far as I know, everything is ready. All we need to do is clean up the dishes and ourselves and get there."

As the bell on the door dinged, the four of them looked up in time to see Melvin and his friend leave. They watched as they crossed the village green to where they had parked their truck in the grocery store lot. Melvin handed the truck keys to Jay who nodded and opened the door for Melvin before climbing in himself.

"I don't know," Tom said. "Something seems 'off' there. When they come back to the event later, I think I will keep an eye on them."

"Great. Do that. But right now, we better get our butts in gear. Don't want to be late for Ben's big morning," Mira said.

"Bossy, bossy," Tom said.

Mira gave him a playful smack, and the two of them headed into the kitchen to see if there was anything they could do to help. Mandy and Grace watched them go and then gathered up the dishes from the tables and followed them.

None of them saw the white Cruze circle the square before heading out of town.

They didn't see it, but Gillian did, and so did Sam.

****

Hannah sat on her bed wishing that the day was over. She wasn't happy with herself for wanting such a thing, but it was true. It was a special day for her new baby brother, and her mom and Evan. Everyone was excited. Everyone but her.

Yesterday, Craig, Sarah, and Leif had arrived and settled into the bunkhouse. Hank had settled into the bunkhouse too, but Hannah hadn't seen much of him yet. She knew he was busy watching for that scary man, Grant.

Everyone was watching for Grant. Everyone but her. Hannah could hear her parents and their guests in the kitchen talking and laughing, and she knew someone would come looking for her soon. She needed to get ready.

Her mom had hung her pretty dress she would wear to the christening in the closet. For the past week, she had looked at it before going to bed.

She loved the dress. It reminded her of a dress she had once before, a long time ago. It had little rose buds on it, and a ladybug appliqué on one of the sleeves. The ladybug made it different than the first one. The ladybug was a special secret between her and Ava.

Ava sewed ladybugs on all of Hannah's clothes. Sometimes they were in hidden places where only Hannah could see. Every ladybug was there to remind Hannah that her mom and dad loved her. Hannah sighed. *I am a lucky girl. I need to be happy today and not worried.*

Hannah heard a knock on the door, and Sarah's voice asked if she could come in. *Oh, no. She is going to know I'm worried.* Hannah thought. But there was nothing to do. Sooner or later she would have to tell someone.

She slid off the bed and opened the door. She intended to let Sarah into the room but instead found herself rushing into Sarah's arms instead.

"Okay, young lady," Sarah said. "Let's hear it. What's going on?"

Hannah reached behind Sarah and shut the door and then led her to her bed.

They both sat there for a minute, as Sarah waited for Hannah to talk.

"If I tell you, can it be between the two of us?"

"It can, but only if it doesn't hurt anyone. However, I will have to tell the appropriate person if there is trouble for you or anyone else."

Hannah paused and then nodded. "Can you wait to tell when it is necessary because it might never be?"

"That I can do, I promise. Now, what's the problem?"

A few minutes later Sarah came into the kitchen followed by Hannah in her beautiful dress.

"Good morning, Hannah. You look lovely," Evan said. Everyone at the table agreed. Hannah looked beautiful.

"Thank you!" Hannah said, kissed Ben on his sticky cheek, and then sat down to eat a big plate of crepes. She could always tell when it was a special day; they had crepes.

Hannah looked over at Sarah who smiled at her and then nodded.

Yes, Hannah thought, *I am a lucky girl.*

Thirty

At precisely 9:30 a.m. everyone was seated in the church waiting for the ceremony to begin. They weren't waiting quietly as might be expected.

Instead, there were giggles, whispers, and people moving between pews to talk to someone, and then back to their seats. Barbara had done a lovely job placing white flowers and twinkle lights around the church, which added to the festive atmosphere. Ava thought the church and everyone in it was beautiful. She loved every laugh and every whispered conversation.

Watching her friends gather to honor Ben's place in their lives was a dream come true. It was more than a dream because it had never occurred to her to want such a thing. Opening her heart had changed her life. The last two years had sped by bringing more blessings than she could count.

For the christening, Ava and Evan had chosen the same stone church where they were married. They loved the arched stained-glass windows and the wooden pews.

It was the oldest church in the village. Some residents claimed that it was over two-hundred years old.

When Ava and Evan booked the church for their wedding, they had discovered that it was owned by the town, and the town was responsible for its maintenance.

Because there was only a small allowance in the budget for its upkeep, many repairs were going undone. When they discovered the problem, Ava and Evan secretly set up a trust for the church's ongoing maintenance and upkeep. Ava considered it a joy and privilege to do good privately.

Since the town was small, the church was used for more than one denominational service. The clerk kept a calendar in the town hall, and each denomination scheduled their service's times with her. On Sunday, the parking lot was full most of the day. Town members greeted each other as they came and went from their various services. Ava thought that the respect they all had for each other's points of view was one of the best parts of Doveland. There was even a non-denominational service, and it was the pastor of that group that they had asked to guide them in Ben's christening.

Tom and Mira were to be the official godparents, but Ava and Evan considered everyone who was attending to be Ben and Hannah's family and had told them so. Ava and Evan figured there could never be too many people to love and help parent Ben and Hannah. They knew that parents don't own their children.

Ben and Hannah had come to them as guests in this lifetime for them to cherish and learn life together. As Ava held a wiggly Ben, she laughed to herself thinking about how much the children had already taught her about patience and understanding.

Ava and Evan wanted the occasion to be very simple without any specific religious connection. It was a chance to mark and celebrate Ben's appearance into all their lives.

Instead of a physical present, each participant was asked to bring a gift of words that they would read aloud as part of the ceremony. Mandy had already collected each person's words and put into a book for Ben.

Ava had asked Hannah if she would like to have an event like Ben's since she had missed out on hers. Hannah assured her that she didn't need it, and Ava believed her. However, she made Hannah pinky-promise to tell her if she ever wanted to have a ceremony of her own and Ava would make sure Hannah got exactly what she envisioned.

Since Hannah didn't want a ceremony, Ava asked everyone to write a special note to Hannah. The notes had already been collected and put into a book just like Ben's. Hannah was to get her book at the same time Ben got his.

At 9:45, the harpist who had played at their wedding began to play, and everyone quieted down. When the song ended, everyone turned their attention to the pastor as he stepped forward. First, he welcomed them and then, glancing at the list in his hand, asked the first person to step forward to read their gift to Ben.

Tom and Mira went first, followed by Hank and Mandy. Everyone read something, even taciturn Sam. By the time it was over, there was not a dry eye in the house. Even Ben had fallen silent, perhaps sensing the importance of what was happening.

As the harpist played softly in the background, Ava, Evan, and Hannah brought Ben to the front of the church. Turning to face their family and friends, they held Ben for all to see as the pastor read a passage from the *Bible* that Ava's mother had often quoted to her. "I know thy works: behold, I have set before thee an open door, and no man can shut it: for thou hast a little strength, and hast kept my word, and hast not denied my name."

Evan held Ben up high for all to see. Mandy handed Ben's book to Ava, then she turned to Hannah, whispered something in her ear and placed her book in her hands. Hannah stared at the book and then at her Auntie Mandy and burst into tears which caused another outburst of happy tears from everyone else in the church.

Then Leif stepped to the front of the church, and everyone quieted down again.

"I'll be brief," he said. "As we celebrate this day, let's remember to be attentive. I know I don't need to tell you why. If you see or hear anything that doesn't feel right to you; please tell someone.

Don't think it's your imagination, or you're being paranoid. Maybe it will be your imagination, but it's better to be alert than taken by surprise. Hank and Sam have assured me that everything is fine today, but they are counting on our awareness. And of course, two of our friends from the Forest Circle are also here watching over us."

At that moment, Ben let out a big wail and everyone laughed. "Sounds as if Ben is hungry. Perfect timing. See you all at the solstice ceremony!"

It was a happy, yet somber group that filed out of the church. They all knew that with everyone in town, Grant was sure to try something to harm some, if not all, of them.

Some of the group headed back to Ava and Evan's house, while others stayed in town to help the solstice committee get set up. Festivities would begin mid-afternoon and last until dark, although it had been rumored that people were planning to camp out all night on the green. On a typical day, it wouldn't be allowed, but the town council was going to pretend it wasn't happening, just this once.

It was all the extra things going on that worried Sam. He couldn't be sure he had every one of the extras under control. He trusted his team, but everyone makes mistakes. He was praying that it was Grant who was going to make a mistake, and not him. He wouldn't be able to live with himself if anything happened to anyone in Doveland because he wanted to do more than recapture Grant. He wanted to take down anyone else that was part of Grant's network. It was risky. It was a risk he had already agreed to take.

He prayed it was a risk that would pay off.

Thirty-One

Melvin held his cap in his hands and watched Jay walk back and forth across the field. Now that he was here watching Jay pace the land he used to own, Melvin remembered more about what had happened thirty-five years before.

The news had been the headline for the local paper. His wife, Sally, had picked up the newspaper in town. When she got home, she slapped the paper down in front of him with tears running down her face. Neither of them spoke. She sat down beside him at the table, and they silently held hands, both of them grateful for their family, and distressed for the ones who had lost their lives.

They hadn't known the family, but it was a tragedy no one could stop talking about. A woman and her child burned to death in their home, the husband coming home from town too late to save them. When it was discovered that it was arson, it became even more of a tragedy.

Every year for many years after that, some reporter would revisit the case, but no one could ever discover why it had happened. They were a small farm family who worked hard to make ends meet. They had no connections to anything that would have caused someone to burn down their house.

Five years later, Melvin read in the paper that the husband had died. He was only thirty years old but had started drinking and using drugs right after his family was murdered, and didn't stop until it killed him. His landlady had found him in his room, dead from an overdose. It was his birthday.

It was hard for Melvin to believe that Jay was that same person. How could he be? No one Melvin knew ever talked about remembering past lives, but there Jay was, looking very much like the man in the paper the night of the fire. Jay looked almost as grief-stricken now as he had looked then.

Melvin tried to understand how it would feel to remember a tragedy like that, and then have a chance to take revenge against the person that caused it. As much as Melvin hoped that Jay would be able to overcome the rage of seeing his family die, Melvin wasn't sure Jay would be able to. Watching Jay pace, Melvin was pretty sure that, given a chance, Jay would take his revenge.

Jay finally stopped walking and sat down on a log that lay near the tree line. He gestured for Melvin to join him. For the next hour, Jay talked about what the farm used to look like. He shared stories about his daughter and how he loved watching her run across the field to greet him at the end of the day.

He talked about his wife, Maggie, the love of his life, then and now.

Melvin had never heard Jay talk so much. At first, it seemed to be calming him down. Jay would pause and run his hand through the grass, look up at the sky, and sigh, and then tell another story.

But near the end of the hour the calmness changed to a steely determination, and as he spoke, he became angrier and angrier. Soon Jay was vibrating with rage.

Afraid for him, Melvin put a gentle hand on his arm which Jay immediately shook off.

"Jay," Melvin said firmly, "This anger will only eat you alive."

"Maybe that's what I want," Jay said, "To be eaten alive; to die again."

Turning to Melvin, he asked, "Do you think we'll see our loved ones again when we die? I don't remember that part from the last time I died."

Melvin took a deep breath. "Son, I don't know. But I am living my life in the hopes that I will see my Sally again, and because she was such a good woman, I am going to have to be the best man I can be to end up in the same place.

"Was your wife, Maggie, a good woman?" Melvin asked Jay.

"The best. Better than I deserved even then. And now since I am not a good man at all, I probably don't have a chance of finding her again."

"I think you do, Jay. I think we just have to be walking the path. Trying to be good would be worth it if you had a chance, don't you think? You might even see your daughter again."

Jay turned to Melvin and searched his face to see if he was leading him on. If there were any chance at all, he would take it. But the rage was eating him up, and he had no idea how he was going to let it go.

"Yes," Jay said. "I would give anything to be with my daughter again."

"You never told me her name," Melvin said.

"Hannah," Jay answered.

Thirty-Two

Frank waited until Pete, Barbara, and all their friends went into the church. *I should have done this last night,* he thought. Now, it's the middle of the day, and someone might see me. But Frank knew Pete was a light sleeper, and he was more afraid of Pete catching him than of someone else seeing him. After he did the deed, he was leaving anyway. As soon as he texted that it was done, the money would be wired into his account. The next step was to tell Lenny how to trace the bank that the money came from. Then he would get even more money. This time the money would be from Lenny.

Win, win for everyone. Well, not everyone. If it goes well, there will be a lot of dead people before the day is over. *What do I care,* he thought. Gathering what he had retrieved the night before, he headed over to the Diner. Instead of walking across the green, Frank went through the back door of the gas station, walked a block to the east, and then circled back around through the alleys until he was at the Diner's back door. As far as he could tell, no one had seen him. Frank took out the key that was in the package along with the vial. Once he had the door open, he pulled out a slip of paper and keyed in the alarm code. *The guy had thought of everything,* Frank mused.

Yes, they would know eventually that the back door had been opened, but it would be long after he was gone.

There was food everywhere. Every table was covered with food wrapped in plastic or sitting in containers waiting to be taken out to the green that afternoon. Frank knew that the ice cream and other frozen delights would be in the freezer. However, it was the potato salad he was looking for, and he found it the refrigerator. Two huge bowls of it. His instructions were to sprinkle the contents of the vial over both.

He took both bowls out, removed the plastic wrap, and dribbled the contents over the first container. However, there was nothing left in the vial for the second one. *Oh, well, must have put too much in the first one.* Frank wasn't worried. He put the undoctered salad in the back of the refrigerator figuring they would only bring that one out when they had finished with the first one. By then it would be too late anyway.

It was tempting to take some food, but it was too dangerous. *What if someone noticed that food was missing?* Instead, Frank reset the alarm and retraced his steps to get back to the gas station.

There is no reason to leave right away. *It might be fun to see the outcome. First things first, though.* Frank texted the word "done" with a picture attached of him putting the contents of the vial into the potato salad, and waited. A few seconds later, he heard a ping also with the word, "done." With trembling fingers, he refreshed the link to his bank account and saw the money in it. *Not bad for thirty minutes of work,* he thought.

Now Lenny. He took out his other phone and sent the account information to him, but not before he had logged onto his computer and transferred his money two more times so no one could trace where it went. All of that took a few hours as he waited to confirm each transfer.

By then, Pete and his friends had left the church and were starting to set up tables on the green.

Frank waited for Lenny to wire the money he owed him, and then transferred that money to another account. *Done is the word of the day,* he thought. *I'm done, they're done, and now Tina is next to being done too.*

To give himself plenty of time before someone started looking for him, Frank put the orange cones out in front of the driveways that led into the station. It would take a while before people realized that although the gas station sign said, "open," it wasn't. It was done. Finished.

****

Frank was wrong. Someone had seen him.

Grant never left things to chance. It was something he prided himself on, and Grant wanted to make sure that Frank carried out the assignment. He couldn't see whether or not he emptied the vial into the potato salad, but he did see him enter and leave the Diner. When Frank sent the text that said 'done,' along with the picture, Grant believed him.

Grant scrambled back from the window where he had watched Frank, and eased himself up from the lying position he had been in for the last five hours. The movie theatre had been easy to break into without anyone knowing it, and a second floor window afforded a full view of the Diner's front and back door.

Grant could have poisoned the salad himself, but he was happy to put one layer between him and the deed so that there was no chance of him being caught. Going back to prison was never going to happen.

It was time to get out of the theater before everyone returned from the christening.

Then it was time to check out of the motel and turn in his white Cruze rental car. A few weeks ago, he had purchased a junker car and hidden it a few blocks from the rental car agency. A stolen license plate would keep anyone from tracking his movements after the disaster he planned started happening.

Not that Grant thought anyone would come looking for him immediately. First, they would try to save everyone. It was possible that not everyone would die. Nevertheless, Grant knew that watching a loved one die instead of yourself would ruin your life, and that is what he was aiming to do. Ruin all their lives.

By the time Frank had left the gas station for good, Grant had parked his new car two blocks from the town green. He had made sure he wouldn't be blocked in by choosing a street that opened into an alley that would take him out of town quickly.

He wasn't going to watch. He was just going to wait for the screams and sirens, and then he would leave.

He pulled his baseball hat low over his eyes and slumped down in his seat. A sunshade advertising beer spread across the front window, a back window piled high with old rags, and side windows covered in dirt, blocked anyone's view into the car.

He had a few hours to kill, so he closed his eyes and sank into a deep, peaceful sleep.

Thirty-Three

Hannah and Ava were the last ones at the house. They were waiting for Ben to wake up from his nap. Evan had taken the truck and headed to town early to help set up the tables and then assist Pete with traffic direction. Ava wanted to drive separate cars so she could come home with Ben when he got tired, and Hannah could return with Evan. Knowing her daughter, she would stay as long as possible.

It was actually a school day, but because of the christening, Hannah had permission to stay home. Hannah was looking forward to meeting up with her classmates when they got out of school and arrived at the celebration.

Ava had suggested Hannah take a nap while Ben was resting. It was going to be a long day. But Hannah was much too keyed up to sleep. Instead, she lay on her bed staring at the ceiling with the same questions running over and over in her head.

Is it a decision that I have to make, or will it be made for me? And if it is made for me, will I like it?

Realizing that there was not going to be a voice that magically gave her the answers she wanted, Hannah decided to stop asking questions that couldn't be answered and enjoy the celebration.

She could trust that all would be well. It was what her mom would say if she were here to say it. *Well,* Hannah thought, *Ava would say the same thing too. Moms are like that.*

She must have drifted off to sleep because she was startled to see Ava leaning over the bed with Ben in her arms.

"Ready to go, sweetie?" Ava asked. Hannah nodded and sat up, feet dangling off the bed so she could admire her new sneakers. She had forgotten to take them off when she lay down. Hannah loved her sneakers because they lit up when she walked. After the christening, she had changed out of her dress, and into soft jeans and shirt. The ever-present ladybug was under the cuff of her jeans and on the collar of her shirt.

She and her mom were dressed almost the same, but Ava didn't have sneakers that lit up or ladybugs on her clothes. *I am going to change that,* thought Hannah. *And even Ben needs a ladybug or two.*

It was a plan that Hannah felt she could cling to because it was something she had control over. She knew how to sew. She knew where Ava kept the ladybugs. It was easy. The afternoon would be hard. It was a turning point. It was just that she was the only one who knew, and she thought she was much too young to be carrying that burden.

The phrase "suck it up buttercup" popped into her head out of nowhere and made her laugh. *Wonder where that came from, but thanks for a laugh,* she said to herself.

Ava watched Hannah go from pensive to laughter and wondered what was going on, but it was too late to ask her. Hannah had grabbed her backpack and was out the door.

If I don't get there quickly she'll start honking the horn, Ava thought. She knew her daughter well. Hannah would have grabbed the car keys, started the car and be buckled in by the time she got to the door.

Right on time, the car horn honked, and Ava laughed. I *probably should stop her from doing that,* Ava thought. *But today is not the day. Today is all about celebration.*

****

Hands on hips, Grace surveyed the town square. Eric stood beside her waiting. "Well, does it meet your approval?" he asked.

Grace turned to answer him but was interrupted by Valerie as she speed-walked towards them. "Grace dear, this is just wonderful," she said grabbing Grace's hand and pulling her into a hug.

"We could never have done this without you. Thank you, thank you, for moving to our town and bringing all your glorious friends with you!"

Turning to look out on the square, she waved her arms at everyone setting up booths and preparing the gazebo for the musicians.

Valerie was right. Many of the people working were Grace's friends. "Thank you Valerie, but I think it's the other way around. My friends brought me here, and your town opened your arms to us. We are the ones who are grateful."

Before Valerie could do any more than nod and smile, someone shouted her name and off she went to see what they wanted. "She's right, you know," Eric said. "It looks wonderful, and they couldn't have done it without you."

"Or my friends," Grace laughed. "It's been a lot of fun putting it together. On the other hand, I'll be happy when the day is over, and it is just you and me."

Eric pulled Grace into a hug, which is how Pete found them a minute later.

"I was waiting until you two were finished hugging, but it didn't look as if it would stop, so here I am bugging you, Grace," he said.

"When do you want us to bring out the food? I have to keep slapping people's hands to keep them from eating it while it's sitting in the Diner. The sooner I get it out on the tables, the happier I will be."

"Not yet, Pete. Keep slapping their hands. We need to wait until all the families have arrived. And let's wait until most of the kids get their faces painted, and make balloons, and then we can set up the food. Can we give it another hour? Perhaps lock the door to the Diner? I'll send people to help you bring it out when it is time."

Pete saluted and said, "Will do captain" as he walked away laughing. He didn't mind. It would give him and Barbara some time to be social before the serving began. Besides, not everyone has arrived. Hank wasn't there yet, and neither was Sam. On the other hand, Pete wasn't expecting to see Sam until the party was over. Of course, Sam is here, watching, somewhere.

Just thinking about Sam watching reminded Pete who Sam was watching for, and he shivered in the warm summer air. *I wish they would hurry up and capture Grant and Lenny too,* Pete thought.

It took only a few minutes before Pete was back on the green, having shooed everyone out of the Diner, grabbed Barbara's hand, locked the door behind them, and headed towards the booth where kids were making balloon animals. The child he was looking for was Hannah. Pete loved that she thought of him and Eric as her grandfathers. *It is hard not to adore her,* he thought. It was also hard not to worry a bit. After what she told them about her dad coming for her, everyone was worried.

Perhaps it was her imagination, but what if it was true? What happens then?

Trying to remember when Hannah said her dad was coming reminded Pete what he had forgotten to tell Ava and Evan for the past few months. It was about that hitchhiker. *Oh well, must have been wrong about him. Otherwise, he would be here by now,* Pete mused.

Barbara pulled his hand, bringing him back from his thoughts. "Come on, Pete. I see Hannah over by the balloons."

Hannah saw them at the same time. "Come play with me," she called, holding up a balloon made into a giraffe. Beside her, Ava stood with Ben, watching the festivities. It was a glorious day, but there was a heavy feeling in Ava's heart. Something was wrong. But there was nothing she could do but wait and watch whatever was going to happen unfold.

Beside her, Suzanne said, "All will be what it must be." Trying not to look as if she was crazy talking to herself, Ava asked, "But, that's the problem. I don't know what must be."

There was no answer from Suzanne. She was already gone, leaving Ava even more troubled than before.

Thirty-Four

While people started gathering in the green, Craig was helping Mandy and Mira with preparations for the party in the kitchen of Your Second Home.

Mandy had decided to try her hand at making a layer cake and was putting the last minute decorations on it. Craig was loading up trays of the pastries that Mandy and Grace had been baking for what seemed like weeks. The pastries had been carefully stacked in the freezer and taken out earlier that morning to thaw.

Grace had rented big coffee serving containers for the party and Mira was busy making enough coffee to last for a few hours. Other drinks, like soda and lemonade, were provided for by the grocery store owners. All the paper and plastic products needed for eating were from the Bed and Breakfast. It was definitely a community affair.

A big block party, Mandy thought. Looking over at Craig, she wondered what was going on with him.

"You are very quiet this visit, Craig," Mandy said as she piped the last of the flowers onto the cake.

"You are," Mira added.

When there was no answer from Craig, they both turned to look at him. He was stoically placing one pastry at a time onto the tray. Where was the upbeat, happy man they knew?

"Craig?" Mandy asked again putting down her pastry bag. "This cake is good enough, and we'll finish the pastry stacking together. Let's sit down for a second."

Mira poured them all a cup of coffee and joined the two of them at one of the round tables at the side of the room. All the blinds to the cafe were down so no one could see what they were doing. The semi-dark room and the silence formed a comfortable cocoon around the three of them.

No one spoke. There wasn't any need to talk. Craig knew that his friends were there for him, whether he told them what was happening or he didn't tell them.

"May I talk about this later?" he asked a few minutes later.

When both of his friends silently nodded, he thanked them with a half-hearted smile.

"Hey, where is everyone?" Hank called, coming in the back door of the shop. At Christmas time, the friends had exchanged keys to homes and stores, so everyone had a key to everything. They loved it that way.

"Out here in the dark," Mandy called. "Grab a coffee and come sit for a second."

Hank didn't need another invitation. Coffee was perfect. He was dead tired. He couldn't share any information yet with his friends, but he could sit and rest for a minute.

After hugging Hank, Mandy grabbed a few pastries off the trays and set them on the table, and the four of them sat in comfortable silence.

They each knew that more was going on than just a solstice celebration. However, no one knew what it was, or what the outcome would be.

"Sam says to tell you he'll see you later, Mira," Hank said. "When this is over, he is going to need a few days of rest."

"We all are, aren't we?" Mira said. "Does anyone know everything that is happening at the celebration today?"

When no one said anything, Mandy piped up. "Well, I do. The kids are going to have a great time. There is going to be a butt load of delicious food, some beautiful singing, a small theater production put on by the first graders, and a whopping big bonfire before the night is over."

"Amen to that," they said together, clinking their coffee cups together in solidarity.

Outside they could hear the giggles and laughter of the children and the band warming up. Mandy's phone pinged with a text message. "Grace says they are ready outside for us."

The four friends stood up and hugged. "I'll be there in a minute or two," Hank said as he left by the back door, locking it behind him. The other three friends opened the front door and began the process of taking out the coffee and pastries. They weren't going to bring out the cake until after the other food was cleared away. Then all the deserts would show up at once.

Mandy turned to Craig and Mira and gave one last sigh. "Ready?" she asked.

"Ready," Craig and Mira answered.

******

It all happened at the same time.

Melvin had parked his truck a few blocks away, and he and Jay were just stepping into the town square at the same time that Hank entered the square from the other direction. Pete and his crew had just finished setting up the food tables, and people were lining up to fill up their plates.

Grant had impatiently stayed in his car waiting for all hell to break out. When nothing happened, he finally decided to walk over himself to see what was taking so long.

A cloud passed over the sun, a hawk screamed in the distance, and a little girl looked up to see happening what she knew was going to happen.

Without thinking, she ran to Hank and leaped into his arms hugging him as tight as she could.

"What's wrong, honey," he asked setting her down on the grass and kneeling in front of her to see her face.

"I love you, Uncle Hank," she said as loudly as she could.

She had made her decision.

Across the green, Jay paled and stumbled into Melvin.

Grant watched the first person take a bite of potato salad. It would take twenty minutes. Only twenty minutes more and he would have completed the first stage of his revenge.

Suzanne and her brother Gillian held hands and prayed. They had done what they could.

Thirty-Five

Jay thought he would pass out.

If it weren't for Melvin standing beside him, he probably would have.

Jay didn't feel the way he thought he would feel. He always thought his rage would take over. He would run at the man who killed his family, and without a second thought, bash his head in until he was dead. He wouldn't care what happened after that. Nothing would matter anymore. He would have had his revenge. And his revenge would bring him peace. He needed peace.

But instead of the blinding rage he expected to feel, he sat panting on a bench with an old man's arm around his shoulders. Jay was sure that the anger was still there, it had to be. Otherwise, he was even more of a crazy person than he thought he was.

"Okay, son, what's going on?" Melvin asked. "Are you sick?

Jay didn't answer. Instead, he kept his gaze on the man and the child hugging each other across the green.

"It can't be," Jay said.

"What can't be?" Melvin asked.

Jay couldn't answer. All he could do was to keep watching as the two of them stood up together, and hand in hand walked over to a woman holding a baby.

Maybe I am wrong, Jay thought. *After all, it was thirty-five years ago. Perhaps I have made all this up in my head. Perhaps it never happened. Maybe I am just crazy.*

Across the green, the little girl had not let go of the man's hand. It was almost as if she was protecting him.

I have to be crazy, Jay thought. *How could she be here? How could she be with him? It can't be him!*

Turning to Melvin, he said, "I do feel sick. Could we leave?"

Melvin nodded and helped Jay to his feet. As they turned to go, Jay looked back one more time, just as the man turned to look in his direction.

"Hank, no!" Hannah yelled, but it was too late. Hank had seen Jay. Hank's heart froze, and Hannah started to cry.

Neither man moved. Both wondering if it was possible.

Seeing Hannah crying, Evan rushed to her as Melvin spun Jay around saying, "Let's go."

Hannah's crying caused Pete to look up and see Melvin leading a young man away from the square. Melvin's friend looks so familiar, Pete thought.

Evan picked up Hannah and put his arm around Hank. "Man, what's going on?"

"Something that doesn't seem possible," Hank replied. "But if it is, my past is here to punish me."

"No, Uncle Hank. I won't let it be that way," Hannah whispered as she turned to watch Jay walk away.

Turn around, she thought. As Jay did, she formed a heart with her hands and then pointed to him, and then Evan, and then Hank.

All Jay could do was nod back and stumble to the truck, blinded by the tears pouring down his face.

"I'll be back for you," he whispered.

****

What the bloody hell was that? Grant thought. He had seen the drama unfold with Hank and that creepy little girl because he was keeping his eyes on Hank. It was Hank who Grant wanted to punish with his plan. He couldn't wait to celebrate Hank's pain as he witnessed all his friends collapse on their way to a sudden and painful death.

Grant had seen what happened but didn't understand it. *Doesn't matter,* he thought. *I'm only here for another twenty minutes, and then I have to go. Probably taking too big a chance being here anyway.* But the thought of watching the carnage and Hank's pain was too delicious to relinquish so easily.

Sam watched Grant watch Hank. Sam was also curious about what had happened between Hank, Hannah, and Melvin's hired hand, but he didn't have time to deal with that one yet.

First, Grant. After capturing his accomplice the night before his team believed that Grant didn't have anyone else working this plan with him.

That meant that the team could begin to close in on their unsuspecting quarry. Finally, we will have this guy back where he belongs, thought Sam.

Sam chuckled to himself as he watched Grant focus on the people eating. I wonder if the food is making him hungry, Sam mused. We'll be sure to withhold food from him for as long as possible once we get him into custody.

A voice in his ear told him it was time. He slipped out of the theater and began his walk towards Grant.

They hadn't wanted to risk taking him in the middle of the crowd, so Sam wondered what had made his director give the order to move in now.

As Sam stepped onto the green, he heard a loud pop and a rocket shot up into the air exploding into fireworks. Everyone turned to look at what was happening. For a split second, Sam was distracted.

When he looked back to Grant, he couldn't find him. Turning in circles to see all around the square, he called to his team. "Anyone see him?"

All he heard was a chorus of "nos." Sam started running to where he knew Grant had parked his car. He arrived to find the two other members of his team who had been assigned to watch the car standing by the car looking glum.

"He didn't come back," one said.

There was nothing for Sam to say. He knew that everything was in place just in case this happened. They had moved to plan B. *But, there shouldn't have been a plan B*, Sam fumed. *We had it covered. What did we miss?*

The night before, Hank and Sam had kept watch from Pete and Barbara's apartment above the Diner while Grace and Eric watched from their apartment across the street. Sam had supplied them all with night vision goggles and burner phones. Every fifteen minutes they checked with each other as they watched for movement in the square.

Part of Sam's team also watched Grant, but Sam was counting on the extra eyes of his friends in Doveland to help.

They knew Grant had someone working with him in Doveland, but they didn't know who it was. Sam's team had seen Grant slip something under the park bench earlier that day and they waited for Grant's accomplice to retrieve it.

At the same time, Sam had people watching over every member of the Circle. They also had eyes on other locations that Grant might target. But they were focusing the majority of their attention on the solstice ceremony. It a perfect venue for Grant because he loved to wreak havoc on a grand scale.

Sam was counting on Grant's ego to make him sloppy. Grant assumed that no one knew what he looked like or was as smart as him. On the other hand, Sam knew Grant had outsmarted them before, and it was possible he would do it again. Sam hadn't wanted to take any chances.

A short time after midnight Eric called Sam. He had seen someone sneak out of the gas station and head to the park bench. Everyone watched the man take out the package and go back to the gas station.

A few minutes later one of Sam's men came to Pete's door along with Grace and Eric. With a hint of pride, he had said, "We know who he is, sir."

"Good job," Sam said. "But make sure the extra cameras we installed are well hidden. We have to catch him doing something before we can charge him. So far, he had just taken a package. Not a criminal offense."

It was Grace who asked the question they all were thinking. "Are you sure this is the only attack Grant has planned? What if more people are helping him?"

Sam considered lying but thought better of it. He knew they would know he wasn't telling the truth. He also needed their extra gifts to help him stop Grant, so he paused while trying to think of the right words to say.

Hank came to his rescue. "You know, Sam and his team. They know what they are doing. But, still, we always need to be alert."

Grace spoke up, "Which means, if the situation is under control, for now, I think sleep would be a good idea, don't you think?"

Last night, Sam had agreed. He had thought the situation was under control. But now, having lost track of Grant, Sam knew that once again he let himself believe that he had the upper hand when he didn't.

He tricked me again. I am the one with the ego that made me sloppy, Sam fumed to himself.

Hiding in the attic of the hardware store, Grant watched Sam, and his men look for him. He didn't even try to stop laughing. It was the most fun he had had in days.

He loved fooling them. He always knew he was smarter than they were. Someday they would figure out that he always had a plan B too. In fact, he had a plan C. Settling down into his hiding place, Grant waited for the screams that should be happening at any moment.

An hour later, Grant was no longer laughing. He was furious. Something had gone wrong. It was time for him to leave town. But he would be back with plan C.

As Grant put plan B into action, he was grateful for his skill at planning. The car he had stolen and hidden a few blocks away was waiting for him. Grant slipped on the latex mask he had had made for him when he had his plastic surgery, and put on the extra clothes he had hidden in the attic. Grant left everything he didn't need behind. He would be long gone before Sam found his stash.

A few minutes later, Grant walked out the back door of the hardware store and casually strolled out to the solstice ceremony. The crowd was watching the children's play, so he joined them, sitting in the back row next to a proud mom and dad.

When the play was over, he joined the crowd as they milled around heading back to their cars.

I suppose I could kill Hank now, Grant thought, fingering the gun in his pocket. *But, I might get caught. I'll just let him suffer wondering where I went and what I am planning next. It won't be long now though, Hank,* Grant promised.

With one last glance at the solstice celebration still going on, Grant melted away through the crowd while laughing to himself. *I guess their superpowers didn't help them this time, did they?*

Thirty-Six

"So what was in the vial?" Pete asked.

Everyone was at Evan and Ava's house hoping to find some answers to what had happened that day. The children had been put to bed, and the grownups were all gathered in the living room. It was a somber meeting. Yes, the disaster Grant had planned fell through. But he had escaped once again.

Then there was what happened with Hannah. However, that seemed even more complicated than what happened with Grant, so they started with what appeared to be the easier question.

"Wait," Ava said. "I know some of you know what happened, but not all of us do."

"Sorry, Ava," Sam said.

He and Mira were sitting together. He was perched on one of the side chairs taken from the dining room table. Mira was sitting at his feet leaning against his legs. Ava thought she looked like a contented cat. All Sam had to do was start petting her head, and she would probably purr.

Ava couldn't blame her for being happy. Sam was openly declaring his love for Mira. Ava knew what that felt like. As if Evan knew what she was thinking, he put his hand on her shoulder while they waited for an answer from Sam.

Sam told them about watching Grant put something under the park bench. He explained how his men retrieved the package, replaced the vial with one filled with water, and returned it to the bench. That night he, his men, Grace, Eric, Pete, and Barbara waited for the accomplice to show up to get it. Once he retrieved the package, they kept him in their sights. In the morning, they followed him as he went into the Diner and sprinkled the contents of the vial over one of the potato salad bowls, and returned to the gas station after texting the word "done" to a burner phone.

After watching him take the vial, one of Sam's men was able to hack his computer, so they watched money transfer to him from two different sources. Then they tracked where he sent the money and let him leave so no one in town would see the arrest. They captured him right outside of Concourse.

"Great," Mandy snapped. "You knew Grant was here. Why didn't you arrest him? What if you hadn't caught what he was doing? What if you hadn't stopped him from poisoning all of us?"

Hank turned to Mandy and tried to hold her hand before answering her. But she snatched it away and gave him a hard stare.

"You knew about this plan? You let us all be in danger? You don't even like potato salad, so he wasn't trying to kill you!"

"Yes, I did know. And no, I don't like potato salad, but Grant wasn't trying to kill me. Grant knows I don't like potato salad. He wanted me to bear the pain of losing all of you because I screwed up. He was aiming for a long, slow, painful death for me. And it would have been."

With those words, Mandy slumped against Tom who had moved over to her as Hank was speaking. "But you knew," she whispered.

"Yes," Sam answered. "We took a considerable risk. But it seemed important to know who in town he was working with, because otherwise, he might have still used that person to hurt you even after we arrested him, and we wouldn't have had a clue how to stop it."

Sarah and Leif had been sitting quietly together waiting for everyone to say what each needed to say. When it was evident that no one was going to ask the next question, Sarah asked. "But you lost him because everyone was distracted when the fireworks went off. You don't think that was a coincidence, do you?"

Sam sighed. "No, we don't. However, we can't prove otherwise right now. The volunteers watching over the fireworks were distracted by the children making balloons. You can't blame them. It was some of their kids having a good time. So either they went off by mistake…"

"Or it was Grant," Craig said.

"Couldn't have been Grant," Sam answered. "Too many people watching him at the moment it happened."

"Which means he probably does have at least one other person, other than the one you captured, working with him in town, and he signaled him somehow," Eric said.

"That's what we think. I have a team analyzing the camera footage now," Sam answered.

"But you believe he has left town?" Sarah asked.

"We do. Somehow, Grant got away. We are hoping the footage tells us how he did that. Here's what we do know. We know Grant hasn't given up. We also know that not only did Grant pay his accomplice, but so did Lenny."

"Wait, haven't you forgotten to tell us who his accomplice was that you captured? Who did he hire to put poison in the potato salad?"

"I can answer that one," Pete said. "It was Frank Jacks."

"What? Mr. Jacks?" Mandy said. "He creeped me out. I should have known there was something up with him. He was always watching us, but I thought it was him being a pervert. Not that I thought that was okay, which is why I stayed as far away from him as possible, but I never thought of him as devious that way."

"We all took him for just a creepy guy, which is not small by any means. However, he wasn't as clever as he thought. Once we saw him take the package, we got warrants for wiretaps and cameras. Everything we needed to take him down.

"It turns out that he is consumed with hate. That made him an easy mark for Grant. We gather that he planned to find his wife, Tina, kill her, and then disappear with all the money that both Grant and Lenny paid him."

"So you believe that Lenny is after Grant too?" Evan asked.

"Yes, we think they are after each other. For now, though, both Grant and Lenny are after Hank. Lenny was aware that Hank had turned them all in last year, but he thought Hank was useful because he would kill Grant for him. Now that Grant got away again, we figure that they are both targeting Hank."

Everyone turned to look at Hank. He was slumped back in his chair, listening.

Life has just gotten worse. I never thought it could get worse than it was, And for a while there, I thought I was going to escape. Doesn't look that way now, Hank thought.

"And then there is what happened with Melvin's hired hand, and you and Hannah. What was that?" Evan asked.

Hank looked at his friends and wondered if after he told them the story whether any one of them would still be his friend.

If Sam wanted to arrest him, he would let him. He would die within days in jail. He knew Lenny or Grant would make sure of that. But he couldn't lie to them. They deserved to know.

Plus he was tired. He was too tired to fight anymore. It was time for it all to be over. It was time for him to get what he deserved. Hell.

****

In her room, Hannah lay awake. She could hear the grownups talking in the living room. She didn't have to hear the exact words to know what they were discussing.

First, they would talk about that man Grant. Then they would talk about what worried her the most—the man she had seen in the town square and her Uncle Hank.

Both events were scary, but one of them was something she could do something about. The question was what? She reminded herself that she was just a little girl, but then laughed to herself. Did it count she remembered being the same little girl twice? It was like a practice session. If she was eight before and she was nine now, then in total she was seventeen. She had at least seventeen years of remembered experience!

I am going to have to do it. There is no choice. Hannah grabbed her robe from the foot of her bed and slid her feet into the slippers her mom had given her for her birthday. This mom, this birthday.

As bravely as she could, she marched into the living room. Hank was barely breathing, and she could tell he was about to say something. She was just in time.

Thirty-Seven

Melvin waited for Jay to come down for breakfast. On the way home from the solstice, Jay hadn't said a word. Melvin was used to quiet, and after being married for most of his life, had learned when it was better to wait than to push.

When they had returned to the farmhouse, Jay went upstairs to his room without eating or saying anything. That was over fourteen hours ago, and Melvin hadn't heard a sound.

Sitting at the kitchen table holding his cup of coffee, Melvin was sure he heard his wife, Sally, tell him to get his ass out of the chair and go upstairs and help that young man.

Melvin listened. Even if it wasn't his dead wife speaking to him, he knew it was the right thing to do. If it were his son lying up there sick, he would do something. It didn't matter if it was sick in the body or sick in the head, he had to do something.

Besides, Melvin wasn't sure if the two things were different. Long years of observation made him think that they were the same thing. The sickness was named by whichever one came first.

He didn't bother trying to be quiet as he came up the stairs. Melvin wanted Jay to have some warning. Melvin knocked quietly on Jay's door and called out.

When there was no answer, he opened the door to find Jay lying on the bed curled into a ball in the same clothes he had on the night before. He hadn't even bothered to take off his boots.

It's worse than I thought, Melvin thought as he called Jay's name again. When there was no answer from Jay, Melvin's heart started thumping in terror. What if Jay had died?

With a trembling hand, and holding his breath, he reached out and touched Jay. He was warm. Alive, but unmoving.

Now, he knew what to do. He started talking to Jay the same way he would speak to one of his animals when they were sick. Soothing words. They didn't have to make any sense. Just let them know you are there to help.

Still talking, he went into the bathroom for a towel. He ran hot water on it, and then wrung it out. Back in the bedroom, Jay hadn't moved. Melvin rolled him onto his back and put the warm towel on his forehead. Jay's eyes remained closed, but his moan told Melvin he was aware that he was there.

It took a bit of a struggle to get his boots off, but once that was done, he brought in a blanket from his bedroom and covered Jay. It was a warm day, but sometimes the weight and warmth of a blanket is helpful.

Jay just lay on the bed, eyes closed, breathing softly, and moaning once in a while.

Back in the kitchen, Melvin got a jug of water and another cup of coffee for himself. Before heading upstairs, he grabbed his *Bible*. He thought he heard his wife laugh, so he said aloud, "Well, I learned this all from you, my love."

He had. He had watched Sally take care of him and his son when they were not well. *Bible* reading always helped; even though he would humph about it, he was still secretly glad she did it. Now the secret was out. *She probably already knew,* Melvin thought.

For the rest of the day, Melvin alternated being reading aloud whatever verse he would turn to and nap in his chair. Once he went downstairs to get himself a sandwich, and twice he took a bathroom break. Each time we would tell Jay where he was going, and then tell him what he had done when he came back.

It was a beautiful day. There were things on the farm that needed to be taken care of, but Melvin knew they would wait. Instead, he gave thanks that in his last days, he had been given something important to do. He could help someone who needed him. Yes, it would get him closer to Sally, but it also had given him a sense of purpose.

He figured that God had to have some fantastic planning skills to arrange for Jay to find his farm. All the things that had to have happened to have Jay come to him were staggering. It was the best place for both of them to be. They both needed healing, and Melvin was prepared to do whatever it took for both of them.

Melvin was surprised how quickly the day went by. He was making plans to bring a cot into Jay's room and spend the night there, when he saw Jay's eyes fly open, and then slowly close again.

"Hello, son," Melvin said. "Are you hungry? I can bring up scrambled eggs and make you coffee or bring you juice. There is water here beside your bed."

With Jay's almost imperceptible nod, Melvin got up. "I'll be back in just a few minutes. We'll have our food up here if you don't mind."

Down in the kitchen, Melvin heard the creak of the bed, and then the flush of the toilet. Listening carefully, he heard water run, and then once again, the creak of the bed.

Smiling to himself, Melvin counted that as a victory.

Jay wasn't running anymore. After a good night's sleep, Melvin would find out what had happened, and together, they would make it right.

Once more, as he had done all day, Melvin raised his eyes heavenward and breathed the words, "Thank you."

Outside the sun dipped down behind the horizon and with a bright burst of red-orange, disappeared for the night. Melvin had always loved the promise that the sun would rise again, and he knew in his heart that this time it was also a promise that he was given another day to do what he had to do.

As he entered Jay's bedroom carrying a tray with two plates of scrambled eggs, and a stack of toast, Jay lifted his eyes and gave him a small smile.

Yep, it has been a good day, Melvin thought.

Thirty-Eight

Evan sat outside drinking his coffee. He hadn't been able to sleep. He and Ava had lain awake for hours after everyone had either gone to their own home or to the bunkhouse. They lay on their backs on the bed staring at the ceiling and holding hands for hours. What could they say? There was so much they didn't understand. To be truthful, Evan wished he didn't have to understand.

Finally, Ava drifted off to sleep. However, Evan knew sleep was not going to come to him, so here he was sitting outside drinking coffee wishing that everything that happened had just been a dream. The problem was, he knew it wasn't a dream. It had happened.

Evan had thought that the year before was the best and worst year of his life. But he and Ava survived it. All his friends and family were thriving. And then this.

That was the problem. What was this?

In the midst of his deep thinking, Evan slowly became aware of Leif and Sarah. He had no idea how long they had been sitting there.

"Wow. You two are either extremely quiet, or I was completely lost in thought."

"I think it was both. We heard Craig moving around so he'll probably be out soon. I think I'll make a pot of coffee if you don't mind," Sarah said.

A few minutes later the three friends were sitting with a coffee in their hands waiting for the sun to come up. They were also waiting for Hank, but no one wanted to mention it.

"You are all uncharacteristically quiet," Hank said, coming up behind them.

"Good grief," Sarah said. "You scared me. Where did you come from?"

"Been walking the woods. Well, more sitting than walking. Looking for some inspiration. Then I saw a light come on in the kitchen and figured the inspiration I am looking for is probably sitting on the deck drinking coffee."

"Well, they say two heads are better than one," Craig said, stepping up on the deck, "And I see five of them right here."

"That's what I am counting on," Hank said. "Have to tell you though, if Hannah hadn't come out last night to tell us what she knows; I was ready to ask Sam to take me straight to prison."

"I am so glad you didn't, Hank, what would we do without you," Ava said coming up behind him and kissing him on the cheek before settling in a chair next to Evan.

"Can we talk about what Hannah told us last night before she wakes up? Craig, you are the one who told us about people that remember their past lives. So is Hannah one of those people called a Jatismar?"

"Well, I don't think she could have made up the story, and now we know who she was waiting for, don't we? It's Melvin's hired hand who was her dad in her past life. Wow."

"And I am responsible for that. I can't stop thinking that Hannah should hate me.

"I burned their house down with her and her mother in it." Hank said. "How can she ever forgive me for that?"

"She doesn't remember the burning part the same way as you saw it, Hank. She remembers living in the farmhouse, and she remembers who her parents were. I think we have to assume that all three of you are here in this place at the same time for a reason," Sarah said.

"What could that be other than to punish me, and take Hannah away from all of you? I deserve the punishment, but you don't deserve to lose her."

"Well, if you are talking about losing her because that man can claim she is his child from his past life, you know that won't go anywhere. He doesn't have a legal leg to stand on," Craig said.

"But, he does have an emotional and love-based one," Ava answered. "Doesn't he have a right to be part of her life now? The problem is, he is most likely out for revenge against you, Hank."

"Which is why I should make it easy and turn myself in now," Hank said. "I'll be out of the way. I deserve his revenge. Let him have it."

"No," said Hannah who had arrived without anyone seeing her. "No, I won't let you, and that isn't the answer anyway. He will try to kill you, Uncle Hank, even if you turn yourself in, because he is drowning in hate. We have to help him."

"Hannah, we didn't mean to wake you, honey. Let's get some slippers and a robe on you, and make some breakfast. Then we can figure out what to do," Ava said.

"I told you what to do. You just don't believe me," Hannah said as she walked back into the house slamming the door behind her.

Well, if they won't do it. I will, Hannah thought. *It has to be done, and I guess I am the only one brave enough.*

Hannah didn't feel all that brave at the moment, but she figured she could talk herself into it.

"Do you want my help?" Suzanne asked, gliding into Hannah's room as Hannah slipped back under covers.

"Can you?" Hannah asked, and then smiled. "Of course, you can, what was I thinking?"

"Well, this is what I think. You need to get back out of bed and go apologize so your family won't be worried. We can talk about what to do later."

Hannah wanted to go back to sleep. She wanted to pout, but she knew Suzanne was right.

Besides, Hannah knew that she needed to act as if everything was normal if she was going to pull off the idea she had. Even with Suzanne's help, it was going to be tricky.

She needed someone who could drive a car. *Oh yes,* she thought as an idea occurred to her, *that just might work.*

Thirty-Nine

The morning after the solstice, the committee met in the town hall as planned. Although, like everyone at the Anders home, Grace hadn't slept a wink, she was still at the meeting right on time as always.

She brought along a tray of leftover pastries and fresh coffee. Grace had learned the value of being an excellent hostess. People told her things without thinking about whether it was wise or not. Luckily, with Grace, it was a smart thing to do. She always had good intentions.

This morning was going to be a good one for information. Grace couldn't wait to hear the reports about the celebration. Although there was an official inquiry going on about the unplanned fireworks, Grace knew that she was likely to find out more by listening to the local gossip, than Sam's men were in their investigation.

She wasn't disappointed. Rumors quickly took over the meeting. Valerie had envisioned a well-run recap of the celebration, but within a few minutes, she realized she was losing the battle. Instead, of fighting the inevitable, Valerie rapped her gavel a few times, thanked everyone for their help and then let the members take over.

The main discussion was speculation over why the gas station appeared to be open, but it wasn't. Rumor had it that Frank Jacks had been arrested. For what, no one was certain. One of the women asked if it had something to do with the fireworks going off in the middle of the afternoon and then immediately afterward a bunch of men, starting to run.

She wanted to know if they were running after the person who set off the fireworks or was something else going on. The group agreed that something else was going on because they were sure they saw one of the high school boys sneak in and light the rocket that caused the commotion.

Valerie asked about Melvin's friend. What had happened to him? Was it heat stroke? It wasn't all that hot that day. Maybe he hadn't drunk enough water?

Grace let the conversation swirl around her, pretending to be absorbed in making sure everyone had a pastry.

One of the members of the committee asked what high school boy did they see. When no one could say who it was, Grace gently stepped in and asked what he had been wearing, because perhaps they could recognize him from his clothes.

When everyone fell silent, she realized that they knew who it was but weren't telling. Why would that be, she wondered. The thought crossed her mind that it might have been the son of someone in the group and no one wanted to tell on him.

Her suspicions increased when she realized that people were having a hard time looking at Valerie, and she had gone uncharacteristically quiet.

Grace knew Valerie had a son in high school. She mentioned one time over coffee that he was in the stage of acting out. *It's possible it was him*, Grace thought. She would have Sam check it out.

But to spare her friend, she said, "Hey, who here didn't make a little mischief in high school? I am sure whoever it was didn't mean for it to be more than a silly prank."

"Of course," someone agreed. "That's all it was. Valerie, you ran a fantastic celebration. All the kids said it was wonderful, and the food was delicious."

With general words of agreement, the meeting broke up. But as Grace picked up the leftover food, Valerie grabbed her arm. "Thank you, Grace. But I do think it was my son, and I think he may be in trouble. Is there any way your friends can help me?"

When Grace didn't answer, Valerie said, "I know that Mira's friend Sam is in some sort of law enforcement. I would rather talk to him than the local police. Could you please ask if we could meet?"

Grace turned to her friend and gathered her in one of her famous Grace hugs. "Of course," she said, releasing her. I'll have Mira set it up. What's your son's name?"

"Johnny. I don't think he meant to do something bad."

"I was serious, Valerie when I said that we all did silly things in high school. And if it was him, then he was manipulated by a master at getting people to do his bidding. Johnny probably had no idea who he was getting mixed up with. Besides, he might be able to help."

Grace told Valerie she would text her with the time of the meeting. Valerie hugged her one more time and thanked her, trying not to let Grace see that there were tears in her eyes.

As she walked away, Grace thought it was good they found out now. Because Johnny was in more trouble than just setting off fireworks as a prank. He had caught Grant's eye, and that was never, ever a good thing.

Forty

Hannah had decided what she needed to do. She figured that Melvin still had a landline, so she found a phone book in the hall closet and located Melvin's phone number.

Hannah didn't call right away. She knew the minute she made the call, she was doing something Ava and Evan would not be happy about. It was a scary thing to do.

But she didn't see another option. So during the school lunch, Hannah escaped into the bathroom and made the call. She hoped Melvin would answer. Hannah had only memorized what she was going to say to Melvin. She didn't think her past-dad would answer, but it was possible.

After all her planning, it turned out it didn't matter because as soon as she heard Melvin's voice, everything flew out of her head. "Hello," he said again.

Hannah cleared her throat and squeaked out a hello.

Melvin knew who it was right away, and felt his heart expand with pleasure. It was the little girl doing what he would have done if he had thought of it. Or been brave enough.

"Is this the little girl I saw at the solstice celebration?" he asked.

"Do you think I am a little girl?" Hannah huffed. "I don't think a little girl would make this call!"

"You are absolutely correct, young lady. You are a brave young lady. Very pretty too, if I may say so."

"Okay," Hannah sniffed, suddenly feeling better. "Can I call you a nice old man, then?"

"You may. Now, young lady, what can I do for you?"

"Well, if you know who I am, I think you might know why I am calling. Do you?"

"Do you mean, do I know the story?"

"Did he tell you? I thought he would be afraid to cause you might not believe him."

"Well, I didn't believe him at first. But I remembered him, so I had to listen."

"Does that mean you remember me too?" This idea had never occurred to Hannah, that someone would remember her.

"I never met you. But, I saw your picture in the paper. That was a long time ago. I am kinda curious. Do you remember where you've been?"

That question took Hannah entirely by surprise. Did she? Should she?

"I'm sorry pretty young lady. I didn't mean to offend you."

"You didn't," Hannah answered, "I just never thought about it. Maybe we could talk about it…"

"When you come see us?" Melvin filled in.

"Yes. Then. May I? I have to talk to him before he does something terrible."

"It's a great idea. When shall we do this?"

"I am thinking tomorrow when I am supposed to be in school. I have a friend who I am going to ask to bring me. Maybe you know him. He used to live in Concourse."

"We'll see. I don't think it is a good idea for you to sneak out, but it sounds like that is what you are going to do. I guess I will have to trust that you know what is best in this situation."

Hannah sighed. "Thank you for trusting me, and helping me, and my past-dad."

"I am grateful you trust me, young lady. By the way, what is your name? Your past-dad—as you call him— told me your name from before. What is it now?"

"It's the same. Hannah. Thank you, Mr. Byler. I will see you tomorrow."

Hannah and Melvin hung up at the same time.

Melvin was grateful that Jay was working in the fields. He had dragged himself out of bed and said that he needed to be outside. Melvin knew that work was an excellent healer, so he gave Jay a list of jobs to do.

He wasn't quite sure what to say to Jay about tomorrow's meeting. Maybe just have Hannah come and let the cards fall as they may. Shaking his head, he headed into the kitchen to start dinner for himself and Jay. It took a few minutes to realize that although he was worried about the next day, he was humming.

Hannah hung up and looked around to make sure that no one had heard her end of the conversation. She had opened every stall door when she came in to check, but during the call, she didn't pay any attention.

The next part of her plan involved Eric and Grace. Hannah figured that she since she had talked them into letting her be at their wedding, she could also talk them into taking her to Melvin's. Eric could pick her up as he always did each day. No one would suspect anything. Hannah reasoned that Grace and Eric were the best people to come. *They don't have any history with either Melvin or my past-dad, and they both are old and full of wisdom.*

That settled, Hannah went back to the classroom and tried to keep her attention on what the teacher was saying, but her thoughts were far away. Luckily, they weren't doing anything she didn't already know, or she might have gotten in trouble for not listening.

When Eric picked her up from school, Hannah gave him her brightest smile and hugged him extra hard. He wasn't fooled, just as she knew he wouldn't be.

"Okay, Hannah. I know when I'm being set up. What do you want?"

"Could we first go see Grace? It's something I have to ask you both."

Eric made a quick call to Ava telling her that he was taking Hannah into town with him. Ava was a bit concerned, but Eric assured her that all was well. He would have Hannah home in time for dinner.

After hugs and cookies, Hannah sat down across from Grace and Eric and told them her plan. "I can't do it without you two, and it has to be done," she said.

After a moment's pause, it was Grace who spoke. "You know this could go so wrong, don't you? Starting with your parents being furious with you, and us, and Hank and …"

"Yes, I know," Hannah said, "But can you believe me when I tell you that it could be so much worse if I don't try?"

Grace and Eric exchanged looks, and then Eric said, "Oh, Hannah, we'll do it, but we reserve the right to get you out of there if things start going wrong. We'll just pick you up and carry you out!"

Hannah threw herself into Eric's arms, hugging him for real this time. Grace excused herself and went to ask Mandy if she would be okay running the store by herself the next day. She and Eric needed to do something important.

Grace hoped that telling a lie of omission for something good to happen constituted the right thing to do. However, she still felt badly about lying, so she turned back to Mandy and added, "I can't actually tell you what we are doing, Mandy, but I believe it is the right thing to do."

Mandy held Grace at arm's length and looked into her eyes. "Are you afraid?"

"A little," Grace answered

"Then I will hold you in a peaceful place in my heart tomorrow, and you will promise to call me immediately if you need anything."

As Grace pulled Mandy into a hug, she thought, *Who would have thought I would be given this beautiful woman to love as a daughter.*

"I love you as a mom too, Grace," Mandy said.

They both laughed as Grace said, "I didn't know you could read minds!"

"I don't really, but anyone with half a heart can feel your love, Grace."

That's what it takes, Grace thought. *I will just love everyone tomorrow with every fiber of my being. That's something I know how to do!*

Forty-One

It was freezing in the cabin. *The middle of June and I am freezing my ass off,* Grant fumed. He hated cabins. He hated camping. Which was precisely why he was in a cabin in Hocking Hills, Ohio. No one would think he would choose to go camping. Everyone knew he hated roughing it, and it was no secret that he hated nature. Too random. Not controllable. Which made a cabin in the middle of nowhere the perfect place to hide away for a few days.

Getting the cabin was just another one of the provisions that Grant had made while still in hiding. Although it was only by chance that he had found out about it.

To keep himself from going crazy while his face was healing from the plastic surgery, he read books. Well, he skimmed books. People that got lost in a story in a book were weak-minded by Grant's account. So he read, but only to keep from freaking out from nothing to do. Therefore, it was serendipitous that in one of the books that he skimmed, there was a character who loved the beauty and remoteness of Hocking Hills, Ohio.

After looking the place up on the internet and realizing it was within the area he wanted to stay, Grant rented a cabin for the summer just in case he needed it. He had a caretaker come to the cabin once a week, clean it, and keep the refrigerator stocked. If Grant hadn't been there that week, the caretaker could take the food home. There was no point in having people smell rotting food and raise the alarm.

Grant had arrived late the night before. And after hiding his rental car, he had gone straight to bed. It had been an exhausting and disappointing day. On the way to the cabin, he had picked up the rental car at the Pittsburgh airport and left the stolen car in the rental car lot. Of course, the new rental car was rented in another one of his fake names.

The first thing he did after waking up was to make a pot of coffee and check his provisions. The caretaker had done an excellent job of getting all his favorite foods, and also some foods that he hated. Once again, he was overly cautious, but it had served him well all these years. His shopping list included hated foods just in case someone was wise enough to check buying practices for foods that Sam and Hank knew Grant liked. Some people would call that crazy, but Grant knew it was the little things that needed to be watched the closest.

On his way to Ohio, Grant had texted the caretaker that his job was done and told him where to pick up the extra cash he had promised him. Then he threw that burner phone away. Once Grant left this hiding place, he would never return. He had prepared other places to hide just in case he needed them.

Grant had no desire to see the beauty of where he was. He was too angry, and it wasn't the kind of beauty that moved him anyway. However, he also knew that if he was going to come up with another idea he couldn't be lost in his emotions. Sam and Hank had stopped his plan again, but he had escaped again, so he was still the winner of this round.

Nevertheless, Grant wanted and needed to be the winner of everything, all the time.

Sure, he could leave the country without doing anything else and live happily ever after, but now it was not just about hating those do-gooders, it was about revenge. *It's about winning. And I always win,* Grant thought.

Which is why Grant decided to go for a walk. He needed a foolproof plan, and his anger was keeping him from thinking clearly. It took over an hour of hiking before Grant's anger calmed down to a simmer, and another hour before ideas started coming to him. Four hours later, and his feet filled with blisters, Grant thought he had come up with something that would work.

The idea was so simple; it was stupid. Today was June 23rd. That gave him eight days to prepare to execute his plan on July 1st. It was an anniversary of sorts.

Thirty-five years before, Grant had asked Hank to do something for him. Hank thought that he was the one who had made a mistake. However, there was no mistake. Grant had sent him to the wrong house on purpose.

It wasn't the first time he had set Hank up for failure in a way that would cause him to suffer. At the time, Grant didn't have anything against Hank. He was his favorite. But Grant loved the power of control. Hank was a tough guy, but it was apparent that his toughness was a result of his abuse as a child. That meant, one day Hank might wake up and stop obeying his master.

Grant was right. That was exactly what had happened to Hank. It had just taken meeting his niece, Ava, to turn him completely against Grant. However, it was inevitable. Something would have turned Hank someday.

Which is exactly why he had Hank burn the wrong house down that day. Sure, Grant knew it was the wrong house. Sure, he knew that the family was inside.

Actually, he thought Hank would get all of them, but after the family had celebrated the man's birthday together, he had gone into town to get something for his daughter's breakfast for the next day.

However, it all worked out for the best from Grant's point of view. Hank was devastated by his "mistake" of killing the woman and her child. Then he was blindsided again when he heard that the man had killed himself with drink and drugs. He died five years after the fire.

Grant had made sure that Hank saw the newspaper that carried the story. As a gift to Hank, Grant had subscribed to Concourse's local newspaper, knowing it was Hank's hometown. Although the fire had happened in Doveland thirty miles away, it was still big news for the local community. It set everyone mourning again, including Hank.

Grant thought it was karma and synchronicity to plan Hank's death on the same day of the fire. Thirty-five years later the town would have another tragedy.

There were a few details needed to figure out how it was going to happen. If Grant did it right, he would kill two birds with one stone, so to speak. He would get rid of Hank and Lenny at the same time. Set up Hank's family for pain, since they were so hard to kill, and then get out of dodge.

Beaches and babes were waiting for him. Grant would never be cold again.

Forty-Two

While Grant was making plans, so were Sam and Hank. However, they weren't as sure about their plans as Grant was about his. Sam and Hank were well aware that Grant had the upper hand. He was on the offense.

Sam and his team spent all their time trying to stop Grant from carrying out his destructive plans. They did prevent the disasters Grant planned, but they never caught him. Grant continued to make them look and feel like complete idiots by getting away.

"You know what the problem is, don't you, Sam?" Hank said. "He's smarter than us. Grant has resources we don't have. He doesn't face any consequences. He just kills and moves on. We follow the rules. We protect rather than harm."

"Are you trying to tell me that being the good guy in this scenario makes us stupider and weaker?" Sam asked.

"I know it doesn't sound right. However, it feels as if it is true. Grant is probably laughing at us."

"Well I am laughing at you," Mira said flouncing down beside Sam on the couch in her house. You two are idiots. What would the Circles say if they heard you giving Evil Ones more power than good?"

"They aren't here, are they?" Sam asked looking around the room. "I have to admit, it freaks me out that they can be two places at one time and just pop in. Wait, that's why we are idiots, isn't it? You wonder why we aren't using the gifts of the people Grant hates. That's why he hates them after all, isn't it?"

"Well, your idiot index just improved a bit, Sam. He hates them because even though Grant struts around as if he is the king of the world, he knows that sooner or later what he represents will be overturned. Otherwise, why bother? His ego is his downfall. Of course, the fact that you two are idiots could be your downfall too. On the other hand, you have me, don't you?" Mira said, nibbling on Sam's ear.

Hank stared at Mira willing her to stop. He didn't resent that Sam and Mira had found each other, it just made him uncomfortable. *Besides, aren't we supposed to be keeping our plans secret,* he thought.

"Well, I second the idiot motion," Sarah said, arriving in the room with Leif. "Sorry, couldn't help overhearing what you were saying."

Seeing the shocked faces of the three people in Mira's living room, Sarah added, "Okay, I see you three would be more comfortable if we came to see you in person. We'll be there in about fifteen minutes. Mandy and Tom are coming too."

Mira used the fifteen minutes to pick up the living room and put on a pot of coffee. Sam got up to help her in the kitchen while Hank paced the living room.

After everyone arrived and were seated, Sam asked Sarah, "So you agree with Mira that we are idiots?"

"Well, that is probably too harsh. You have saved everyone twice, and your intention has always been good, but you aren't using all the resources at your disposal, including your own creative thinking.

"Sam, you are thinking like a lawman, and Hank you are thinking like a guilty man."

"What do you suggest we think like then," Sam asked. "I am a lawman."

"And, how can I not think like a guilty man?" Hank said. "I am guilty. I did all those terrible things. How can I step away from that?"

"I'm afraid that I am not much help either," Mandy said. "I did all those terrible things too. Maybe Hank is going to say I didn't kill anyone or hurt people on purpose, but I'm not sure that it matters. Guilty is guilty. I still feel guilty."

"Yes," Leif said. "As humans we make mistakes. It's impossible not to. Fighting our mistakes takes up a lot of energy and keeps us locked into the past, or the box we have put ourselves within. It's an effective prison of our own making.

"Instead, surrender to it, so your mistakes lose their grip. Let them drift into the past. Are any of you doing any form of meditation and prayer?

"Well now. I see that you aren't. And why not? Do you like living in your human perceptions? Are you willing to be free from them?

"Not only would you begin to release yourself from the stories you are living, but you will expand your awareness and see what others don't. That will include a solution to whatever you need right now.

"All five of you have shifted your stories quite a bit this past year. Think of what last year was like for you. Imagine what the future can bring if you actively surrender and move into your true spiritual nature?"

Seeing everyone's bewildered expression, Sarah added. "You think we have gifts because we do things most people don't do.

But everyone has these possibilities because everyone is an expression of the Divine Infinite. Being here on earth gives us the chance to express that, and experience the divine in all the ways it presents itself."

"Everyone?" Mandy asked. "What about the Evil Ones, like Grant and Lenny. How can they be the expression of the Divine Infinite?"

"Well, they aren't, are they?" Sarah answered. "They aren't expressing their unique spiritual nature. So either the individualities called Grant and Lenny are not there at all, or it is hidden beneath the prison they have built for themselves. They both have let themselves be driven by evil.

"If you keep thinking of yourselves as guilty humans, in a way you are letting yourself be driven by evil. It is a false representation of who you are. Let it go. Things will become clearer as you do."

"Let's take a moment, and all of us sit in silence, knowing that there is a solution, and letting the idea of our humanness drift off for a moment," Leif said.

For Sam and Hank, this seemed impossible. But Mira, Tom, Mandy, and Sarah had already put their coffee cups down and closed their eyes. Looking across at Leif staring at them with intent, Hank and Sam realized that they didn't really have a choice, and did the same.

"Just let your thoughts float by," Leif said. "Don't fight. Just feel."

For Hank, it was torture. Thoughts of all the things he had done kept erupting. The house burning was the worst. He had been told that the woman and her daughter were dead from smoke inhalation before the fire reached them. But he could see the flames.

He saw the man run out of the truck screaming for them. Hank saw himself fall to his knees in disbelief and terror at what he had done.

However, he did his best to disconnect those thoughts from himself. Hank imagined snipping the ties that connected him to the thoughts and let them float away. For one brief second he felt something different, and then it was gone. But it was enough to show him it was possible.

No one spoke. Silence filled the room. And then there was a light knock on the door, and they all heard Grace ask, "May I come in?"

Sarah had ended up sitting on the floor in a meditation pose. Over time, this had become the most comfortable for her. She untangled her legs and silently opened the door to Grace.

"Oh," Grace said. "I didn't mean to interrupt."

"I don't think this is an interruption, Grace. I think this might be what we were waiting to arrive," Sarah said, leading Grace over to the chair beside the couch.

By then everyone had opened their eyes, and begun the adjusting to being present in the room.

"That was harder but more interesting than I thought it would be," Sam said. "Not quite as woo-woo as I imagined."

Sarah laughed, "Oh, it's plenty woo-woo. I love woo-woo! Thank you for starting this practice."

Seeing Sam's face, Sarah added, "Yes, practice, lots of practice. We've had years of practice being human. It will take dedication to practice letting it go."

"I don't know if I like that answer," Hank said, "But I know I don't like living with myself now this way, and for a moment I felt something different."

Sarah smiled at him, and Hank smiled back. This is what I have been given, Hank thought. I will not let it go.

"Okay, I'll practice. But what do you mean that Grace arriving might be a solution?"

"Were you all meditating together?" Grace asked. When she got positive nods in return, she said, "Wow. Who would have thought that would happen. Mandy, perhaps we can set up regular times together? Maybe Eric will join us."

Mandy looked at Grace with love and answered. "Absolutely."

"Okay, woo-woo time is over," Sam said in exasperation. "What solutions?"

"Grace, you want to tell them why you are here?" Sarah asked.

"Oh, yes. Wow. Okay, I can only stay a minute anyway. I called Ava to talk to Sarah, and she said Sarah was visiting Mira and Sam, so I popped over. It was Sam I wanted to see anyway.

"We had a meeting this morning to wrap up the solstice celebration, and Valerie asked me to talk to you, Sam. It's about her son, Johnny.

"She thinks he was the one that set off the fireworks. She wants you to look into it instead of the police. She doesn't want it to turn into a legal problem if that is possible. If he made a mistake, she doesn't want him to be punished his whole life for it."

Sam and Hank exchanged looks. It was an opening they hadn't expected. A solution. Out of nowhere.

"I think I will start practicing," Sam said.

"Thank you, Grace, for telling us. I understand how one bad choice can ruin a kid's life," Hank replied.

Grace gave Sam the information Valerie had told her. Everyone hugged, and Sarah and Leif accompanied Grace outside.

"Do you know what Hannah wants us to do?" Grace asked them.

"Yes," Sarah answered.

"Should we?" Grace asked.

Both Sarah and Leif nodded yes.

Another adventure, Grace thought and gave thanks for being in the right place at the right time.

Forty-Three

"Let me check with you one more time, Hannah," Eric said as he pulled out of the driveway. I could still take you to school if you have changed your mind."

Grace turned in her seat and added, "It won't be a failure, Hannah, it just might be better to do something else."

"I know you both mean well," Hannah said. "And I know I look like I am just a little girl, but I remember my dad, and I know that I am the only one who will be able to talk to him about Hank. I have to help him!"

Grace reached back and patted Hannah's hand. "Okay, honey, we'll do it this way."

For the next twenty minutes, they traveled in silence, each of them doing the best that they could not to be too nervous.

"Oh, I forgot to tell you," Hannah said, "Suzanne is going to meet us there, but since you can't see her, I thought I should tell you now."

"Do you think Melvin or your dad will see her?" Eric asked.

"I don't know," Hannah answered, "but if they can't, should I tell them that she is there?"

"It may be too much information, but let's play it by ear, and see what feels the best."

Grace directed Eric until they could see Melvin's truck parked beside an old farmhouse sitting on a slight rise back from the road.

"They know that we are coming, right?" Eric asked.

"Melvin does," Hannah answered. "We agreed that it would be best for Jay not to know."

"Not so sure that was a wise decision, young lady, but it's done now, and perhaps you and Melvin know your dad best."

As they pulled up beside the farmhouse, Melvin stepped out of the back door and walked over to open Hannah's door, extending a hand to help her out.

For a long moment, they both stood looking at each other and then Melvin knelt down beside her and Hannah wrapped her arms around him.

"Another love at first sight," Eric whispered to Grace. She nodded with tears in her eyes. No matter what, they were going to make a new friend today.

Taking Hannah's hand, Melvin led them back to the house. He said he would ring the bell for Jay to come in from the fields when Hannah was ready to see him.

"How much did he tell you?" Hannah asked.

"He told me what he remembers from before. Jay's been in pain for so many years he wants to hurt someone. He thinks that will make the pain go away. But he saw that you love that man even though he burned the house down and killed you," Melvin answered.

"I don't think he can understand how you can love that man after all that. Now Jay is stuck between not wanting to hurt you, and wanting his revenge."

"Does he know I recognize him?"

"He thinks that you do, because of what you did at the solstice.

"But Jay is worried that he has made it all up and is just going crazy."

The four of them were sitting at Melvin's kitchen table. "I think we had a table like this in our kitchen," Hannah said.

"That's what Jay said too," Melvin told her. "He said it reminded him of good times. We probably both got it from the Sears store. I could never get rid of this table; it reminds me of all the good meals my wife, Sally, made for us."

"You know, Melvin. I used to live in Concourse. I worked at the free clinic in town," Eric said.

Melvin smiled as wide as his wrinkled face would let him. "I thought I recognized you! We donated some of our fresh vegetables there once in a while. Why did you move away?"

For the next few minutes, Eric recapped the story of Hank leaving his sister at the free clinic after killing his abusive father. Hank knew he had to run away. He knew his sister would be better off without him.

Eric told about his moving away and raising Abbie as his daughter how she had died in her twenties from cancer. Last year, to Eric's thinking, divine intervention returned a part of Abbie to Hank.

"Hank found Ava and her daughter Hannah and turned his life around because of it. Now Hank is working to capture the man called Grant who is trying to harm Ava and her friends and family, including Hannah."

"Wow," Melvin said. "That is quite a story, and I know there must be more, but perhaps Hannah is ready for the next chapter in that story?"

"I am," Hannah replied. "But I think it would be better if I went to my dad myself. Maybe you could ring the bell. When he starts walking this way, I'll meet him outside. Outside always seems better, doesn't it? Perhaps the trees will help him be calm."

As Hannah spoke, she glanced up at the corner behind Melvin causing him to turn around to see what she was looking at. "Do you see anything?" Hannah asked.

"No, should I?"

"Okay, I'll try it," Hannah said to what appeared to be an empty corner as she touched Melvin's hand.

"Do you see anything, now? she asked.

Melvin turned to look again and almost jumped out of his seat, releasing Hannah's hand. "Well, I thought I did. Scared the begeezus out of me. Who was that?"

"A friend of ours. She lives in another dimension, but she comes to help a lot. Do you want to meet her?"

Melvin shook his head, "Ya never know what some folks can do. Since Jay showed up, I've had to change my mind about many things. Yes, I think I would."

Hannah touched Melvin's hand again and introduced Suzanne. Melvin nodded at Suzanne with as much grace as he could muster and said, "Hello."

Suzanne glided over to stand by the table and said hello to Melvin. Melvin's face turned white under his farmer's tan. "We can talk?"

"Indeed we can, but I think Hannah is most interested in talking to Jay first. I'll walk out with her and keep her safe. Although I don't think there is anything to worry about. By the way, Hannah, perhaps Grace would like to see me too. Would you try it?"

Hannah reached out and held Grace's hand. Grace's gasped and said, "Nice to meet you, Suzanne. I have wanted to meet you ever since I met Ava."

"It's a pleasure, Grace. You have been a blessing to everyone, including your handsome husband over there."

Eric smiled. "Suzanne, you are giving it away."

"You can see her?" Grace stuttered.

"Yes, I have been able to for a few months. I have a feeling why. But whatever the reason is, I am grateful."

"May I go now please," Hannah asked. "I know you grownups want to keep talking, but I need to go see my dad now."

"Of course," Melvin said. He went to the back door and pulled a string hanging beside it to ring the bell hanging off the eaves of the back stoop. "I rigged this up for my Sally so she wouldn't have to go outside to ring the bell in bad weather."

Hannah smiled at him and walked out being careful not to bang the screen door behind her. In the distance, she could see a man walking towards the house.

She waved, and he stopped and stared, and then waved back. Slowly at first they continued to walk toward each other until Hannah broke into a run,

He paused and then started running toward her, tripping over the rough ground. Just twenty feet from the house, they met. Hannah leaped into his arms, and everyone in the farmhouse could hear her say, "Daddy, daddy."

The three people watching from the back door looked at each other. Each of them overwhelmed by what they were seeing and wondering what was going to happen next.

Forty-Four

Ava was doing her best to be calm. She breathed in and out, trying to let the emotions out that threatened to explode. She stared at the three people seated at the dining room table with her and wondered if she was capable of carrying on a decent conversation.

When it became apparent that she was not going to be able to talk without yelling, she simply pointed at Hannah and said "room."

Hannah stared at her mom without remorse, which only made Ava angrier. "Now!" Ava said. "We are going to talk about this, but not right now. I am calling a meeting, and then you can tell everyone what you told me."

As soon as Ava heard Hannah's door close, Ava turned her full attention to Eric and Grace. "You two don't even look ashamed!"

When neither Eric nor Grace answered, Ava added, "I know she would have gotten there one way or another, so I guess I should thank you for being the ones. But right now, I am just too angry."

Grace stood up and motioned for Eric to join her.

"Ava, dear, I think you will find that it's not so much that you are angry, but that you are afraid. Call a meeting for tonight. In the meantime, try not to be frightened."

Ava didn't answer, just watched the two of them leave without even walking them to the door.

With Ben asleep, and Hannah in her room, Ava didn't move at all. She just stared at the wall and wondered if her world was falling apart again.

An hour later, Evan found Ava still sitting at the dining room table. Ava jumped when Evan touched her shoulder. "Ava, what's the matter? Is everything, okay?"

Ava looked up at Evan as if waking up from a deep sleep. "I don't know. Maybe not. But then, maybe everything is going to fall apart, and I don't know what to do to stop it."

Evan didn't have a chance to find out what was wrong because Ben started crying and Ava left to feed him. As she walked out of the kitchen, she said, "Call everyone. We need to have a meeting tonight. Make it as soon as possible, and be sure Hank is here."

By the time Ava returned to the kitchen, Evan had contacted everyone. It turned out that Grace had already alerted most of them, and they were all bringing food.

"Are you going to tell me what is going on, Ava?" He asked.

Ava shook her head. "No. I don't want to talk about it until we can all talk about it together. And please, don't ask Hannah either. When everyone gets here, she can come out of her room, but not until then."

"It's that bad?" Evan asked.

"Yes, it is," Ava answered.

****

After Hannah and her friends left, Melvin wasn't sure what to say to Jay, so he didn't say anything. Instead, he made dinner. Sally had taught him how to make biscuits, so while Jay sat outside on the stoop staring at nothing, Melvin baked.

He wasn't sure if he should make comfort food or celebration food, but settled on mac and cheese from a box. Before Jay came, he would make it for himself for dinner at least once a week. It reminded him of meals with his son when he was a child.

It was not wise to question why the cheese was so orange. Maybe that's why kids like it so much, he thought to himself.

When the biscuits were done, he opened the back door and joined Jay on the stoop.

"Want to talk about it?" Melvin asked.

Jay turned to look at Melvin as if he had never seen him before. "Melvin. Why are you so kind to me?"

Melvin didn't answer him. Instead, he handed him a beer and took a swig from his.

"Let's eat. Then we'll talk. After that, maybe you will see why it's easy to be kind to you."

Jay gestured at the worn out picnic table sitting under a tree in the backyard. "How about eating there?" he said.

This time it was Melvin who stared at Jay. He wanted to ask him if Sally was in his head too because he had just heard her suggest that very same thing to him. But he didn't. There would be time for that kind of discussion another time.

Instead, they went inside and loaded up the old trays that Sally kept around for such things. Sally had purchased what she called pretty trays, but Melvin and his son had always reached for the old battered ones. That's what happened this time too.

Jay had the one with a can of Budweiser pictured on the bottom, and Melvin took the one that advertised shaving cream. It reminded him of the Berma-Shave signs that used to be along the roadside. The whole family would always read them out together when they traveled.

Now everything is flashy and shiny. Much harder to remember anything. Everyone who had seen those old signs remembered them.

They were so popular that by the time they were phased out in 1963—because people drove too fast to read them—there was no longer a need for a product name. Melvin still remembered that sign. "If you / Don't know /Whose signs / These are / You can't have / Driven very far."

No one remembers the big billboards that pollute the countryside now.

Outside, Melvin and Jay didn't say anything. They were both lost in their thoughts. After eating and taking everything back in the kitchen the two of them went to the front porch. Jay sat in the swing and Melvin in his old chair that Sally had kept threatening to throw away.

Melvin was grateful that she never got around to doing it. The chair fit him like a glove, and without knowing it, he drifted off to sleep.

When he woke, it was getting dark, and Jay was still sitting on the swing, looking out over the farm.

"Hey, old man. I see you got your beauty sleep," he said.

Melvin snorted. "When you get this old, it will happen to you too."

Jay turned to look at Melvin. "That's just it, Melvin. I don't think I will make it to old."

As Melvin started to protest, Jay added, "And I am beginning to think that's not a bad thing."

"Okay. Let's say it's not. But why do you think that you won't be growing old?"

"It's a feeling I have. I guess we will just have to wait and see."

Melvin waited, and when Jay didn't continue he asked, "Are you ready, son, to tell me what happened between you and that pretty young lady?"

Jay looked up at the darkening sky and sighed. "I guess I better, because you are involved in the plan."

"Is that a good thing?" Melvin asked.

"It's another thing we will just have to wait and see," Jay answered.

Forty-Five

Ava watched her friends and family laughing and eating and wondered how they could be doing something so ordinary when the whole world was turning upside down.

Then she remembered that they didn't know. Only Grace and Eric remained subdued. Evan had gone to Hannah's room to get her. Since then she hadn't left his side as he filled his plate and suggested things for her to put on her plate.

Everyone had come to the meeting except Sam who was working with his team to find Grant. Although Sarah, Leif, and Craig were scheduled to fly out in the morning, Ava was thinking of asking them to stay. Maybe after they heard what was happening, they would decide to anyway.

I wish they all lived here, Ava thought. Sarah turned and smiled at her and walked to her side. "We're thinking about it," she said.

"Listening to my thoughts?" Ava asked. "But really it would be wonderful to have all of the Stone Circle here along with the rest of the friends we have gathered.

"Do you think Craig and his wife would ever think about moving here?"

"Craig, maybe," Sarah answered.

Ava turned to look at Craig and for the first time realized that he had not cheered up since he had arrived.

"I can't believe I haven't noticed. Have I been too selfish? Is there something I can do?"

"Talk to him, and listen to what he wants to say," Leif answered, coming over to the two of them.

"But not now. It's time to discuss why you have brought us all together," Sarah said. "You are going to have to step up and take charge."

Ava looked at her two wise friends and realized that they were right. She couldn't be hanging back hoping it would all go away. She thought she had stopped running, but here she was running from what needed to be discussed.

Grace had been watching Ava talk to Sarah and Leif. As soon as she saw Ava look up at her, she knew what Ava was asking her to do. "Okay everyone, it's time for a meeting. Ava, do you want us inside or out?"

"I would love to go outside, and I would love to gather around a fire," she answered.

"Your wish is my command," Evan said and headed outside to start a fire. Everyone followed after grabbing their favorite drink.

Twenty minutes later, with everyone seated in a circle, Ava said, "Okay, Hannah. Tell people what you did today. And then, tell us what you think we ought to do about it."

Hannah looked around the circle and then lifted her eyes to look south to where Melvin and Jay also sat in the semi-dark. She could see them there, and she could hear what they were saying. Melvin had agreed. The first step was complete.

Turning to everyone, Hannah smiled and began. "It's about my past-dad, Jay. It's also about my present-dad, Evan, and my Uncle Hank."

Ava gasped and turned white. Hearing it out loud was worse than she thought it was going to be.

"Don't be afraid, mom," Hannah said. "I have a plan."

Forty-Six

Lenny had heard what happened in Doveland. Once again, Grant had escaped. That was not good news. Lenny had hoped that not only would Grant's plan succeed, ridding him of all those do-gooders in Doveland, but Grant would either be killed or put in jail in the process.

Lenny knew he didn't have all of Grant's resources. However, that was only because Lenny hadn't been around long enough to build them up. If he could get rid of Grant, he would have time to get everything he needed. He would become an even greater leader than Grant had ever been.

Yes, most of Grant's contacts were rounded up in the fiasco from last year. Most of them went to jail, where they had each met their demise. Everyone knew it was Grant who was behind all their deaths, but what good did that do if they couldn't catch him?

The few men that had escaped the roundup last year were skittish. They figured Grant or Sam would be coming after them. Lenny wondered which one would be worse. At least with Sam, they had a chance to live. With Grant, it was over. Grant was getting rid of loose ends, and they were all loose ends.

Even so, the remnant of Grant's team still ran many influential world organizations. They were the invisible power, always working behind the scenes.

Lenny was in the right place at the right time. Most of the men who remained from Grant's group were old. Either Grant would kill them, or they would die of old age. Still, Lenny needed them for now. During the past year, he had contacted every one of them. He offered his services. He told them that he could be as ruthless and brilliant as Grant. They wanted proof, and the proof they wanted was the death of Grant.

Lenny agreed. Killing off Grant was imperative. If Lenny could also kill Hank at the same time, it would be a double whammy. It would prove that Lenny could lead them. What Lenny had going for him was that everyone thought he was just dealing drugs, and that was all that he was good at doing. Yes, he was selling drugs. However, drugs were a cover. What he was really doing was buying power. Sometimes he bought it with money. Other times he used bribes.

He had a collection of damning evidence against almost everyone in power, not just in the United States, but much of Europe. He was working on bribes and fear with leaders of other countries now. Soon he would have the world in his hands. He would have ultimate power, and he would use it too. Lenny laughed to himself. He was close to winning, and no one even knew he was in the game.

He would be a leader greater than Grant ever had been. First, he had to get rid of Grant. Lenny knew that Grant was coming after him. Lenny was going to use that against him. Let Grant come. They would see who was the most powerful.

******

Johnny Price was trying to look tough. Watching him through the two-way mirror, Sam chuckled. In spite of Johnny's black clothes and pierced nose and eyebrows, Johnny was a scared kid way in over his head.

The year before, Sam had made a few friends in the Doveland police and they were doing him a favor by letting him use their interrogation room. Actually, it was usually the room where the few members of their force would meet for coffee and the ubiquitous donuts. When Your Second Home opened, they had moved up to a higher fare now that Grace and Mandy brought them croissants and coffee each morning.

All of meant was the police owed Sam a favor. They hadn't asked why Johnny Price was sitting in their station looking like his life was over. If Sam could scare the kid straight, they would be grateful. They liked Valerie and Harold Price. When relatives came to visit, they often stayed at the Bed and Breakfast. Valerie and Harold always made them feel welcome and comfortable.

Many of the old-timers remembered Johnny as a sweet little boy. However, once he got to high school, he made friends with kids that just liked causing trouble. Lately, they had been doing more than just being rowdy. Johnny was heading for a disaster instead of the life his parents had dreamed for him. Therefore, if Sam could help Johnny turn away from the path he was traveling, it would be a good thing.

It had been over an hour since Johnny came to the station with his mother and father. They had walked him in and left without saying a word, just as Sam had requested. Johnny had watched them go with fear in his eyes. Sam knew that the longer he left Johnny in the room by himself the more his fear would take over. Johnny's mind would make up scenarios about what they knew and what would happen to him.

Sam and Hank had reinforced the fear by having a conversation right outside the door, making sure that Johnny heard every word. Hank had argued for leniency, saying he knew how persuasive Grant could be. "Give the kid a break, won't you," he had yelled at Sam while trying not to laugh.

Sam had yelled right back. "Hell no. He helped Grant. A stone cold killer only just begins to describe how evil Grant is. I can't give Johnny a break. They would have my badge for it at headquarters."

"Shit, man," Hank replied as they shuffled away from the door.

That was thirty minutes ago. Every minute since then Johnny had wilted more and more. Sam waited until he saw Johnny's lip tremble and then he walked in slamming a folder full of papers down on the table.

Sam pulled out a chair and sat back on it as if he didn't have a care in the world. "I have all the paperwork ready to transfer you," he said.

Johnny's eyes opened so wide Sam thought that they might pop out.

"Whaaa? Where? Where am I going?"

"Didn't your parents tell you? You committed a federal crime. You'll be going to a prison far away from here. They are going to have to sell their business to pay your legal fees. It won't be doing them any good though. Nothing is going to save you," Sam said.

In his heart, Sam hated doing what he was doing to Johnny. However, he knew that if he didn't try this tactic, Johnny might be lost forever. Someday Johnny might even be grateful for what Sam was doing. For now, though, it was painful for both of them.

None of that showed on Sam's face though. Instead, he fixed Johnny with a cold stare, picked up the folder, and stood up.

"Good luck, kid," he said as he started out of the room.

"Wait. Wait. I didn't know I was doing something that bad. That man offered me a hundred bucks to set off the fireworks if I saw you start to walk towards him. That's all. I don't know what you are talking about."

Sam turned and leaned on the door. "Oh, that's a good one. Just a hundred dollars. Why did he pick you? You've been working with a dangerous criminal for a long time. You need a better story than that!"

Sam started to turn the doorknob when Johnny burst out crying.

"Okay. I'll tell you everything I know. But I swear that I didn't know that he was a dangerous criminal. Please, please, help me."

Sam looked away to compose himself. He couldn't look like a softy now. His face granite, he replied. "Okay. Let's try it. But if you lie to me all bets are off for you. Your life is over, and you are only seventeen."

"Sixteen," Johnny said softly. "Only sixteen, and I promise. I'll tell you everything."

Forty-Seven

The next few days were relatively peaceful. Tom thought it was probably because everyone needed time to rest and reflect on everything that had happened during the last week. While it was quiet, he and Mandy decided to use the time to spruce up his house. He had bought it after falling in love with Doveland when he visited Ava and Evan the summer before.

Mira had bought her own house at the same time, but unlike him, his sister went to work immediately transforming her new house into a home for herself.

He had done nothing but move a few possessions into his. Then he had gone off to travel the world again. Tom knew he was trying to capture a time that was probably over. But he had loved his carefree days traveling the world and doing good on a whim.

Now his Good Old Dudes (G.O.D. for short) group was becoming more formal, and he didn't like it. He still enjoyed the good they were doing. He just didn't like that it was becoming an official organization. Sometime soon, he would have to decide what to do about it.

Tom knew there was another reason he had left town. He had been afraid of his feelings for Mandy.

She seemed so damaged when they met. However, over the past year, he realized he had been wrong about that. Yes, she had been emotionally and physically exhausted, but as the Circles opened their arms and hearts to her, she bloomed.

Every time he came home to visit and check on his house, he and Mandy got to know each other a little bit better. Finally, he gave up hiding from his feelings and came home to stay. The Stone Circle needed him, and he needed Mandy.

Mandy loved her little apartment above the store. However, when Eric and Grace got married, Tom asked Mandy to come live with him. He pretended that it was the most practical thing to do. It meant that Eric and Grace could expand into more rooms.

Truthfully, it was his heart that wanted it to happen. The very first day Mandy moved in, she took over. She brought the furniture she had carefully purchased for her apartment. Ava had told him that Mandy had style, and he was beginning to understand how drastically that style would affect his life.

They set up the living room first, so their friends had a place to sit. Up until then, Tom had been using the unopened boxes as chairs.

However, Mandy didn't have enough furniture to fill the rest of the house, so they used the quiet days as an excuse to shop. Tom had to admit that he loved every moment of it. They agreed on almost everything, and when they didn't, Tom knew Mandy was right.

Looking at his home, he was grateful for the time he lived with his sister, Mira. She had pushed him into not being such a slob. Tom hadn't liked the nagging at the time, but now realized Mira was training him to be part of a couple. Perhaps it was what he had been looking for the whole time. Just the thought of it made him smile.

Tonight, Mandy was making a red curry dinner. If the smell wafting in from the kitchen was any indication, it was going to be delicious. Mira and Sam were coming over for dinner. If Tom had anything to say about it, they were not going to discuss Jay, Grant, or Lenny. They were going to be just two normal couples enjoying a beautiful June evening with friends.

******

Pete handed Barbara a sweater. The evening was cooling down, and he didn't want her to get cold. Both of them were enjoying his excessive attention to making sure she was comfortable.

His over-attentiveness began when he retired from driving a truck. However, it reached full bloom when they moved to Doveland.

At first, Barbara was amused. She had been used to Pete being gone for weeks at a time and fending for herself, so the new attention was interesting.

Then she became annoyed.

She thought he was doing it because he believed that she was still not well.

"You're going to make me sick, Pete, if you keep this up," she had complained. "And don't pretend that you don't know what I am talking about. Why are you fussing over me so much? I'm not sick anymore!"

Barbara's outburst had shocked Pete, and instead of saying anything, he had walked out of the room. Barbara watched him go with a sick heart. He was the love of her life. She hadn't meant to hurt him. When he returned a few hours later, he found Barbara sitting on their bed looking at pictures of their wedding.

He sat down beside her and reached for her hand. "No, Barbara, I am not fussing because I think you are sick. I am fussing because I realized that my whole life it was what I wanted to do. But truckers don't fiddly fuss around with blankets and tea and flowers for their wives.

"At least that is what I thought. Besides, if I thought about how much I was missing you while I was traveling, I would never have been able to go. I loved trucking, and I wanted to make sure you had security for life. Now that I am home, I'm myself, you see. I am a fiddly bits husband. I hope you will accept me this way."

Barbara felt the impact of what he said so deep inside of her it left her speechless. Pete, misunderstanding her silence started to get up from the bed until Barbara grabbed his wrist and pulled him back down to sit beside her.

When she turned to face him, Pete saw tears running down her face. "Happy tears?" he asked.

"Happy tears," she had answered.

Now, months later, they were both happy with the new rhythm of their life. Pete fussed, and Barbara drank it in. She hadn't realized how thirsty she had been for his over-the-top attention. *Someday it might end,* she thought. *In the meantime, I will soak it up.*

Therefore, Barbara wasn't surprised when Pete brought her a sweater. It meant he had checked the temperature and knew it was a little cooler than she would be comfortable in without it.

Walking hand in hand they strolled around the square until one of them decided to sit. "Shall we talk about the dinner?" Barbara asked. "Why are we having it at the Diner instead of Ava's?"

"It was Hannah's idea," Pete answered. "Everything is Hannah's plan.

"She set up the dinner, and she chose the Diner. I gather it is because she thought our place was the most neutral one in the group.

"She's right," Barbara answered. "We don't have as much to lose as everyone else. Besides, we don't know him."

When Pete didn't answer, she knew something was wrong. "Pete?" she asked.

"That's the thing, Barbara, I do know him. In fact, he's here because of me. So if something goes wrong, then this is all my fault."

"I don't know much, Pete Mann, but I do know this. It could never be your fault. This happened because it did, and you don't know if it is a bad thing anyway."

Pete turned to look at his wife and kissed her on the forehead. "You're right," he said, "Let's go home and watch something sweet on the TV."

Barbara laughed and swatted at him. "Aren't you the most wonderful husband in the world."

"Yep," Pete answered.

Inside, he wasn't so sure. He would just have to trust that it was going to work out for good.

Barbara was always saying, "All things work together for them that love God." Sometimes she substituted the word good for God since she said it helped her understand the concept better.

He knew he and his friends loved good. That meant that all things would work out for good, he just didn't know how that was going to happen. For a minute, Pete thought he heard, "Knowing how things are going to happen is not your job."

In the past, he would have thought he was going crazy. Since meeting Ava the year before, he had discovered that there were people around that he couldn't see.

He assumed that's what just happened. "Okay. I'll go with it," Pete whispered, hoping Barbara didn't hear.

Barbara did hear. She just shook her head and smiled. She heard it too, but since he didn't say anything, she would keep it to herself.

Instead, she nodded in the direction of the voice, and whispered, "Amen, to that."

Forty-Eight

"I can't believe we're doing this, Evan," Ava said. They were in their bedroom getting ready for the dinner that Hannah had planned.

For the past ten minutes, she had tried on one outfit after another. Nothing felt good. Everything made her uncomfortable or look too fat. Finally, Evan came over and put his arms around her.

"Stop, Ava. It doesn't matter what you wear, and we don't have a choice, do we? We have to meet with him one way or another. This seems like the most civilized way. Not to mention the safest way."

"But how can we let Hannah make all these decisions? She is just a little girl."

"Ava, she looks like a little girl, but as she insists on telling us, for this, she is the wisest of us all. She remembers him. It's part of her gift. We have to let her lead us on this one.

Other things, we know best, but this time. I think Hannah does."

Evan looked down on Ava's blue eyes and brushed her hair out of her eyes. It had grown since last summer when she had cut it into a pixie cut.

She kept asking him which way did he like her hair, and he kept telling her in every way and every hairstyle she was beautiful to him.

Even though she didn't believe him, it was true. She could be bald, and he would think she was beautiful. Kissing her on the nose, he pointed out her favorite T-shirt and jacket with sparkles on it and said, "What about that?"

"Lucky me," Ava answered. "A fashionista in my house. Would you check on Hannah to see if she is ready?"

"You are not fooling me, Ava. Nevertheless, I will go and check on her, and I'll get Ben ready. We have to leave in ten minutes."

Ava pulled the shirt over her head, fluffed her hair, and stared at herself in the mirror.

Breathe in, breathe out. How many times did I say that to myself last summer when I thought I had lost everything, and look at what happened. It all worked out. We have Hannah, Ben, and friends who have moved to Doveland to be with us. That didn't all happen so that we would lose Hannah now, she reasoned.

"That's my girl," Suzanne said as she drifted into sight. Remember what you decided to learn how to do?"

"Trust?" Ava asked.

"Yes. Trust," Suzanne said and was gone.

Slipping on her jacket and picking up her purse, Ava looked in the mirror one last time and said to herself, "Trust!"

****

In the bunkhouse, Hank was hyperventilating. How was he going to get through this dinner? How was he going to explain what happened? And even if he was able to explain, how could he ever make it right?

Hannah, Hannah, he said to himself. *How can you be put in the middle of this?*

Maybe I should just run away and save everyone.

"You can't, Uncle Hank," Hannah said.

"I didn't hear you come in, Hannah," Hank said kneeling beside her and holding her hands. It was like looking at his sister Abbie the last time he had seen her. Now her grandchild was stronger than he could ever be. This time, instead of hurting someone to make things right, he would have to talk to the man he destroyed thirty-five years before and beg for forgiveness to make it right.

To be truthful, Hank couldn't understand this at all. That man had died. Now he was alive again. His child had died, and now she was alive again.

"No one really dies, Hank," Hannah said reading his mind. "They just go somewhere else. Some people go to the light and stay. Other people, at different times, come back here or go elsewhere.

"Some people know how to leave this life by choice and go to another dimension like most of the Forest Circle did. It's rare, but it happens.

"Most people that die don't remember anything about their past lives when they come back. My past-dad and I do. Didn't Craig say that those people are called a Jatismar?"

Hank nodded. "Do you like remembering?"

"Do you like being tall? Or white? It just is what I am this time. Whether I like it or not it won't change anything. But I think I remember so I can save Jay."

"Save Jay?"

"Yes, save Jay because he just remembers the pain, and he wants and needs it to go away. He thinks hurting you will make that happen. I know it won't.

"So by saving him, I am saving you."

"How are you going to do that, Hannah?"

"You'll see. Trust me, Uncle Hank."

In the corner of the room, Suzanne smiled.

******

Melvin stood in front of Jay and straightened out Jay's tie. It was a plain dark blue one that Melvin had pulled out of his closet for Jay. "When is the last time you wore a tie, son?"

"When Maggie and I got married? Or maybe it was when she would drag me to church."

"I know the feeling," Melvin answered. "Sally always made me slap on a tie when she dragged me to church. I guess I would give anything to have her make me put on a tie again."

The two men stared at each other. They had both lost their wives. They understood each other. They both knew they had been given a rare gift, but at the moment Jay was too worried to do more than grimace at Melvin,

Melvin grabbed the sports jacket he had found in his son's closet and held it out to Jay. "I know you're scared, but you might as well look good for your daughter."

"My daughter," Jay grumbled. "What good does it do me to have found her? I can't keep her. I can't go back and be her dad again with Maggie. She belongs to another family now. I don't have any rights at all."

"Don't be a jackass, Jay. Some people would give their right arm to find a loved one they thought they had lost. You don't own her. You never did.

"She and her new family are offering you a place in their life. They don't have to. They could keep you away from her. Instead, they invited us to dinner so you can meet her family and friends.

"If you can't see this as a gift, you don't deserve her. Because that wouldn't be love would it? Depriving her of a life filled with family and friends?"

Melvin tossed the coat to Jay and walked away. If Jay could have seen Melvin's face, he would have been astonished because Melvin was smiling. He had just felt Sally's warm breath and heard her say, "And that's why I love you, Melvin."

No matter what, Jay, Melvin said to himself. *You have been a gift to me giving me a chance to practice love and kindness. I am making Sally happy. So I am sticking with you until I have to go. We'll see this out together.*

Jay caught the coat and sat down on the closest chair. Closing his eyes, he tried to calm down. But Melvin was right. He was scared. He was afraid because he was still angry. What if he did something that would harm Hannah? *What if no matter how friendly people are to me I do something bad? I am an evil man now. What if I am doomed?* Jay thought.

Jay moaned and put his head in his hands. Something tapped on his bedroom window. Looking up, Jay saw a rufous hummingbird hovering outside, its copper throat glowing in the sun. Tapping. Astonished, Jay watched it hover and tap. "Are you trying to get in?" he asked.

"Good god, boy, hurry up," Melvin called up the stairs. "You don't want to be late for your daughter's dinner do you?"

"Hold on," Jay answered. He opened his wallet and took out a picture.

Melvin had gone to the library and looked up the story of the fire on the internet. Somehow, he had printed out a picture of Jay's wife from the article and brought it home for him. Staring at her picture, Jay said, "I'm going to see our daughter now, Maggie. For better or worse, but I promise you, I'll try to make it for the better."

Looking up, Jay caught a glimpse of himself in the hall mirror. He looked different. He had cut his hair and shaved his beard. That was Melvin's doing.

All of this is Melvin's doing, Jay thought, admiring the coat and tie Melvin had made him wear. *I look like a new man so I can act like a new man and just maybe it will come true.*

With a last glance at the window where the hummingbird still hovered, Jay flung the coat over his shoulder muttering, *and now I am talking to pictures and birds. Maybe that's a good sign, and maybe it ain't.*

Forty Nine

Pete flipped the sign over the door from open to closed, hoping that it wasn't symbolic. *We all need to have open hearts and minds,* he thought. *No matter what happens, this is going to be a dinner party no one will ever forget.* No one knew exactly what would happen, but everyone hoped it wouldn't turn into a fight.

Pete turned from the door and surveyed what he and Barbara had done to turn the Diner into a place that would seat everyone. They wanted it to be welcoming and comfortable and for everyone to be able to see each other. It would have been hard to do that if they were sitting in booths, so he and Sam had pushed all the freestanding tables together to make a big square. Mandy and Grace had somehow come up with a big white tablecloth, that covered the whole thing. With the lights dimmed, the Diner appeared transformed.

Pete had also wanted to borrow pretty plates and utensils from Your Second Home, but Barbara had said that would have made it too fancy. She said that Hannah had chosen the Diner because it was homey, and they should stick with the plan. Pete smiled at the memory of Barbara correcting him.

They were a real team now. Not just the wife at home and him on the road, but a partnership that worked together and lived together. *As long as I remember who is in charge,* Pete chuckled to himself.

"Whoa, nice," Eric said as he and Grace came into the room from the back of the kitchen. Everyone knew to use the back door, including Melvin and Jay. Barbara stayed in the kitchen with Sam who was doing the cooking for tonight. Their extra cook, Alex, was given the night off, explaining it was a family affair. Before he had gone for the day, he had made a huge salad that Grace was now looking at as if she could eat the whole thing by herself.

As their guests arrived, Barbara directed them to the drinks and asked them to take a seat while they waited for the guests of honor. Hannah had asked to be seated between Evan and Hank and across from Melvin and Jay. She had also drawn a little picture showing where everyone else was to be seated. To make it easy for everyone to find their seat, Mandy had made pretty place cards for the table.

Those that could see Suzanne were happy that she was also there. Having the Forest Circle around always gave everyone a sense of comfort.

At precisely 6:00 p.m. Hank arrived by himself looking as if he was a condemned man going to the gallows. If asked, he would have said that was precisely how he felt. Hank found his seat and noticed he was sitting between Hannah and Ava. *Hannah is being protective,* he thought.

"Where are they?" Tom asked. "What if they don't come?" Just then, they heard the gurgle of baby Ben as Ava and her family entered the room. Ava had wanted to leave Ben home with a babysitter, but Hannah said that it was important that Ben be there.

Sarah and Leif had agreed, so she reluctantly consented. Hannah had placed Ava and Ben beside Grace and Eric. Evan sat on the other side of Hannah.

No one spoke until Hannah broke the silence. "People," she said, "be yourselves. You'd think it was the end of the world. I promise you that it isn't!"

Grace took the hint and started a conversation about Valerie's plan to hang flower baskets around the town square. By the time Melvin and Jay arrived, everyone was in full conversation mode. Before they came in the door, Hannah knew they were coming and had gone to the kitchen to wait for them. She led them both into the room holding their hands and paused until everyone noticed them.

"Everyone," she said, "This is my new friend, Melvin and my past-dad, Jay."

No one spoke until Pete jumped up and rushed over to Jay to shake his hand. "Man, I'm happy to see you again, Jay. I am glad you found your way here."

Eric joined Pete in shaking Melvin and Jay's hands. The women all waved hello. Jay shook hands as prompted by Melvin but couldn't take his eyes off Hank, who was keeping his head down.

When Hannah seated Melvin and Jay in front of Hank. Hank looked up trying his best not to show his terror. In all the years, that he had done terrible things, and dealt with Grant and his horror show, Hank had never been as frightened.

Jay was staring at Hank too, his hatred blazing. However, looking closely, Hank was surprised to see that Jay's eyes were hiding the same kind of terror that he was feeling.

Once everyone was seated, Hannah stood beside her chair and once again waited for everyone to look at her.

"I wanted you all to be here so you can all hear what I need to tell you at the same time. I don't have big words to say. It's simple. I love all of you. I can't choose between you. I can't stop loving one, so I can love another.

"I know you all love me too. So, I have a request to make. Please be friends. Let me love both Jay and Evan without splitting me in half.

"I was there, dad," Hannah said looking at Jay. "I know what happened. It was a terrible thing. However, what I learned when I was elsewhere was there is nothing to forgive when we are not in this human world. We are all one."

Looking at the rest of the room, Hannah said, "Yes I remember parts of my past life like Jay does. I also remember the other place where love is in charge. I want love to be in charge here too."

Turning to Hank, Hannah said. "I know you didn't mean for my mom and me to die. Grant set you up. He sent you to the wrong house on purpose. It was how he wanted to control you. You have been punishing yourself for a long time for what you did. But you didn't know."

"How do you know this, Hannah?" Hank asked, trying to keep his voice steady.

"Before my grandma, Abbie, left, she told me. Remember she was watching over you and Ava your whole lives after she died. She saw what happened."

Turning to Jay, Hannah said, "Dad. It wasn't Hank's fault. It wasn't your fault either that you weren't home. Besides, it was a momentary discomfort before the door opened and mom and I left here to go to that other place. Mom is happy there. She watches over both of us. You haven't lost her. You just can't hear her because you are so hurt and angry."

No one said anything. Ava's heart felt as if it had stopped, and Evan started crying when Hannah put her hand on his shoulder and said, "This is my daddy this time, Jay. It's not either or. It's both."

Jay looked across the table at the two men sitting beside his daughter. Both of them were openly crying. Between them, Hannah stood with her hands on her heart, staring at him with a deep burning love.

"Please, dad," she said.

Jay slowly stood up. For a moment, everyone thought he was leaving, but instead, he walked around the table to Hank who stood to meet him. It was Jay who extended his hand. Only Hannah and Evan heard him whisper as they tentatively shook hands, "I am going to try and not hate you. Not for you—for Hannah."

"Thank you," Hank whispered back. "For Hannah."

From the kitchen, Sam called, "Food's on."

Gratefully, everyone at the table rose to fill their plates; the tension broken.

Only Evan, Hank, and Jay remained in place, staring at each other. It was Evan who broke the silence by saying, "For Hannah."

"For Hannah," was echoed by the other two men.

Hannah stood in the corner watching with Suzanne. "Is it enough, Suzanne?" she asked.

"It's a beginning," Suzanne replied.

Fifty

"Why are we bringing up this pain again, Grace?" Hank demanded. Sam, Hank, and Grace were sitting on a bench in the town square outside the Diner. The rest of the group had gone home, leaving Eric, Barbara, Sarah, and Pete to clean up.

Before her mom dragged her off saying it was time for bed because Hannah had school the next day, Hannah had made the rounds hugging everyone and thanking them for coming.

As they packed up all the baby things, Hannah asked Ava if Jay could hold Ben. With only a momentary hesitation, Ava had lifted Ben and placed him in Jay's arms.

Jay was startled by the gesture and felt awkward holding a baby. However, the awkwardness lasted only a moment. He turned his back on Ava and looked down at the baby in his arms. Hannah's brother. Hannah had a life. It was what she was trying to tell him.

"Thank you, Ava," he said turning to place Ben back in her arms. "And thank you for being such a good mother to Hannah."

Ava looked up at Jay with tears in her eyes. "It is a joy to have Hannah in our life, Jay. Please know that we want you to be part of our family, in whatever way you choose.

I can't imagine what it would be like to lose my child. Let me make it better for you."

Jay had turned away then, leaving Ava to stare after him.

"It's a lot to take in, isn't it?" Sarah said coming up beside Jay, "Especially when you have been feeling alone for so long."

Jay turned to look at Sarah and nodded. For a moment, he had an overwhelming urge to hug her but stopped himself in time. Melvin arrived and asked Jay if he was ready to go home. As they walked away, Melvin turned back to Sarah and Ava and waved. They waved back with smiles on their faces. Jay was in good hands.

"Wonder what those three are cooking up,'" Ava said, looking over at Sam, Hank, and Grace sitting on the park bench.

"We'll know soon enough," Sarah had answered.

****

"Alright, Johnny," Sam said. "It's time to decide."

Five days had passed since he had let Johnny go home with a warning that he would be called back, and when he was, Johnny would have a choice to make.

Sam knew that the choice was not going to be easy for Johnny. Either way, things could go wrong. Coming up with the idea made Sam heartsick. However, he had a village to protect. More than a village, he thought. Grant on the loose was a danger to everyone.

Sam looked at Johnny sitting across from him at the back table in Your Second Home. He hadn't wanted to meet him at the police station and terrify him into a decision. Sam needed Johnny to choose to do the right thing because it was the right thing, not because he was afraid.

On the other hand, Sam couldn't let himself be fooled into thinking he was not using fear to some degree. If Johnny chose not to help, he would have the local police charge him with a crime. Experiencing consequences for your actions was something Sam believed in passionately.

The consequence he was offering was more dangerous than going to jail but would be more life-affirming for Johnny. Sam hoped it would give him a sense of purpose, and honor. They were qualities that could be built upon.

So although Sam looked calm as he stared at Johnny, in his heart, he was pleading with him to take the hard way. To say yes. To be part of the plan to capture Grant.

Sam had not told Valerie and Harold what he was offering their son. They didn't want to know. They were wise enough to understand that they might choose the wrong thing for him out of fear. Instead, they told Sam that they trusted him to do the right thing for Johnny. It was a trust that Sam took seriously.

Please say yes, he said to himself again.

Johnny had aged in the past five days. No longer a boy of sixteen, but a young man of sixteen. Life was no longer a joke. Johnny had thought long and hard about why he was running around with boys that would get him in trouble.

His little brother, Lex, looked up to him. His parents loved him. They worked hard to make a nice home for him and Lex. Why was he running away from them?

Grace had come to see Johnny a few days before at his house. Johnny's grandmother had died before he was two years old, so Grace asked if Johnny minded if she adopted him and his brother, Lex. She didn't have any children she explained. Her first husband, Jim, hadn't wanted children. They both loved being free to travel and explore.

Now that Eric had brought a big family into her life, she had discovered a gift for being a grandmother. She would like a few more kids to look out for, would he be willing to be one of them?

At first, Johnny wanted to laugh at her. He tried to act tough and say he didn't need anyone. But she just stood there and let him feel all those things, and once they had flowed out of him, Johnny felt something else flood in to fill the space. Johnny would never have said aloud what he felt, but he thought it must be love. And bravery. He felt brave.

So now he looked across at Sam and realized he wouldn't mind growing up to be like him, and he wouldn't mind that Grace, watching over them from the kitchen, would be his grandmother. So he nodded and said, "Yes."

Sam reached across the table to shake his hand, then changed his mind, and stood up. He walked over to Johnny and hugged him instead. "Okay, young man, let me tell you the plan."

Fifty-One

"I still don't like it, Sam," Hank said. "I don't like it at all."

Sam and Hank were sitting in Hank's room in the bunkhouse discussing the plan that Sam had put into motion. Actually, it was Grace who had set it in motion the night before, and now it was a matter of managing what was going to happen.

Hank was terrified. Sure, they had stopped Grant from his destructive plans at Ava's wedding, but now they were going to have to stop him again at another party.

To Hank, it was tempting fate. But Sam was sure it was going to work. As he explained to Hank, it had to work because they didn't have another option. If Grant planned the next attack, they would be on the defensive. If they designed it, they would have greater control.

"You have to have perfect control to make this work, Sam, and you really can't guarantee that you will," Hank argued.

"I agree with you in principle," Sam replied, "but we have the upper hand here."

"I think you are fooling yourself, Sam," Hank replied. "And it could cost lives if it fails. Including Mira's."

Sam paused. "Low blow, buddy," he said. "But you're right. That's why we have to have all the details worked out."

"Okay, tell me exactly what is happening." Hank said, "If I can't stop you, I can at least do everything possible to make sure it goes well."

Listening to Hank and Sam discuss their plans, Suzanne turned to her brother Gillian and asked, "Aren't they taking a huge risk doing this? Will it work?"

"We can't stop it," he said. "We can only be there when it is over."

****

Grace wasn't thinking about attacks, she was thinking about joy. She envisioned all their friends and family gathering together on the big green lawn. In her mind's eye, she saw blankets and picnic baskets, and children running and playing.

She knew the risk of having it at Jay's old place, but she thought that if she spun it right, the picnic she was planning could become a healing event.

Perhaps they could help Jay buy the property and build again. She planned to have the picnic on Jay's birthday. It seemed like a perfect way to welcome him into the family.

A part of Grace was worried. When she discussed the idea the night before with Hank and Sam, Hank had hated the idea.

Of course, he would, she thought. Neither Jay nor Hank could be expected to be comfortable at first. The place held terrible memories for them both. However, Grace was sure that once she told them about her idea to help rebuild the house for Jay, Hank would come on board.

Sam loved the plan. He had been looking for an idea that would tempt Grant and Lenny to come back to Doveland at the same time.

This event was the perfect bait, and since it was going to happen within a few days, neither of them would have a chance to make elaborate plans.

Of course, it meant that he wouldn't have much time either, but he and his team were already in town. Plus he had a few aces up his sleeve, like Johnny.

Grace had listened in on Sam's meeting with Johnny, and once Johnny agreed, Grace drove herself out to see Melvin and Jay. She had to admit to herself that she didn't tell Eric because she wasn't sure he would approve of her plan. However, once she had it set up, Grace knew he would support her.

Melvin and Jay were surprised to see her but invited Grace in for tea or coffee. Seeing Melvin's old coffee maker, Grace chose tea. She had brought a tin of fresh cookies that Mandy made, and the three of them dunked and sipped for a few minutes before she told them her idea of a picnic.

Melvin was worried about the plan, but he waited to see what Jay would say before agreeing. Jay reacted the same way Hank had. Jay hated the idea.

But eventually, Grace won him over the same way that she had won over Hank. "Healing has to continue," she said. "Why not get the worst over now with a celebration of freedom. Everyone will come. It will be a family gathering. A new beginning. It will give us a chance to celebrate your new life with us."

Jay wanted to jump on his chair, pound his fists and yell at her, "Never, never, never will I have a new life with you!" But he kept silent. Melvin noticed that Jay's face was flushed, but Grace appeared to be choosing to be oblivious to the depth of Jay's feelings.

After at least a half hour of persuading on Grace's part, both Melvin and Jay finally reluctantly agreed.

"For Hannah," they said. They would come to Jay's old homestead for a picnic at 1:00 p.m. on July 1st.

Grace made them promise. She told them Hannah would be grateful, and happy to see where she used to live. She asked Jay to see the celebration through Hannah's eyes. It would be a beautiful moment.

Grace could see Jay visibly melt at Hannah's name, and she held out hope that a full healing would take place, and there would be a new beginning for Jay, Hannah, and Hank.

While Grace was meeting with Melvin and Jay, Sam and Hank were reviewing all the details of the plan. The protection was complicated, but the plan was simple.

Johnny had agreed to send Grant a message and tell him about the party. He made sure to ask for both money and a guarantee that he never had to do another thing for Grant again. It would be what Grant expected him to ask.

At the same time, another one of Sam's men embedded into Lenny's group had mentioned the celebration to him. "Why not get rid of the Circle and Grant at the same time," he had whispered to Lenny.

"Why not?" Lenny had replied. "It will be a new beginning."

In his cabin at Hocking Hills, Grant had also decided that it was the perfect plan. He figured it was a setup.

Nevertheless, Grant knew that Sam still wasn't as smart as he was and never would be, as hard as he might try. Grant would get rid of them all, including Lenny. He was sure that Lenny was preparing to kill both him and Hank. The idea made Grant laugh. When will they ever learn that I am the smartest one? It's my turn to win, and win I will.

It would be a new beginning for him, and it would be darkness for everyone else.

Fifty-Two

"No, no, no, a thousand times no!" Ava shouted. "Have you lost your mind? I won't allow it. I won't let Hannah come anywhere near this insane picnic you are planning. I can't believe you convinced anyone else that this is a good idea."

Ava burst into tears, grabbed Ben, ran back to Ben's bedroom, and slammed the door, causing Ben to start wailing at the top of his lungs.

"This is a mess," Evan said. "I agree with Ava. What were you thinking, Grace? And Sam. Good god, this is not something I ever thought you would do, put us all in danger like this."

Grace, Hannah, and Sam stood in Evan's kitchen waiting for Evan's rant to be over.

The three of them knew this was not a popular plan. In fact, they were the only ones who believed a picnic on Jay's old land was a good idea. Everyone else had capitulated to Grace's plan and were doing their best to appear enthusiastic. But not because of Grace; it was Hannah who convinced them. Not with fancy words, but with just six words, "It has to be this way."

Now the three of them were down to the last holdouts, Ava and Evan. Grace moved to Evan and reached out her hand.

"Evan, dear, this is a hard thing to consider, but something is moving us all to this event. If we resist it, whatever is going to happen is going to happen differently. At least this gives us a chance."

"What chance, Grace?" Evan demanded, his eyes burning into hers. "What kind of chance are we talking about?"

"For everyone to find peace. Isn't that what Jay and Hank are both yearning for, and you too? It's a managed release instead of an unexpected explosion."

Evan paused, thinking it over. "Yes, that part is probably true, and I would be much more willing if it didn't also involve putting everyone present in danger from Grant and maybe even Lenny. How can that be a good thing?"

"That's something I'll answer," Sam said. "It's a managed risk. If we don't set it up, it will be set up for us. All of you will be protected. We will have drones overhead, and back up around the perimeter of the property. If either Lenny or Grant shows up —and we hope that they will—we will be waiting for them.

"We have a chance to put them both away forever. That can happen at the same time as both Jay and Hank find a way to get past the pain of the fire. Imagine how different everyone's life will be after we accomplish these two things."

Evan nodded, but added, "Imagine how different everyone's life will be if either one of these things doesn't happen the way you plan it. People could be killed. Hank and Jay could hurt each other. Hannah could witness a tragedy."

All this time, Hannah had been standing beside Grace holding her hand. "Dad," Hannah said, "I already witnessed a tragedy. I want to live this life without bringing the past one into it any more than I have to. There is one more thing you all should know. I am not sure if it makes it better or worse. It just is."

"Okay, Hannah. We'll do it for you. I'll convince your mother. She's just worried about losing you. But you better tell us what else we need to know."

"Well, you know the picnic is planned for Jay's birthday in this lifetime. He'll be thirty. But it is also Jay's birthday in his past life, and it was on his twenty-fifth birthday that our house burned down, and it was on his birthday that he died, thirty years ago."

Grace gasped. She didn't know about all the coincidences of that date. Sam and Evan stared at Hannah as if she had grown another head.

"How can this be a good thing, Hannah? It's more tempting of fate," Hank said having come into the kitchen just in time to hear her tell everyone about the dates.

"Time is not a circle or a past or present or future, Uncle Hank. You know that. Everything is going on at the same time. So what will happen at the picnic will feel like completion but only because it already happened, and already didn't happen."

"Wait. I don't understand what you just said at all, Hannah. However, I guess I don't need to. But, I do need to know what's going to happen at the picnic," Sam asked.

"No, you don't need to know, because it doesn't matter. We can't do anything about it," Hannah said. "We just have to be there."

****

The morning of the picnic dawned bright and clear.

Tom and Mandy had gone out for a walk and ended up at Evan and Ava's house. They had cut through the woods using a path that Evan had cleared in the fall. It wasn't an accident that their land was adjacent to each other.

Mira's property was on the other side of Tom's. They wanted it to be easy to walk to each other's homes. Put together, all three properties stretched almost to town.

As they walked, Mandy talked about her idea of a bike path leading from the village out into the country. Perhaps they could buy the land on the other side of Evan's so it could go for miles? They would build the path using their own money, but then donate it to Doveland. It would run parallel to the road but with a buffer of trees and plants. Maybe someday the path could connect Doveland and Concourse?

Tom turned to look at Mandy as they paused outside of Evan's property. "I love this idea, Mandy, and I want to do it with you, but right now, we just need to get through this day."

"That's what I am doing. Getting through this day by planning what's next. By giving us all something that looks into the future. I'm afraid, Tom. And planning is one way I get over being afraid."

Tom looked at Mandy and realized once again that she had gotten more and more beautiful in the past year. He couldn't imagine his life without her, and the picnic frightened him too. She was right. They needed to plan something beautiful and look forward to what was coming next. A bike path to town sounded perfect.

Ava came out on the back deck and waved at the two of them. "Come on in and have some coffee and muffins," she called out to them.

From his room in the bunkhouse, Hank watched the four of them sipping coffee on the back deck and hoped that he would see them all there again the next day. He and Sam had worked long into the night preparing the protection and putting the plan into place. But as much as Hank hated to admit it, he was afraid that Grant was probably smarter than all of them.

However, Grant had a weakness. He was alone. People only worked with him because they were afraid of him.

Hank was counting on the fact that he wasn't alone to win the day. He was part of a Karass, a community, a gathering of friends. There was always strength in numbers. Plus they loved each other, and Hank knew that love is stronger than fear.

On the way to his car, Hank stopped in the house to get coffee and a hug from Hannah. He had to help Sam, but when he had completed his part, Hank would meet everyone at Jay's place for the picnic.

Hannah followed him to his car. "Thank you for trusting me," she said.

Hank knelt down and hugged her. "If this brings peace to your past-dad, and happiness to you, no matter what happens, I will be happy."

Hannah hugged him back and then watched him drive away, waving the whole time. She looked up to see Suzanne standing near her. "It will be okay, little one," she said.

"I know," Hannah replied. "It's just not what everyone would want, even me. I wish it could be different."

Neither of them spoke. Suzanne and Hannah knew it couldn't and wouldn't be. By the end of the day, everything would be different.

Fifty-Three

Grace said she would make macaroni salad for the picnic. Everyone was a little leery of potato salad after the solstice celebration. Eric said it wasn't the potato salad's fault. But he agreed that perhaps it would be best to wait until next summer before making another big batch. By then people would have forgotten.

"If things don't work out, do you think they will forget that I forced the issue of this picnic?" Grace asked.

"I don't know, love," Eric answered. "Why did you do it, anyway? It seems as if it is only you and Hannah that feel that this is important."

Eric waited for Grace to answer him. But she didn't. Instead, Grace had put the bowl of salad down and was staring at him. "Eric, what's wrong?"

"What do you mean what's wrong?"

Grace didn't answer with words. Instead, she reached for both his hands and held them, waiting for him to tell her. When he didn't say anything, Grace knew she had her answer.

What was she going to do? Everyone was upset with her for a good reason. She had pressured, pleaded, and cajoled them all until they said yes to the picnic. She couldn't even explain why.

She was afraid too. However, as she had told Melvin and Jay, something was guiding her to do it. She hoped that what was guiding her was not evil.

The thread of hope she was holding onto was that Hannah had felt that guidance too. The two of them had talked and texted over the past few days working out the plans for the picnic. They were an odd couple, an old woman and a little girl. *Perhaps that's why we were chosen to do this,* she thought. They were at the opposite ends of the journey.

And now, Eric. He was not telling her because there was nothing to say that would make her feel better. *When the day is over, I am going to make him tell me everything. I need to know how much time we have,* she thought.

Eric and Grace sat together quietly for a few more minutes before Eric said, "Best be going, love. I promised Pete and Barbara we would help set up the blankets. You and Mandy are coming separately with more food?"

She nodded, and then hugged him as hard as she could, pressing every bit of his body against hers feeling how thin he had become. They stood together a few more minutes, hugging as if it was the last chance they would have to be together. Grace knew that what they were doing was dangerous. She knew something was going to happen. She just didn't know what.

Hannah had told her that all would be well, but that didn't quiet Grace's fears. Grace had been around long enough to know that all will always be well, but sometimes there are terrible things that have to happen first.

****

Ava and her family pulled up to the picnic site at precisely 1:00 p.m..

Hannah had insisted that they not be either early or late because the timing was crucial. Since Hannah had been guiding the entire event, they decided to do what she asked, even if it did seem strange to be following a little girl's directions for something as important as this gathering.

For both Ava and Evan it was often hard to remember that in many ways Hannah was not a little girl. She had returned to this lifetime with memories. It made her wiser than her years. She had also returned with gifts that connected her to other dimensions and the people that inhabited them. Ava had asked Hannah if the Forest Circle was telling her what to do, but Hannah had only answered that Suzanne was often around.

"I see that everyone has followed Sam's instructions," Evan said. It was a strange sight. Everyone had pulled their cars up onto the property and then circled them with the back end of every vehicle facing the middle, forming a big circle. Ava thought it looked like what the covered wagons used to do at night.

"That's exactly what it is, isn't it?" Evan said, reading her mind. "Sam has set up a barrier and having everyone back in it makes it easier to quickly get away if we have to.

"I see our spot, up there," pointed Hannah. "It's at the top of the hill, right beside Melvin's truck. Well, his truck will be there because they are right behind us. Perfect timing."

Evan glanced in the rear-view mirror and raised his hand to say hello. Melvin waved back. Jay didn't move.

Both vehicles worked their way around the circle and then backed into their spot. As soon as they were parked, Hannah jumped out of the car and rushed to Jay. He scooped her up and swung her around. They both remembered doing that very same thing on that very same hill, many years before.

Putting her down, she grabbed his hand and walked him towards the picnic. Evan knew what she was doing, and he was proud of her. Hannah was the peacemaker. It was what she wanted to do, and he was going to do everything he could to support her.

He flipped open the back gate of the car and pulled out all the stuff a baby needs. At first, he was going to let the gate stay open, but remembered Sam's words to be prepared to go quickly if necessary. If they had to get out fast, they would leave the stuff. Stuff was replaceable. People were not.

****

Sarah thought that if there was ever a perfect setting for a picnic, this was it. The ring of vehicles blocked some of the views, but the grass was green, a gentle breeze kept the bugs away, and there were just enough clouds in the sky to be beautiful and to filter some of the blazing sun's rays.

Eric and Pete had borrowed blankets from everyone, and Barbara had laid them out in a lovely pattern around the circle. Baskets of food and ice chests were on a few long tables set in the middle of the blankets. Grace was the perfect hostess, helping everyone get the drink that they wanted, and keeping the food covered when necessary.

Someone had been wise enough to bring a few big umbrellas. They were stuck in the ground providing shade for the food and the people who wanted to be out of the sun. Everything was perfect. It was definitely a day everyone would remember.

Sarah missed having Leif by her side. Instead of coming to the picnic, he and Craig were helping Sam's team by using their remote viewing skills.

Leif thought that perhaps they would see things that Sam and his men might miss. Sarah had been fitted with an earpiece so she could hear Sam's instructions and keep in touch with Leif. She wasn't the only one. Hank had an earpiece as well as Tom and Pete.

Sam had handed the earpieces out with the admonition that they probably weren't necessary, but just in case he needed to reach them, he would have a direct line to the picnic. Sam also had everyone's cell phone set up in a text message that he would send if necessary. Everyone hoped it wouldn't be.

The plan was to find Grant and Lenny long before they came close to the gathering.

For now, the most important thing going on was the peacemaking that Hannah was doing with Jay and Hank. She had brought them both to a blanket, and the three of them were talking. Well, not talking. Hannah was speaking, Hank and Jay were staring at each other.

Sarah prayed that both of them would find peace in forgiving each other and forgiving themselves. If anyone could start that process, it would be Hannah.

Fifty-Four

Hannah sat in front of Hank and Jay smiling at them both. "Dad, would you believe me if I told you that the most important thing you can do right now is to forgive Hank?"

Jay looked at his Hannah. Well, not his Hannah. She looked different. Hannah was more grown up now than she had been when she was his daughter, even though she was just a year older than the last time he saw her. That day, she had rushed at him on the way out the door to give him a good night kiss and wish him happy birthday one more time.

Before Hannah, Jay had thought that the most beautiful thing that ever happened to him was finding his wife, Maggie. Then Hannah came along, and both he and Maggie felt that heaven had opened up and bestowed upon them the most precious gift of all. *Only eight years later and everything was ripped away from me,* he thought.

"No, it wasn't, Dad," Hannah said reading his mind. "Look, here I am. The only reason it feels that way is because you won't let go."

Jay looked across the blanket at Hank. He appeared as miserable as Jay felt.

Since the dinner a few days before, Jay had done nothing but think about what Hannah was asking of him. He and Melvin had sat up an entire night talking about it. Well, not always talking. Sometimes they just let the silence seep in.

Melvin had turned out to be the dad Jay had always wanted. Melvin shared stories about his life and some of the lessons he had learned. Hannah had told Melvin Hank's story. Using what Hannah had told him, Melvin helped Jay see that Hank was a victim too.

Does Hannah know how happy she is making Melvin? Jay wondered. Looking at Hannah, Jay realized that she did. Hannah's heart was big enough to include everyone. What about his heart?

Hank spoke up. "I'm sorry, Jay, I know that nothing I can say will ever make up for what happened, and I don't mind if you hate me forever. But for Hannah, I hope we can make some form of peace between us."

As Hannah reached out and touched Jay's hand, something happened. It felt as if his insides were melting from her touch. All thought about the past and revenge were gone, and for the first time in this lifetime, he let love do the thinking.

"I forgive you, Hank. Let it go." Jay said, surprising himself.

At that moment, Jay heard a voice that he hadn't heard for thirty-five years. He heard Maggie say, "I love you." Startled, he glanced at Hannah.

She smiled at him and said, "She's been here the whole time."

****

Sam was not as calm as he was letting on. In fact, inside he was a teeming mass of emotions.

However, there was no way he was going to let his team know. They needed to stay focused to find Grant and Lenny.

It was appalling to Sam that both of them had disappeared over an hour ago. Both of them. Not just Grant, not just Lenny. Both of them.

The plan had started well. Just as Sam's team had done a year before, they raided Grant's old headquarters where Lenny and his team were supposed to be. However, they weren't there. All they found was a sign that said, "Really?"

Well, yes, really. Sam didn't expect Lenny to be there, but he did expect to find the evidence that he needed to convict Lenny and put him in jail for a long time. Sam did expect to shut down Lenny's operation. Instead, all they had was a sign that said, "Really?"

Disappointing and humiliating as that had been, Sam hadn't been too worried. His team had eyes along every highway and back road leading into Doveland, and a few hours before, his team had found both Grant and Lenny. Although they were taking separate routes, they were both heading straight for Doveland.

Once they were spotted, his team started following them. They used a variety of cars and even a few trucks to keep track of them. They were experts.

However, Sam knew that Grant and Lenny would expect to be followed, so when Grant pulled into a gas station, a member of Sam's team pulled in behind him. While filling his tank with gas, placed a tracker on the underside of Grant's car. Sam's team did the same thing with Lenny. Both vehicles were tracked for fifteen minutes, and then—nothing.

Both Lenny and Grant had disappeared. The trackers stopped working, and the cars were gone.

An hour ago, his team had found both vehicles. Each car was parked behind abandoned buildings. No sign of either Grant or Lenny. Sam figured they had preplanned vehicles waiting for them. It wasn't surprising. That wasn't what was making his stomach feel as if he had swallowed acid. After all, they all knew where Grant and Lenny were headed.

It was the fact that they had both done the same thing at the same time that terrified Sam. They were working together. They were both heading to Doveland to attack the Stone Circle and their friends and family.

Where they were now, Sam didn't know. Although every available resource was being used, no one had seen them. The only evidence they had that Grant and Lenny were planning something big was that they were risking their freedom by coming to Doveland. It had to be worth it to them.

If it could be worse than not knowing what they were planning, and not knowing where they were, Sam didn't know what it could be. If his team didn't find Grant and Lenny within the next thirty minutes, he would have to close down the picnic. Even with all the people he had watching over his friends, Sam couldn't take any chances.

He also had to assume that he had a leak in his organization. Otherwise, how did Grant outsmart him? Well, he won't outsmart me in the end, Sam said to himself, hoping against hope that it was true.

****

Every ounce of Grant's being was alive with the excitement. He was outsmarting Sam again. It was a delicious feeling!

Sam expected a big complicated plan. What Grant had devised was simple.

He would go to the picnic and kill Hank along with as many friends and family as possible. Nothing fancy.

No one would be expecting such a simple plan. They were all prepared for something dramatic. Instead, Grant would walk into the picnic, and everyone would be happy to see him. Why? Because he would look exactly like Sam.

Even Sam wouldn't be able to tell them apart if he was there. But Sam wouldn't be there, would he? Grant knew that Sam was overseeing his team from his temporary headquarters in the town hall.

Grant had gotten the idea of being Sam from an old Star Trek show. When Grant was stuck doing nothing after his surgery, he had watched TV. It had turned out to be productive. He loved the storyline where there were two Captain Kirks, and the crew had to tell which one was fake and which one was the real Captain.

Grant would be Sam. At least long enough to kill Hank and anyone else in the line of fire.

In the ensuing confusion, he would escape once again. Lenny would be waiting outside of town for him. In return for providing misdirection while Grant was busy killing people, he would give Lenny the keys to the kingdom, so to speak.

Grant chuckled to himself as he applied the last bit of makeup to his face. Yes, he would turn over the keys to Lenny. But what the keys were for would not be what Lenny was expecting.

Fifty-Five

Did Grant think he was stupid or something? Lenny asked himself. No way was he going to play along with what Grant wanted.

Sure, Grant had promised to turn over all the information Lenny needed to run the organization and collect the billions of dollars that flowed through it. But did Lenny believe Grant? Not for a moment.

Lenny played along with Grant because that's what Grant expected. Grant still thought of Lenny as a young kid learning the ropes. He was not young, he wasn't a kid anymore, and he already knew the ropes.

Lenny knew how Grant worked. He knew he was lying. Yes, Lenny would have one of his crew do the misdirection that Grant wanted and set off an explosion.

However, it would not be where Grant wanted it to be. Lenny didn't get the pleasure out of killing people that Grant did. He didn't mind; it just wasn't a driving force as it was with Grant. Instead, he would have a member of his crew blow up something less important. There was no need to hurt people just because it gave Grant a thrill. In fact, it was a good reason not to.

Lenny was going to the picnic just like everyone else. He wasn't going specifically to hurt those woo-woo do-gooders. If they did get hurt, it was because they got in his way; but they weren't his focus. He was going to the picnic to get rid of Grant once and for all. Grant had taught him a few tricks and Lenny was going to use every single one of them against him. *This day was the beginning of a new era, the Lenny era.*

For a moment, Lenny sobered. He was a little disturbed that some of the people at the picnic could be injured or killed, but he couldn't do anything about that. He hoped that no children got hurt. Lenny liked kids. However, that wasn't going to keep him from doing what he had to do. He had to rid the world of Grant. Everyone would thank him for it in the end.

Lenny laughed to himself as he traded out the car Grant had left for him for another car. He was sure Grant had put a tracker on the first one. Grant always wanted to know where everyone was. It would look like Lenny was precisely where he was supposed to be—in Concourse causing a commotion by blowing up buildings downtown—because one of his crew would drive that car to where Grant would be looking for it.

However, because Lenny needed the misdirection too, another member of his crew would blow up something else. Melvin's farm. No one was home. Everyone was at the picnic. No one would die. He might even be doing Melvin a favor. Lenny figured that the guy was too old to be farming anyway.

After the bomb went off, Lenny would be right behind Grant at the picnic. While Grant was causing chaos, Lenny would do the simple thing. Kill Grant when no one was looking. It was going to be both easy and incredibly satisfying.

Yes, it would be the beginning of the Lenny era. It wouldn't be long now.

****

"Are we doing any good here?" Craig asked Leif. "It feels useless. Less than useless. Maybe we should be at the picnic with everyone else."

Leif and Craig were in the church where Ava and Evan had been married, and where Ben was christened. It was quiet, and that's what they needed. If they discovered anything, they had three ways to contact Sam and the members of his team. Leif and Craig each had an earpiece that connected them directly to Sam. They also each had a burner phone, and they shared a satellite phone.

Sam had said that Grant might try to shut down cell signals, so they had more than one way to reach each other in case that happened. Leif had joked that perhaps a bonfire out front and smoke signals would be a good idea. For a moment, Sam considered the idea and then realized that Leif was joking. Even then, he had considered it; he was so worried about the communication between him and his team somehow being shut down.

As one last precaution, even though they were only a few blocks away from each other, Sam stationed a runner outside the church. And a driver. One way or another, Leif and Craig would be able to get through to Sam.

"Seriously, Sam," Leif had said. "Aren't you going to extremes here?"

One look at Sam's face and he understood. He would go to any length to protect them. Plus, Mira was at the picnic.

And that's why Leif and Craig were in a church trying to remote view what Grant and Lenny were doing. Sam was ready to try anything.

However, it wasn't working. Neither Leif nor Craig were getting the slightest hint of anything.

"What's blocking us," Craig asked. "Are we doing it to ourselves, or is there something else going on?"

"Both," Suzanne said as she attempted to sit in the pew with them. "But that doesn't matter right now. It would be better if you were both at the picnic. If you leave right now, you'll be there in time.

"In time for what?" Leif asked, fear making his voice crack.

"Just go, Leif. Sarah is fine. Let Sam know. Craig, you go too. They will need your expertise as a doctor."

****

Later Sarah would relive those last moments. She would slow them down until she could see every detail. She would ask herself if there had been something she could have done to stop it. Suzanne assured her that there wasn't, and that eased her heart a bit.

However, when it was happening, when the shots rang out and the bodies fell, it felt as if a movie had sped up and everything tunneled down to one thing: Leif running towards her, and Hannah picking flowers and handing them to Hank and Jay.

They both still had them in their hands when it was over.

Fifty-Six

Grant could see the picnic in the distance, so he pressed down on the accelerator. He needed to squeal to a stop and make everyone look at him. That's what Sam would do if he were rushing to the scene. Grant was driving the same kind of car that Sam drove. No one would question if it were Sam or not. Of course, it was.

Sam squealing to a stop would start a panic. People would stop thinking clearly.

Although he would leave the doors open, he had no plans to drive the same car out. He would take one of the vehicles parked in the circle on the hill. Everyone knew to leave their keys in the ignition for a quick getaway. They just didn't think it would be his.

Sam's team would assume what Grant wanted them to. They would think that Sam had arrived at the picnic because it was an emergency.

Grant would make sure no one would believe differently because he would be running and yelling at Hank to come quick and help him. It would be chaos.

Grant loved chaos.

****

Ava and Evan played with Ben on the blanket while keeping an eye on Hannah. "It looks as if she has brought peace to the two of them," Evan said. "She is brave and kind just like her mother."

Ava smiled at him. "I think she is much braver than me because I am still worried that something bad is going to happen."

They both saw Hannah hand flowers to Jay and Hank who received them as if they were being given the most precious gift in the world. As Ava watched, the three of them moved further into the field outside the ring of cars.

It increased Ava's fears, but looking around she could see everyone else seemed relaxed and was having a good time. *Nervous over nothing,* Ava thought.

A shadow moved over Ben, and Ava glanced up to see Grace and Eric. "May we sit?" Grace asked.

Evan jumped up and unfolded two chairs for them and then two more for him and Ava so they would all be at the same eye level. Grace picked Ben up off the blanket, placed him on her lap, and made funny faces at him. He giggled and reached for her hair as it tickled his belly.

"You did a wonderful job of setting this up, Grace," Ava said. "And Mandy's birthday cake for Jay looks delicious!"

They all turned to look at the table set up in the middle of the blankets. In its center was a beautiful cake with a sparkling glass cover over it. A big blue umbrella stuck in the center of the table protected it from the sun.

"Perhaps we should have the cake now?" Grace said. As she handed Ben back to Ava, a boom sounded in the distance.

Everybody looked up, no longer relaxed. Sarah was standing at the buffet table helping to serve food, so they all turned their attention to her. Sarah raised a hand to ask them to give her a minute and listened to the voice in her ear. A long minute passed before Sarah nodded and then addressed the group. "Sam says not to worry, it has nothing to do with us."

Relieved, everyone waved and turned back to what they were doing. Sarah continued to stand at the table, trying to keep her expression neutral. However, she was worried. Sam had told her more. He had said it was an explosion near Concourse and he was sending a few men to check it out, and he was on the way to the picnic.

Leif had called her just seconds before the boom. He and Craig were also on their way because Suzanne had told them they were going to be needed. In spite of his calm tone, Sarah knew there was more to it than what he was saying.

Sarah was contemplating rounding people up to go home when a squeal of brakes interrupted her thoughts.

Sarah watched Sam jump out of his car and start running towards Hank, yelling for Hank to help him. It made no sense to her. *How did Sam get here this quickly,* she thought.

Outside the ring of cars, Hank turned to see Sam running towards him waving a gun.

Waving a gun? Sam would never wave a gun. Hank pushed Hannah down, yelled at Jay to stay with her, and started running towards the man with the gun.

Hank knew who was coming at him. It looked like Sam, but he ran like Grant.

Part of Hank was relieved. He deserved to die. He had expected to die many times in his life, and it was finally here. He welcomed death. But he didn't want anyone else to die.

He reached behind his back for his gun and remembered that the gun was in the glove compartment of his car. He hadn't wanted to have it around the kids. Besides Sam was supposed to be protecting the gathering.

Stupid! I'm an idiot! I have to stop Grant somehow.

As Hank ran, he yelled at everyone to stay down, hoping that no one would question why he was running at someone that looked like Sam.

Hank knew he had to get Grant before anyone else realized that it was Grant, panicked and did something that would put everyone in danger.

However, Jay was faster than Hank. Running full speed, he pulled in front of Hank and headed straight for Grant waving his arms so that Grant's attention was on him.

"No!" Hank screamed.

Two shots rang out. Hank was still running towards Grant when he saw Grant fall. Grant fired his gun just before he hit the ground, missing Hank. It took Hank only a split second to realize what happened. Jay had saved his life. On purpose.

Hank was still yelling, "No!" as he reached Jay.

Jay was lying on his back with a glazed look in his eyes and a smile on his lips. In his hands, he was still holding Hannah's flowers. On the front of the blue shirt that Melvin had bought for him, a red rose was blooming.

Hannah got to Jay next. Hank tried to pull her away, but she pleaded with him, "I have to be here, Hank."

Realizing the truth in what she said, he moved to let her in. Jay reached out and held Hannah's hand, as his shirt became redder and redder. Hank was frantically holding his hands over the hole in Jay's chest and yelling "Don't go."

Seconds later, Sam arrived with Craig and Leif. Sam went to check on Grant while Craig did what he could for Jay as they waited for an ambulance.

If Grant had been alive, he would have appreciated the irony of it. He had forgotten that the crew knew who the Captain Kirk impostor was and had killed him.

Craig knelt beside Jay trying to hold back the flood of blood. Hannah looked up to see Suzanne and Gillian watching and waiting. "He's going to die, isn't he?" Hannah asked tears running down her face.

There was no need to answer her. The three of them already knew the outcome. There was nothing they could do, but be there for Jay.

What happened next was spoken of in hushed tones for many years afterward. Although only a few people actually saw what happened, everyone present felt the after effect.

Jay moved his head enough to see Hank who was crying harder than he ever thought possible. "Why, why did you do it? I deserved to die," Hank said.

"No," Jay whispered. "No one deserves to die. Hannah was right. There is nothing to forgive. I need you to take care of Hannah and her family for me until I see her again."

A long sigh escaped his lips, and then Jay asked, "Can you see her?"

"See who, Jay?"

"Maggie. I see Maggie. She says I can come to her now. "

"Mommy," Hannah breathed.

Everyone saw a light. Everyone felt a rush of well-being. But only Hannah saw her parents meet again. Jay was still carrying the flowers that Hannah had picked for him.

Hank sobbed as he laid his flowers on Jay's chest. Jay had found his peace.

Hank had a long way to go. "I promise," he whispered.

Turning to Hannah who was still holding Jay's hand, Hank picked her up and carried her to Ava and Evan who had been frantically trying to get to her. They sunk to their knees as she flew into their arms.

Hank had one last thing to do. He had to make sure that Grant was truly dead. Grant had saved him from the streets, but instead of teaching him how to be a good man, he had made him into a pawn of his evil.

Grant was lying face down in the grass yards away from Jay, surrounded by the men who had been chasing him for years. Each man was savoring the moment.

Hank leaned over Grant to see if he was breathing. He wasn't. For Grant, it was over. For Hank, it was a relief.

Fifty-Seven

It wasn't over for Sam and his team. Grant had a bullet in his back. They needed the answer to the question, who killed him?

Sam's team told everyone to remain at the picnic until they could question them. What had they seen? Did anyone in the group have a gun? Sam didn't really believe anyone at the picnic had killed Grant, but perhaps someone had seen who did.

People waited on their blanket or in their cars. Sam had asked them not to sit together in groups and not to discuss what they had seen. He didn't want their memories influenced by something someone else said.

Besides the need for questioning, everyone knew they couldn't leave until Sam said it was safe. Sam's team wanted to make sure that Grant's killer was not still present.

Sam used the last bit of his mental and physical energy to keep his team engaged and his friends feeling secure. Both his body and his mind wanted to shut down. What had happened was too close to a disaster. He wasn't sure how much more he could put into the Grant and Lenny debacle.

The whole ordeal of the past year had been a long slog. Sam couldn't wait until it was over. Part of him didn't give a crap. Whoever had killed Grant had done the world a favor.

However, Sam knew that loose ends would come back to haunt him, so he pushed himself and his team to resolve what happened.

His team was searching the woods and the roads out of town. He prayed that Lenny would be found soon, so he could wrap the investigation up and go to Mira's and sleep for more than the three hours a night he had been sleeping the last three months.

Sam assumed Grant's killer was Lenny. However, if it wasn't Lenny, he didn't know what he could do about it. He was just too tired to go after someone else.

Hank and Leif stood together on the edge of the circle watching all the activity. Hank was still shaking. Someone had brought him a bottle of water, and he sipped at it only because he knew it would help. "Did you know what was going to happen, Leif?" Hank asked.

"Would it matter if I did?"

"I suppose not," Hank said hanging his head and scuffing his foot in the grass.

"If it helps, Hank, no, I didn't know. But I think Suzanne and Gillian did."

"And Hannah?"

"Yes, I think Hannah knew too. Now that it is over, perhaps she can go back to being a little girl."

"Is it over?"

"For her, I believe it is. For us, perhaps not. But Hannah and Jay have peace now, and that is what Jay had been searching for this whole lifetime."

A few tense hours later, Sam told them they could all go home. They had caught Lenny on his way to New York. Although they hadn't found the gun, they were reasonably sure that he had been the one who had shot Grant.

It was an exhausted group of people who hugged each other and headed home. Before leaving, Mira stood in front of Sam and whispered to him. She knew he wouldn't appreciate a hug from her at that moment, but she wanted him to know she would be waiting for him.

Sam watched Mira head home with Tom and Mandy and wondered if this would be a good time to change careers.

That night Hannah knelt beside her bed to say her prayers. It wasn't something she had learned from Ava.

She remembered that Maggie used to pray with her every night. It was their special time together. They would take turns saying what they were grateful for that day. Tonight Hannah's prayer was very simple. "Thank you for taking care of my daddy, Jay, and for giving me another daddy to grow up with."

Ava stood outside Hannah's door and silently wept. She had a prayer too. She prayed that Hannah would only remember the love that had been given her, but be able to forget the past lifetime and just live in this one.

"I am not sure that is a prayer that can be answered, Ava," Suzanne said materializing by her shoulder. "In fact, I am not sure she should forget. But the part about living in this lifetime, that you can help her do."

"Am I up to it, Suzanne?" Ava asked.

"Why do you think you are her mother?" Suzanne said as she faded away.

Ava waited until Hannah had finished with her prayers and then stepped into the room to tuck her in.

"I'm going to be ten soon, Mom. I'm growing up," Hannah said.

"That you are my sweetheart," Ava said, smoothing Hannah's hair away from her forehead, and kissing her goodnight on her nose.

"Sweet dreams, lovely one," Ava said snapping off the light. Hannah was already asleep, hugging her grandmother, Abbie's, well-loved stuffed rabbit.

****

The Stone Circle gathered on the back deck waiting for Ava to get Hannah to bed. Ben had fallen asleep an hour earlier, and Ava was hoping he would sleep all night. It hadn't happened yet, but she thought this was a good night for it to be the first time.

Evan had started a fire, not that they needed one because it was a warm evening. He had started the fire for the sense of community and warmth that it represented. Each member of the Stone Circle had gone home to clean up, but without being told, or asked, had come to their favorite gathering place. They knew there were plans to be made, and things to discuss.

However, no one was talking when Ava made her way to her chair. Everyone was lost in their own thoughts. Looking around the circle, Ava thought about all that they had gone through the past few years. It was only two years ago that they had found each other in this lifetime. Last year, they had helped Ava find her daughter and her Uncle, and the friends that were repopulating the village of Doveland.

Jay's death was profoundly sad, and yet at the same time extraordinarily beautiful. It reminded them once again that what is called death is just another door. Yes, Ava thought, life is eternal, and love does transcend time and space. We keep seeing that over and over again. Whatever comes next, we will do it together.

Fifty - Eight

They were back in the chapel, this time for Jay's funeral.
However, it wasn't a day of mourning. It was a day of
celebration.

The town of Doveland had asked Ava and Evan if they
would hold the service on July 4th. That way they could all
celebrate the idea of freedom, by celebrating Jay's freedom.
Valerie was instrumental in suggesting the timing of the service
and all of Hannah's family and friends were grateful to her for
arranging it.

Instead of being draped in black, each pew had a multicolor
bow attached to it. At the front of the chapel, Ava had placed
arrangements of wildflowers. She and Hannah had spent the
morning the day before collecting them.

It had given them both a chance to talk about what had
happened. It was Hannah's idea to sit in the field for a few
minutes just listening to nature speak to them. It was a reminder
of the cycle of life. As they left the meadow, Hannah slipped her
hand into Ava's, and Ava felt the power of love washing away all
her anxiety.

At the chapel, Melvin, Ava, Evan, and Hannah sat in the
front row representing Jay's family.

They couldn't believe how many people had shown up for the service. Every pew was filled, and still there was a line out the door as people waited to write in the guest-book.

News of what had happened traveled quickly through Doveland, and Jay's story seemed to touch the hearts of many people. Besides, he had saved one of their own. Because, to Hank's great surprise, the town had embraced him. He didn't understand why they did. But he was making great strides in allowing himself to feel accepted.

Some old timers who remembered Jay from the first time around had also come to the chapel to pay their respects. No one tried too hard to explain how he could have died twice, on the same day and at the same age. They just knew he was gone again. However, this time he had been able to save someone. He was not a victim. He was a hero.

After everyone was seated, a small group of children led by the school's music teacher sang "Amazing Grace." Sarah thought that the message of the song was the perfect symbol of why the community had embraced Jay and Hank. Many understood what it felt like to be given a second chance and to find their way to grace.

It was a simple ceremony. Leif read a few passages from the *Bible*, and each of Jay's family from this lifetime spoke briefly about what they had learned by having him in their life.

Hank tried to thank Jay for saving his life, but broke down and couldn't finish. Melvin closed the service. "I hope you are listening, Jay, because you rescued me from living out my life waiting for death. Now my life overflows with friends. And Jay, if you see Sally, would you take care of her for me? I have a few more years and a few more things to do, and then I'll be along."

After the service, a long line of cars made the trip out to what had been Jay's property. Evan had found the current owner of the land and made him an offer he couldn't refuse. He and Ava planned to turn it into a sanctuary for birds and animals to be held in trust for the people of Doveland. Nothing formal, just a place anyone could come and walk, or sit and find peace.

Hannah had said that Jay would like his ashes released over the meadow, and everyone agreed if anyone knew what Jay would have wanted, it would be Hannah. This time instead of a circle of cars on the hill, it was a circle of people who stood and watched as the wind took the ashes and spread them across the land.

There was no sign of the violence that had erupted a few days before, or thirty-five years before that. A rift had been healed, and everyone could feel it.

Instead of a wake, the town had something else planned. An old-fashioned barn raising. The explosion they had heard while at the picnic was Melvin's barn blowing up.

When Melvin heard what had happened, he laughed. "That barn was ready to fall down anyway."

Privately, Melvin decided to send Lenny a thank you note once he found out what prison he was going to. Melvin knew Lenny could have blown up his house. Instead, he had given him a gift and taken down the barn for him.

The raising of the barn had taken some planning, but Hank made it happen quickly. He gathered his old construction crew, and they planned it out together. He intended to pay for it himself, but Valerie had spread the word about what was happening, and a fund was started with almost everyone pitching in.

Melvin said that he might never use the barn for farming again, so perhaps it could be used for parties and barn dances.

Without Jay, Melvin knew his heart was no longer into farming, and his vegetable garden was all he needed.

The barn raising was also a chance to have a party. As Valerie said to Sarah, Doveland was a town that loved to celebrate. Even though Melvin's property was closer to Concourse, they were adopting it, and Melvin, as their own.

Mandy made another birthday cake for Jay since no one had been able to eat the last one. Pete made another salad and brought along a grill for hamburgers and hot dogs.

Alex from the Diner was teaching Johnny how to grill. Pete had decided he could use more help at the Diner and asked Johnny if he would be willing. He and Barbara had discussed how they could help the community, and being available for kids like Johnny felt right to them.

Johnny was given a choice. Work at the Diner or pick up trash along the road. Although Johnny had helped them catch Grant, Sam and Johnny's parents wanted him to understand there were consequences to bad choices. Johnny knew a good thing when he saw it. Besides, he really liked Pete, and he loved to eat. It was an excellent second chance, and Johnny had no desire to blow it.

Grace had not been the one to plan this particular party. Instead, after the service, she had gone home with Eric. He had finally told her the news. There was nothing that could be done for him. At first, she cried. And then they both cried. Then, after asking him if he was absolutely sure, she asked him what he wanted to do. He had a plan, but neither Grace nor Eric knew if it was possible, or how to accomplish it if it was.

"Leif and Sarah will know," Grace said, and then the two of them sat on her couch and watched the sun go down over the town square, each lost in their own thoughts, wondering how many more sunrises and sunsets they would share together.

Fifty-Nine

Sarah and Leif sat on the bed in the bunkhouse as they waited for their ride to the airport. Their suitcases packed and stacked by the front door. They had stayed much longer than they planned to, and now that the emergency was over, it was time to go back.

Evan had rented a town car for them and Craig who was also returning to his home. They were both looking forward to having some private time with Craig. With all that had gone on, they never had time to focus on him, and whatever was bothering him.

Sitting, or pretending to sit, on the chairs in the room, were Suzanne and Gillian.

"I know you aren't happy, Sarah," Suzanne said.

"How could I be?" she responded. "If we decide to do this, I would not see you and Gillian again, and Leif would be..."

Sarah couldn't continue. She and Leif were sitting as close together as possible. She was doing her best not to cry.

"We have to go, Sarah," Suzanne said. "We are needed in many places. Gillian and I have stayed close to you to help these last few years, but we need to help other Circles too. And it's not *never*. You know better than that, Sarah. Anything is possible."

Sarah nodded. "I know I am supposed to know better than that, but at the moment my heart doesn't seem to be catching up with the logic of it."

"Leif doesn't have to do it," Gillian said.

"That's the other part I understand," Sarah said. "I understand that he doesn't have to. But I also understand that he will probably decide that it would be best."

"You don't have to decide, yet," Suzanne said. "Go back to Sandpoint. We will still be near. Eric has a little time, but not much. So decide soon."

In the silence of their leaving, Leif turned to Sarah. "I won't do this if you say not to."

"You know I can't ask that of you, Leif. I would hate myself for the asking, and you would have less faith in me if I did. Besides, there are Grace and Eric to think about. It's not just about me."

"For me, Sarah, it is always just about you."

Sarah laid her head on his shoulder and held his hand until they heard Ava call out that the car had arrived.

Leif kissed Sarah, used his handkerchief to tap the tears off her cheeks, and said, "Let's go home."

****

The ride to the airport was a somber one. Sarah and Leif sat quietly holding hands until Craig spoke up.

"Big decision?"

They both nodded.

"I have one to make too," he said.

Sarah reached across to Craig and held his hand. "Forget about us at the moment. We never had a chance to ask you about what is going on with you. Is it Jo Anne?"

"It is. Leif, since we met, I have grown and changed, and it seems Jo Anne has changed in the opposite direction. I feel as if I want to turn the healing center over to the doctors working there and scale down to a small private family practice. I want to bring in holistic ideas, and prevention. The corporate culture of health care is not for me anymore.

"Jo Anne likes the city. She loves social gatherings and being part of that culture. The one I want to leave.

"To put it bluntly, Jo Anne hasn't been happy with me for years. However, when I was a little rowdier and making lots of money, she liked me more. "Now. Not so much. She asked for a divorce a few months ago."

"I'm sorry, Craig," Leif said. "Is there anything we can do to help?"

"Well, when I arrived for the christening I was just going to stay for a few days. Then all that drama happened, and now a few weeks later I have had time to get to know Doveland. I see why you like it.

"What do you think of me moving here, and starting that little holistic practice here?"

Sarah smiled. Her first real smile in days. "I think the town would be honored and overjoyed to have you. Besides, that would mean the whole Stone Circle would be here."

Craig stared at her. "The whole Stone Circle? Are you and Leif moving to Doveland? Oh, that's the decision?"

"Part of it," Sarah answered. "If it were just that, it would be easy. Suzanne has said the Forest Circle is fine with us selling the house and moving here.

"In fact, it was her suggestion. Last year, Evan sold the one he bought, so there is no need to stay. The rest of the decision is much more difficult. Eric would like to join the Forest Circle, but there is only one way to do that."

"Someone has to take him," Craig said.

"Yes," Sarah whispered.

"And that would be Leif?" Craig asked.

"And that would be Leif."

Sixty

"We keep meeting at this cemetery, Ava," Hank said.

The two of them were sitting on Hank's father's grave. Ava thought that perhaps it was a little morbid, but they knew it was a place to lay things to rest.

Hank had come to see his father not only as a monster, but also as a man who had somehow gone wrong, and no one had stepped in to help.

Hank knew that he could have ended up just like him, and in fact had lived a worse life for many years. Then his family had saved him, and friends had embraced him in spite of what he had done.

Pete and Barbara had talked to Hank about Johnny, asked if he would be willing to mentor him and perhaps some of the other boys from Doveland, and perhaps Concourse. He had said yes without hesitation.

Sam had managed to get Hank released from any more obligations to the FBI, so he was free to do as much good as he could. He hoped that it would make up for so many of his past bad choices.

The hawk was sitting on the same limb it had been on the first time he found his father's grave.

Ava told him that Sarah and Leif had a hawk that watched out for them too.

"Have they decided what they are going to do?" Hank asked.

"Not officially. However, you know what they will probably decide. Sarah said she would come live in Doveland if Leif takes Eric to the Forest Circle."

"I don't get how they can do that, do you? Instead of letting Eric die, he is choosing to leave instead. How does that work?"

Ava looked at Hank. "Don't know. All I know is that what Leif is choosing to do must be what love for others looks like. The good news is that Leif and Eric will still be around, just not physically present."

"The way that Suzanne and Gillian have been present?"

"Yep, just like that. Both of them just left too. Well, Gillian only left after I was found, but it's still weird that they can shift to another dimension like that. What if everyone could?"

They both looked up as they saw Melvin's old truck pull up beside Ava's car. He opened the door and yelled out at them both.

"I'm too old to be chasing after the two of you. Get your butts off that grave and come over to my house. We have a birthday party to plan!"

A few minutes later the three of them were standing outside of Melvin's barn looking at the sign he had hung over the door. It said, "Jay's Place."

"Do you think Hannah would like to have her tenth birthday here?" Melvin asked.

Hank turned to Ava, "How many kids do you think we could invite?"

"As many as you want, Hank," she said. "It's a new beginning."

Author's Note

All characters in this book are fictional. Some are composites of people I have known. Some are entirely made up. As this series goes on, the characters become more and more just my imagination.

I decided that in this series I wanted to write about a town where I would love to live. Years ago, my husband, Delbert Lee Piper Sr., and I traveled to small towns to find the one in my head. I had a list of things I wanted in a small town.

Although we did discover a few that we loved, we never found the one that was perfect in every way. Perhaps that's not possible in real life.

So instead, I am making one up. Doveland has become that perfect town for me. It is a combination of a few towns we know, and a few we have lived in or read about.

As I write this series I am populating the town with people I would love to spend time with. Sometimes they are composites of people I already know, and some are people who just live in my head. Yes, I am aware that in someways this is the same thing.

I often have conversations about these characters now as if they were real. I hope they become that way for you, too.

May I ask a favor of you? If you have a second, please review *Jatismar*. Books go out in the world and authors never know where they go. It's like sending your kids off to school and never seeing them again. Reviews help in so many ways! I thank you in advance!

I hope that you are enjoying this *Karass* saga. The next one in the series is called *Exousia*.

As you read this series, let me know what you think! Find all my books on Amazon and many of your other favorite places to buy books.

I would love it if you followed me to keep up to date with what I'm writing. You can do that on Amazon from my author's page. Amazon will let you know when the next book comes out.

Or come sign up for my email at https://becalewis.com, and you'll hear from me a bit more often.

Connect with me online:
Twitter: https://twitter.com/becalewis
Facebook: https://www.facebook.com/becalewiswriter
Pinterest: https://www.pinterest.com/theshift/
Instagram: http://instagram.com/becalewis
LinkedIn: https://linkedin.com/in/becalewis

ACKNOWLEDGMENTS

I could never write a book without the help of my friends and my book community. Thank you Jet Tucker, Jamie Lewis, Diana Cormier, and Barbara Budan for taking the time to do the final reader proof. You can't imagine how much I appreciate it. A huge thank you to Laura Moliter for the last look editing.

Thank you to the fabulous Elizabeth Mackey for the fantastic book covers for the *Karass* series.

Thank you to every other member of my street team who helps me make so many decisions that help the book be the best book possible, Cheryl Kirk, Diane Solomon, Shawna Hixton, Corinne Pierce, Linn Moffett, Tiffany Loosvelt, Merri McElderry, Fay Christie, Joanna Pieters, Barbara Best, Kathleen Piper, Rosemary Serafin, Nicole Petzolt

And always thank you to my beloved husband, Del, for being my daily sounding board, for putting up with all my questions, my constant need to want to make things better, and for being the love of my life

OTHER BOOKS BY BECA

The KARASS Series - Fiction
Karass
Pragma
Jatismar
Exousia
Stemma
 - Keep watching for more!

The Shift Series - Nonfiction
Living in Grace: The Shift to Spiritual Perception
The Daily Shift: Daily Lessons From Love To Money
The 4 Essential Questions: Choosing Spiritually Healthy
Habits
The 28 Day Shift To Wealth: A Daily Prosperity Plan
The Intent Course: Say Yes To What Moves You

Perception Parables: - Fiction - very short stories
Love's Silent Sweet Secret: A Fable About Love
Golden Chains And Silver Cords: A Fable About Letting Go

Advice: - Nonfiction
A Woman's ABC's of Life: Lessons in Love, Life and Career
from Those Who Learned The Hard Way

ABOUT BECA LEWIS

Beca writes books that she hopes will change people's perceptions of themselves and the world, and open possibilities of things and ideas that are waiting to be seen and experienced.

At sixteen, Beca founded her own dance studio. Later, she received a Master's Degree in Dance in Choreography from UCLA and founded the Harbinger Dance Theatre, a multimedia dance company, while continuing to run her dance school.

After graduating—to better support her three children—Beca switched to the sales field, where she worked as an employee and independent contractor to many industries, excelling in each while perfecting and teaching her Shift® system, and writing books.

She joined the financial industry in 1983 and became an Associate Vice President of Investments at a major stock brokerage firm, and was a licensed Certified Financial Planner for more than twenty years.

This diversity, along with a variety of life challenges, helped fuel the desire to share what she's learned by writing and talking with the hopes that it will make a difference in other people's lives.

Beca grew up in State College, PA, with the dream of becoming a dancer and then a writer. She carried that dream forward as she fulfilled a childhood wish by moving to Southern California in 1969. Beca told her family she would never move back to the cold.

After living there for thirty years, she met her husband Delbert Lee Piper Sr., at a retreat in Virginia and everything changed. They decided to find a place they could call their own which sent them off traveling around the United States for a year or so they lived, and worked in a few different places before returning to live in the cold once again near his family in a small town in Northeast Ohio.

When not working and teaching together, they love to visit and play with their combined family of eight children and five grandchildren, read, study, do yoga and taiji, feed birds, work in their garden, and design things. Actually, designing things is what Beca loves to do. Del enjoys the end result.

77672508R00163

Made in the USA
Middletown, DE
24 June 2018